THEY WILL FALL

USA TODAY BESTSELLING AUTHOR
RACHEL LEIGH

Dear Reader,

They Will Fall is the third, and final, book in a three part series. It is highly recommended to read the first two books first. You can start with We Will Reign!

Please advise, this is a dark college, why-choose romance with content that may be triggering.

xo Rachel

Copyright © 2023 Rachel Leigh

All rights reserved. No portion of this book may be reproduced in any form without permission from the copyright owner. This is a work of fiction. Names, characters, businesses, places, events, locales, and incidents are either the products of the author's imagination or used in a fictitious manner.

For permissions contact: rachelleighauthor@gmail.com

ISBN: 978-1-956764-27-7

Cover Design by Ya'll That Graphic

Editing by Fairest Reviews and Editing Services

Proofreading by Rumi Khan

www.rachelleighauthor.com

For the girls who love hard,
and fight harder.

BLURB

After a rocky start to my freshman year at BCU, I was confident the threat was gone.

The murders ended, and my name was cleared. All the while, three unsuspecting men took me by surprise...

Ridge, my stalker turned lover.

Maddox, prince charming who swept me off my feet.

And Lev, my villain who climbed out of the black hole he'd been living in, showing me a version of himself no one thought they'd ever see again.

Then everything changed.

Campus Alert: Shelter in place. Homicide suspect at large.

That suspect...it's me.

I'm not innocent by any means, but I didn't commit the crimes I'm being accused of. Someone is out to get me, and it's apparent they'll go to depths unimaginable to ensure my demise.

But I was born a survivor, and I'll rise from the ashes, even if it means I have to burn first.

Playlist
Listen Now on Spotify
Stop and Stare by One Republic
Better Man by Pearl Jam
Whatever It Takes by Lifehouse
Someone You Loved by Lewis Capaldi
Lips of an Angel by Hinder
Hanging by a Moment by Lifehouse
If The World Was Ending by JP Saxe
If You're Gone by Matchbox 20
Shattered by O.A.R
CHECK OUT THE PINTEREST BOARD

PROLOGUE
MADDOX

Thirteen Years Old

MY FINGER TREMBLES over the lever of the rifle. The smooth steel glides against my sweaty hand as I move the rifle into position. I stare down the sight, draw in a shaky breath, and hold it in my lungs to stop myself from shaking. My dad's heavy breath rings in my ear. It's so loud, a constant roar that drowns out everything else.

"Eye on the target, Maddox. Never take your eye off it."

Hunting, or even just shooting, is supposed to be a sport —a journey of conquest. Something to do that gives you an adrenaline rush and takes you to a place where you are completely present, while proving that you are in charge of your own destiny. It's the thrill of the hunt.

At least, that's the way I look at it. My dad, though, to him, it's a power trip. Proof that humans are more powerful than animals.

We're not hunting. I'm staring down the sight at a target on a plastic deer set about one hundred yards away.

"Now," he quips, giving me his permission to release the bullet.

My finger inches forward, pulling it back before the rifle fires at the target...missing it by a good inch.

Dad sighs heavily, making his disappointment in me known.

"Almost," I tell him, hopeful he'll see I'm trying my hardest.

"Almost doesn't count, son. You either hit it, or you don't. And you didn't." He grabs the barrel, pulling the rifle off my shoulder. "Give me the damn thing." He points, pulls, and shoots, hitting the target before I can even take in my next breath.

I'm not sure whether to congratulate him or tuck my tail between my legs. But he doesn't allow me the chance to do either as he slams the gun to my chest and stalks behind me. The sound of the tall grass scratching against his rubber boots rings in my ears. His exit is more deafening than his presence.

Giving it a good five minutes, I wait until he's gone then I shoot again, and again, and again. Never giving up as I try my damnedest to hit the target.

After thirty minutes of missing every shot, I'm down to one bullet left in the magazine.

My last shot.

The realization that my heart is no longer pounding, my palms are no longer sweating, and my breath has steadied has my confidence soaring. It's crazy what one can do when no one is watching. When the pressure is off—it's just a man and his target.

I aim.

I pull.

I fire.

"Yes!" I shout, my voice ringing with excitement. The empty barrel clatters against my thigh as I spin around, hoping he saw.

"I did it, Dad," I holler, but I know he can't hear me. He's already back at the house a quarter mile away.

I quickly empty the magazine, stuff the rifle in the bag at my feet, then toss it over my shoulder. Galloping through the field, I shout the entire way. "I hit the target, Dad. I did it."

My feet don't stop moving until I'm at the front door, and once I pull it open, I shout again as it slams closed behind me. My eyes search the open space, stopping in the dining room as I approach him, breathlessly.

Dad is sitting at the table with his reading glasses perched on the bridge of his nose, a cup of steaming coffee to one side. The newspaper is spread out in front of him. "Dad," I say, my voice barely a whisper, "I did it."

He pulls back his sleeve and looks at his wristwatch with a blank face. He glances at it for a moment before his eyes meet mine, the expression on his face unreadable. "That deer would've been long gone by now, son." Then he pushes his glasses up on his nose, and he returns to his paper.

My shoulders slump in defeat as I turn around, letting the strap of my rifle bag slide down my arm. With each step, it ricochets off the floor as it creeps downward.

I look forward to the day when I'm no longer a failure in his eyes. All my life all I've ever craved is my dad's approval.

I'm almost fearful of the extremes I'd be willing to go to, to get it.

CHAPTER 1
MADDOX

I RE-READ the text that was sent hours ago as we struggle to keep warm in Lev's old cabin.

> Campus Alert: Shelter-in-place. Homicide suspect at large.

"We can't stay here forever," Riley says through chattering teeth. "It's...it's so damn cold." She drags the words out as if each one is momentarily frozen in time. Ridge pulls her closer, holding on to her so tightly, the Jaws of Life couldn't pry his arms away.

It's unreal how quickly the weather changed. A couple days ago, we had clear skies and tee shirt weather. Now, fluffy white clouds cast shadows over the mountains, threatening snow. The air is cold, below freezing, and it's only going to get worse since we're smack in the midst of an arctic storm that's rolling through. Fortunately, we've got the cabin for shelter, even if there is no heat or electricity.

I watch Ridge and Riley. Listening to their conversation while gnawing on my fingernails like they are my last meal. And they could be. It's a great possibility because everyone knows Cade is dead. They don't know I did it, though—that I killed him. According to my father, The Elders think it was Riley who took his life. Eventually, the truth will come out because there is no way in hell I'd ever let Riley go down for what I did. Then, my life will be over. I'll be banished, a Punisher will be assigned to me, and any chance at having a normal life will cease to exist. Every chance encounter, he'll be there, ready to make my life more miserable than the day before.

I killed a member of The Society.

An innocent man.

I'm screwed.

But if I go down, I'm taking Lev with me. All the time we thought it was Cade who snuck in her room, sexually assaulted her, then killed Zeke. Turns out, the real assailant was living under our thumbs the entire time.

I'm not sure where Lev is right now. No one knows. And I really don't give a shit where he's run off to. At least, not yet. I'll find him when he's useful to me.

Riley, Ridge, and I have been hiding out for nearly twelve hours. It's now eight o'clock in the morning and we should all be heading to our morning classes, but classes were canceled for the day and the shelter-in-place rule is still in effect.

Ridge and Riley dozed off for a couple hours, but I haven't slept at all. It's damn near impossible when my mind is running rampant. I've got no fucking idea how this shit is going to come together. We're all out of our league on this one. Should have just left well enough alone. Fuck me. Fuck all of this.

There's one option. I could fess up. Just open my mouth and let it all come out.

'Be a man, Maddox. You're a Crane, and Crane's don't cower.' That's what my dad would say right now. He has this way of making me feel as if I can conquer anything. Now I'm starting to wonder if it was more of a curse than a blessing.

In this case, the wisdom of his words wouldn't be directed at me confessing the truth. They'd be telling me to keep what I did to myself. I'm not him, though. This is my chapter—my story—and I'm writing it my damn self.

Wonder what dear ol' Dad is going to think of me once the truth about what I did is brought to light.

"We've gotta get the hell out of here," Ridge says as he emerges from beneath the blanket he's huddled under with Riley. His bare chest is exposed because his main focus right now is keeping his angel warm. I get it. I want her warm, too. But I'd rather her be safe, and he's been going on and on about how we need to leave the cabin. I beg to differ because leaving means the risk of getting caught, and once she's caught, it's game over.

With his legs still kept under the floral-printed fabric that looks like it's hasn't been washed since the late nineties, he runs his fingers down the side of his face. Stroking his chin, he stares off into the air. His eyes glaze over for a moment as he speaks his thoughts into existence. "We've got no food. There's no fucking heat in this place. Hell, we can head back to Glendale, if needed. We've still got the lease on the apartment. No one will even consider looking for Riley there."

"It's too risky," I tell him from my seat at the kitchen table that's pointed in their direction. I lean forward, my elbows pressed firmly to my knees. "The campus, and surrounding areas, are swarming with The Elders right now. Everyone is looking for her and this is the last place they'd think to search." An idea comes to mind that has me on my feet. "Lemme go get food. And more blankets. Anything we need to hole up in here a little bit longer until this is all settled and her name is cleared."

Ridge tosses the blanket off him aggressively and gets to his knees. "And who the fuck is out there trying to clear it?" he shouts. "No one! Not a single fucking person, so it's up to us! We're not doing her any good here."

"Would you guys quit it?" Riley jumps in. "Stop talking as if I'm not even here. I'm right fucking here!" She places an arm on Ridge's shoulder, pulling him back toward her, though he resists and continues to scowl at me like I'm the enemy right now. "Ridge is right. We can't stay here forever, but I can't stand the thought of either of you going out there and facing repercussions for being with me." She chokes on her words as they slip through her damp lips. Her eyes are downcast and she speaks softly. "Maybe it's best for all of us if we part ways for a while. Just until this is over."

My heart pangs with remorse. I get to my feet and move to sit behind her. Taking her hair in one hand, I move it to the side so I can press a warm kiss to the back of her neck. "There isn't a chance in hell we are leaving you."

She turns her head to look at me as I run my fingers down the sleeve of her hoodie. "It's not safe for you guys. I don't want your names connected to me in any way until this is over."

Ridge scoots closer, his hand now resting on her leg overtop the blanket. "We are connected to you, Angel, and I don't give a fuck who knows it. Consequences be damned, you are stuck with us."

Massaging her shoulders, I speak tenderly in a way that I hope calms her nerves. "Right now, our whereabouts won't be questioned since we're on lockdown. Everyone assumes we're in our dorms. We've got time."

"He's right. We've got some time," Ridge reminds her. "No one will suspect we're with you, and if they do, then fuck them. None of us are guilty. We didn't do a damn thing wrong."

I look at him, wondering if he truly believes the lies he's saying. "Not a damn thing, huh?"

He scoffs. "What's that supposed to mean?"

My shoulders rise and fall rapidly. "I just don't think any of us are free of guilt right now, and I certainly wouldn't want you walking around campus with a bout of confidence and wind up getting your ass in deep water."

I've had my suspicions for a while, and I don't think Ridge is as innocent has he's letting on. Cade and Zeke aren't the only ones who died—there are others, too. Others who I originally thought Riley killed. It could have been Lev, but I've put together a timeline of the events that took place, and Ridge's whereabouts aren't accounted for during any of the other murders. I'm not saying he's guilty, but he's on my list of suspects, along with Lev.

"We need to find Lev," Riley pipes up. Her shoulders draw back and she inhales a deep breath. "Maybe we can talk some sense into him and get him to confess to what he's done."

A humorous chuckle bubbles up my throat. "Lev, confess? Not a chance in hell. Lev only cares about saving his own ass."

"I agree," Riley says solemnly. Her face pulls into a frown as she looks down at her finger that's wrapped with the blanket threading. "Lev has no intention of helping any of us. He's not the man I thought he was."

"For what it's worth, you made him want to be better," Ridge tells her. "I saw the way he looked at you, and it was a look we haven't seen from Lev in years."

I hate that Ridge is sugarcoating this for her. I know he's trying to ease the fall from the high she was on with Lev, but it's only going to give her something to hold on to, and she needs to let go of him. Of course, Ridge and I have his back, and we'll do everything we can to help him once he allows us to. But Lev isn't relationship material. He needs to fix himself before he can be trusted with our girl's heart.

Riley's eyes lift, dancing from mine to Ridge's and back. "If only it was enough. I just don't get it." She averts her gaze, staring off in thought. The corners of her mouth twitch as a smile slowly spreads on her lips. "Toward the end, Lev was gentle. Kind. Compassionate, even. It was nothing I'd ever imagined I'd ever feel from him, but everything I'd hoped for." Her smile quickly drops. "I guess it was all for nothing."

Ridge and I share a look of displeasure because we both knew this thing with Lev was going to end with Riley brokenhearted. Fortunately, she'll have Ridge and me to mend the shattered pieces.

Or, at the very least, she'll have Ridge. I might have to disappear for a while if I decide to tell my side of the story. Head to the East Coast. Change my name. Riley and the guys will be mad at me for a while, but I hope one day they'll understand why I did what I did. It was all for her.

I was given an assignment to keep an eye on the Kappa Rho brothers—Cade being one of them. Thanks to Lev, I thought Cade assaulted Riley. In my heart, I believed I was avenging what he did to her by taking his life. But I was wrong. So fucking wrong.

"You're right," Riley exhales heavily. "Lev isn't who I thought he was, and now he needs to be a man and face what he's done."

Be a man. As opposed to a coward who hides behind his own secrets, while others feel the wrath of his mistakes.

"There's something you both need to know," I fess up, ready to unleash this dreadful burden from my shoulders.

A sudden knock at the door grabs all our attention. My eyes shoot over my shoulder as Ridge and Riley jump up from the floor. I remain crouched, hands dangling over my knees.

"Fuck," Ridge blurts. He looks left, then right. "We gotta hide."

This is it. They're here for her. It's now or never.

I stand up, straightening my back before crossing the room to a trembling Riley. "You need to hear what I have to say."

The pounding grows in intensity and Riley pulls me by the hand, lugging me into the bathroom. Standing in the doorway, she whisper-yells to Ridge, "Get in here!"

Refusing to listen, Ridge slides his back against the wall, inching slowly toward the window. The air escapes him with a heavy sigh as he passes the window and reaches the door. He stops in front of it, puts his hand on the knob, and his eyes bolt over his shoulder, while Riley and I wait impatiently for an inkling as to what he's doing. "It's fucking Scar." He pulls open the door.

Riley drops my hand and rushes out of the bathroom to greet her best friend, while I press the heels of my palms to the doorframe and drop my head in defeat. *I tried.*

CHAPTER 2
RILEY

"I DIDN'T DO IT," I cry as I throw myself into Scar's arms. Crew, Jagger, and Neo stand behind her, arms crossed over their chests and stern looks on their faces. Well, two of them, anyways. Neo is wearing a prominent scowl with his lips set in a firm line, and I wouldn't expect anything less from him.

"Sure, you didn't." Neo scoffs and I just roll my eyes at him. He dresses like he doesn't want to be seen, but that doesn't stop everyone from looking. He's always sporting that bad-boy persona and I've learned to just ignore anything that comes out of his cocksure mouth. And often, it's warranted.

Scar's forehead creases in contempt as she glances over at Neo. Slow strides bring her closer to me before she takes my shoulders in both hands and gazes into my eyes with a reassuring look. "*We*," she emphasizes, "know you didn't."

My lips press into a thin white line as I swallow the lump lodged in my throat. "It was Lev," I blurt out, immediately wishing I could take back the words because now that I've said them, with witnesses, there is no going back.

Jagger's eyes perk up. "Lev Pemberley?"

"No," Ridge says from behind me. "Riley's confused. The last twenty-four hours have been draining for her. We don't know who it was." His hand rests on my hip as he stands behind me. "Isn't that right, Angel?"

My thoughts elude me as I try to decipher why Ridge is covering for Lev. After everything Lev's done, why is he protecting him? I turn my head to look at Ridge, losing Scar's hold on me, as a cold wave washes over my skin. Eyebrows knitted, I question what he just said. "I'm confused?"

"That's not what I meant."

"But it's what you said. No more lies, Ridge. No more secrets. It's time everyone knows what Lev has done because I sure as hell am not going down for his crimes."

"What exactly did Lev do?" Neo asks, suddenly piqued with interest.

"None of your fucking business," Maddox tells him as he takes me by the hand, pulling me away from the group. He leans close, his voice a whisper in my ear. "We need to keep everything under wraps for the time being. Incriminate no one."

"That's bullshit." I huff loud enough for everyone to hear. I jerk my hand away, annoyed that both Maddox and Ridge are defending Lev's actions. "This is all Lev's fault. Why the hell should I protect him? And why are you?"

"I'm not protecting him. I'm just..." Maddox's words trail off as Ridge steps beside us.

"We need definitive proof before we bring any of this to light." His eyes remain pinned on Scar and her guys as he speaks. "Please, just let us handle this before you start spreading rumors."

I clench my fists as I slam my foot to the floor, rattling an empty pop can on the scuffed kitchen table. Every muscle in my body tenses with rage. "Scar," I bellow, as I push past Ridge and Maddox. "Can I talk to you, please?"

I grasp the bathroom handle with one hand and slowly open the door. Scar steps inside, her eyes wide at my outburst. Slamming the door shut quickly, I create an echo that reverberates off the walls of the small space.

"I have to find him," I tell her, really hating that I'm putting her in this position of knowing what I might have to do. "I have to leave campus and find Lev."

"Ry. Babe. I dunno. This shit you're in is deep. I think you need to just come forward and let The Elders handle it. I mean, they've got a fucking Punisher assigned to you. This isn't some little thing that's just going to blow over."

"I know." I exhale a pent-up breath. "It's a fucking mess." Tears prick the corners of my eyes and I aggressively jab my fingertips into them because I don't want to shed a tear over what's going on...or over Lev.

I miss him, though. I hate the fucking bastard. But, I miss him.

"This all stemmed from Governor Saint's death. If only I'd just stayed out of it."

"Don't." Scar grabs my hands, pulling them away from my face. "Don't you dare go there. That son of a bitch got exactly what he deserved, as far as I'm concerned, and to anyone else who knows what really happened, you're a hero, Ry. You saved us all."

"A hero?" I laugh dryly. "Hardly."

"You are! And if the truth ever comes out about what happened, I'm hopeful The Elders will see it that way, too. Because if one truth is revealed, we're going to make damn sure all truths are revealed."

"Thank you," I tell her, pulling her in for a hug. "You

always have a way of pulling me out of the darkness. I don't know what I'd do without you."

"You never have to find out. I promise you that." She takes a step back and runs her thumb under my eye because one stupid tear broke free. It was a tear of happiness, though, because moments like this prove how unbelievably blessed I am to have such amazing friends and boyfriends.

Thinking of boyfriends, and almost ex-boyfriends, or whatever Lev was to me, Scar needs to know my plan. It's not actually a plan because it literally just popped into my head a few minutes ago, but it might be the only way I can get two steps ahead of The Elders, and The Punisher assigned to me. "Well," I begin, "there is only one way to ensure that we will never be without each other, and it weighs heavily on Lev."

"Whatever you're thinking, no." A look of displeasure washes over her face. "I love you, babe, but you're your own worst enemy when it comes to getting yourself out of the mud you're stuck in. Do I need to remind you of the time you got gum stuck to the bottom of your shoe?"

A smile draws on my face and an airy chuckle escapes me. "That was some sticky-ass gum, okay?"

"I only had to cut a chunk. Just saying." My hand sweeps through the air as I spin in a circle, coming to a stop at the free-standing sink. With my palms resting against the porcelain, I heave a sigh. Looking down, I absorb what she said. Not the part about the gum, or my hair, but me being my own worst enemy. She's right.

"I don't know what else to do," I tell her. "I have to find him."

Scar inhales deeply, and while I can't see her face from where she's standing behind me, I imagine she's chewing hard on her bottom lip. It's something she does often when she's deep in thought.

I raise my head, ripping my gaze away from the sink. Casting a sidelong look at her, I'm proven correct. Sure enough, her lip is sucked between her teeth, and her nostrils are flaring as she breathes deeply.

"I'll be safe. I promise."

Her eyes close momentarily before she reaches into her pocket and pulls out a phone. It's not just any phone, though. It's one of those old flip ones. "Take this."

She sets the phone in my palm as I watch her with quizzical eyes. "What's this for?"

"You've all had your phones turned off. I knew I'd find you here today, and I brought this so we'd have a way of keeping in touch while you're hiding out. It's a burner phone that can't be traced."

She's right. Ridge, Maddox, and I shut our phones off to not risk anyone tracking our whereabouts. It's been tempting to turn it on, just to get an update on the situation, but I know it's a risk. I tap my fingers to the phone she handed me, smiling. "Always thinking ahead."

"As a member of a fucked-up society, we sort of have to."

"Scar," I say softly as I tuck the phone in the side pocket of my black joggers. "There's one more thing."

"For fuck's sake, Ry," she sighs. "What else could there possibly be? You're wanted for murder and you're going on a manhunt for a deranged psycho. I swear to fucking God, if I see you on *America's Most Wanted*..."

"Shut up." I punch her shoulder playfully. "It won't come to that. At least, I hope not. It's just that, I'm not telling Ridge and Maddox I'm leaving. The last thing I want is for two innocent guys, who I care deeply about, to get in trouble for something they didn't do."

"You mean, in the way that you've been set up to fall for something *you* didn't do?"

"Exactly. I don't want them to get hurt."

"You're really falling for these guys, aren't you?"

This time, I'm the one gnawing on my bottom lip, but I do it with a sly smile creeping up on my face. "Harder than I thought it was possible to fall."

"And Lev? Are you two just...done?"

With my eyes downcast, I release my lip from my teeth. "Lev and I were nothing but an illusion. A budding relationship built on fraud. Not only is it over, it never even had a chance to begin. Now, it never will because Lev Pemberley is going down and I sure as fuck am not going with him."

"I'm sorry to say this, but it's probably best you learned the truth about him before your heart was too invested."

But my heart was invested. So much more than I'm letting on. I can still see his face in my memories and taste him on my tongue. If I think hard enough, I swear I can remember what it feels like to be wrapped in his arms, and it was probably one of the best feelings in the world. Lev doesn't attach himself to people or things easily, yet he did to me. I felt special. Now, I feel like a joke.

My mouth goes dry and a boulder rests on my chest. "It is what it is."

"You always go with the easiest response."

"It's the only one I've got." I shrug.

"Scar," Neo hollers. "Come on, baby. We're leaving."

Scar's eyes roll. "There's always that one that can't play nice with others."

I chuckle. "Gotta love him."

"Oh, I do." She smirks as she pulls the bathroom door open. "More than life, but it doesn't mean I don't wanna smack him sometimes."

Neo's voice rises to a near shout. "And you keep that fucking maniac away from campus, and my girl. I don't care how close you assholes are. He comes near us, or her, I'll take care of him myself."

Ridge shoves Neo out the door then slams it shut before Crew, Jagger, and Scar even have a chance to make their exit.

"Keep in touch," Scar whispers as she pulls me in for a hug. "And be safe."

"I will," I tell her. "This will all be over soon."

If only I could believe the words leaving my mouth because I'm scared as hell, and something in my gut tells me, this is only the beginning of my descent into the fire.

CHAPTER 3
RIDGE

"DON'T LET her out of your sight for a second," I tell Maddox quietly as my sweaty palm wraps around the door handle. "I get the feeling she's plotting something."

"Don't plan to take my eyes off her." He glances at Riley, who's writing in her notebook on the couch. Her knees are bent, feet pressed firmly to the cushion, and the spiral book is resting on her upper thighs.

After Maddox mentioned going back to campus for supplies, I volunteered myself as tribute. I didn't really expect him to agree so quickly, but he did. So here I am, lacing up my boots with a wool beanie pulled down over my ears so I can fill the two oversized backpacks strung over my shoulders with enough food to last us a few days.

It's a gamble to venture out, considering it's a fucking ghost town back on campus with everyone still sheltering in place. Everyone but The Elders, who are lurking around. Jagger mentioned that there's at least a dozen and said they've been having countless meetings—all about Riley. He was helpful and told me a route they've been taking on a back trail to get to and from the places they need to be, so I was grateful for that bit of information. Crew, Jagger, and especially Neo can be real assholes, but so can we, so I don't judge them too harshly.

Lost in his gaze, Maddox smiles unknowingly as he watches her. "How'd we get so fucking lucky?"

"Luck has nothing to do with it. We create our own destiny."

And in my case, I created a future with Riley in it because when I want something, I take it. I've never wanted anyone or anything, the way I want her, and even as I have her, I want more and more of her. I will never stop wanting her.

I snap out of the memories of everything I did to get to where I'm at today with my angel. If I think too much about those days, I raise walls to protect myself and my secrets, and my only quest right now is protecting Riley.

"I'm out. Don't," I emphasize, "fuck this up."

I pull open the door slowly, taking care to silence the creak so I don't distract Riley from her writing. It's the first time she's opened her notebook in days and I'm happy to see she's releasing some of the aggressive thoughts running rampant in her mind through her poetry.

Maddox gives me a sailor salute, then shuts the door behind me. There's an itch inside me I can't scratch. This uneasy feeling that Riley is up to something. Maybe it's because I know her so well, inside and out. I swear to all that is holy if Maddox doesn't keep her within arm's reach, he will become my prey. Best friend or not.

Instead of rushing this trip, I take my time. I absorb the chill of the fresh evening air, run my fingers over the crisp leaves, scooping up a bead of frost, and most importantly, I think about my next move.

Right now, Maddox and Riley are convinced Lev killed the men I took care of. They think he did it just to set Riley up. Her being set up was news to me because Maddox never once mentioned it, and now that I think about it, I still need to tear into him for that.

How dare he forget to tell me such pertinent information? If I had to guess, it was his dad's doing. Maddox has always been his dad's little puppet. Lev and I watched for years as he did everything he could to gain his father's approval, coming up short every time. His father always made him feel like a failure when, in reality, he never failed at all. He just didn't measure up to his father's impossibly high expectations. It still pisses me off that Maddox thinks he needs to.

Before I realize it, my thoughts have distracted me and I've only got about five more minutes before I reach the back of the campus. I need to think. *Fuck.* I need a plan.

Obviously, I won't let Lev go down for what I did, but I sure as hell don't plan to go down either. There are so many speculations circulating around us. Lev killing Cade and Zeke. Me killing the men who threatened Riley's future. Then, of course, there's Riley killing the governor. The scary thing is, they aren't just speculations—they're the truth.

I'm actually proud to admit that we're all a big mess of flawed and complex fuckery. Wouldn't have it any other way either. It's proof that there is no limit to how far we will go to protect those we care about.

Riley's happiness is my top priority. I'd take on the whole world if it means keeping her happy and safe.

I tiptoe toward the backside of the main building on campus, my boots crunching lightly on the mixture of dried leaves and gravel. Voices in the distance hit my ears and I rush behind it and flatten my body against the stone-cold structure, daring myself not to breathe.

The voices grow louder, but thankfully, no one has spotted me yet. My hearing is sharp and clear, so I pick out each one's voice in stark clarity.

One is most certainly Maddox's dad, Stanley Crane. The second is, without a doubt, Lev's uncle—Cade's dad. The third is a female and I can't quite figure out her identity, yet.

"We all have our own motives here, so don't play the holier-than-thou game with me, Marta,"

Marta. That's Lev's aunt.

I suppose it makes sense, considering Lev's uncle is here, but it's not often wives accompany their husbands when they're doing The Society's work. Then again, they did just lose their son.

I creep forward, careful not to make a sound, and peer around the corner of the building. I spot Lev's uncle in a black tee shirt that hugs his biceps. His arms wave in animated conversation as he speaks to the others who are out of view.

"Guess we're just not understanding why you're so hell-bent on blaming someone for Sebastian Saint's death. It was ruled a suicide. Let that be enough, Stanley."

He's referring to the governor, and for once, I agree with him. I wish everyone just let it be enough. Then my angel would be safe.

"Austin's right," Marta says. "It was an open-and-shut

case that was handled with the same care as any other member. Governor or not, he was no better than us."

"Where was that logic during your brother's murder?" Stanley asks. "You sure as hell didn't allow that case to be open and shut so quickly."

My jaw drops as the conversation shifts to a heavy one. It's been years since I've heard anyone talk about Lev's parents, who were brutally murdered in their home, along with Lev's two little sisters.

"As if I had a choice," Austin snaps. "Everyone knows that fucking rotten governor closed that case before anyone could even look at it."

I've always known the killer was never caught, but I had no idea it was because Governor Saint ended the investigation. The question is, why?

"With good reason." Stanley scoffs. "That bastard got what he deserved and I can pretty much guarantee his wife and girls were just in the wrong place at the wrong time."

I watch as Austin's face twists with rage. He steps forward, his long fingers lunging at Stanley's neck. Once he's got a good grip, he seethes, "Who the fuck do you think you are?"

I quickly return my back to the building. Is this really happening right now? Two Elders going at it, over what? A murder that took place years ago?

And how fucking ironic that I'm here witnessing this shit unfold. A devilish smile creeps across my face at the realization that we're only as fucked up as our predecessors.

Like father, like son.

If only I knew mine.

I bet he's a badass motherfucker. I imagine him as someone who parts a crowd when he enters a room. Or someone that stacks the bodies of his enemies—much like I do.

In reality, my father's a fucking coward who ran away when times got tough, but if I dwell on that, I can't help but feel that his cowardice is embedded in my veins. It's so damn difficult to accept that I'm related to a man who couldn't stand up and face his problems.

Peering around the corner again, I listen to the string of insults coming from both men.

"Now is not the time for this," Marta gripes, using her body as a wedge between Austin and Stanley. "Donald did what he had to do. You of all people should know how serious we have to take our assignments. It's nothing personal."

Donald is Lev's dad. Just the mention of his name sends chills down my spine. Donald and his wife, Becca, were hands down the kindest people in the world. Everyone loved them, which is another reason their murders came as such a shock to our small town of Glendale.

The words coming from Marta come as no surprise. I didn't know it at the time, but Lev's dad was a Punisher, just like Lev is. It's very common for sons of The Society to take on the same position as their fathers. In fact, it's extremely odd for them not to. Needless to say, my male ancestors are all Sleuths. I can only ascertain that Donald was killed out of revenge for a punishment he enacted.

"But what happened to him is more than personal," Austin snaps, giving Stanley a shove and freeing him from his vise grip. "Donald was a good man, and now all that's left of that family is my good-for-nothing nephew. And for you to open your fucking mouth and say he got what he deserved."

He jabs his middle finger in the air, directed at Stanley. "Fuck you."

What a fucking lying scoundrel. He's standing there defending his brother when he's been drugging his brother's son, just so he can take all his damn money.

It's taking everything in me not to round this corner and end Austin Pemberley myself. If anyone is good for nothing, it's that abusive narcissist.

"Donald was a good man, but Helen Foster was a good woman. And we all know what happened to her."

My lungs restrict at the mention of my mom's name. I hold my breath, and my eyes dart from person to person, searching for clues. My heart pounds as if it's trying to break through my rib cage.

To this day, I still don't know who took my mom's life, but with any luck, one of these assholes will throw a name out.

I know it was a member of The Society. A Punisher, perhaps? I've lived with the guilt of her death my entire life, knowing it was because I killed that man in our home. The Elders sealed the case, and she told me she got off scot-free after pleading self-defense. But he was still a member, and I took his life. Even if she did take the blame. When she went missing a few days later, I knew exactly why.

All because of me.

It's the number one reason I will reign over The Society one day. Why I will call the shots and I will punish everyone who wronged my family by taking my mom's life and forcing my dad away.

The Sleuth will become The Punisher.

"What's Helen have to do with this?" Marta asks, as oblivious as I am.

There's a beat of silence before Austin speaks up. "I never mentioned it because it wasn't necessary, but Donald is the one that was assigned to her case. It was the last case he had before his life was cut short. So myself, and others, have naturally assumed his demise was a revenge tactic for her death."

My muscles tense and I hold my breath as if the air has been stolen from me. My vision blurs and my head fogs up. His words echo in my mind, and I fight to make sense of his shocking revelation.

Donald Pemberley—Lev's dad—killed my mom?

How is this even possible? Does Lev know? Did he have time to even figure this one out? At the time, Lev didn't even know his dad was a Punisher, so I can't imagine he's aware.

But Donald? No way! The man was a saint.

I guess all saints have a past, but still. This doesn't make any sense.

I'm not sure what this means for Lev and me now. I don't know how I'll confront this, or if I even should. My mom is gone. Donald is gone. Years of plotting my own revenge on the man who took her life has just come to an abrupt stop.

Because his fate has already been sealed. Someone else killed him to avenge her. But who?

My mind swirls around a million different questions, while I try to process the information. I gasp for air, feeling like I've been submerged underwater and I'm now resurfacing.

Shock shifts to clarity. And this newfound knowledge sends heat rising from my stomach, as if a raging fire had been sparked.

I regain my focus and return to listening, hoping for more information.

"What about that morbid boy of hers, Ridge?" Marta asks, and any sympathy I felt toward her for being married to a fucking dickwad has diminished.

Stanley will defend me. I'm confident he will have my back. He raised me after I lost my mom. He's a second father to me.

"I've thought about that," Austin chimes in. "But he and my nephew are like brothers. Have been since they were tots. I don't think it was him."

Although I don't like the asshat, I'm grateful he's relieved me of suspicion because he's got one thing right. Lev and I are like brothers. However, had I known then what I know now, I would've got to Donald Pemberley—and Donald alone—before anyone else had a chance to end his life.

"Anything's possible," Stanley says, and my jaw returns to its dropped state. "I've considered Ridge for a while now. If he caught wind of Donald taking out his mom, I don't doubt for a second, he'd take matters into his own hands."

Un-fucking-believable! It feels like the floor has been pulled from beneath me. Fire burns the backs of my eyes, but I refuse to let these assholes have any power over me anymore.

Maddox's dad practically threw me under the bus. Lev's dad killed my mom. And an unknown person killed Lev's family out of revenge.

Is it possible this all stemmed from something I did when I was eleven years old? Did all these people lose their lives because I killed a man out of anger as a child?

"How about a deal?" Stanley says, and my ears perk up.

"A deal with you? Not a chance in hell."

"Might be easier to put all this shit behind us if we work together."

I hold my breath and lean in, not wanting to miss any of his words. I can feel in my bones the gravity of what he's about to negotiate for. My eyes dart among them and I try to get a read on Austin. His guard is up, but he looks intrigued.

"If it benefits you, fuck no. If it benefits me, let's hear the terms."

"You want your nephew found, correct?" Stanley asks him, and Austin's response is a stern nod. "And I want that Cross girl. I know damn well she's behind the governor's death, and chances are, she's holding on to a lot of information that could harm other members. We can't let that happen."

My teeth grind together and my fists clench into tight balls as I listen to them speak with such familiarity about the woman I love. My vision goes red with anger at the realization that this man, who I thought was a good, honest Elder, is just as crooked as the rest of them.

"So you want me to help you find the Cross girl, and you'll help me find Lev?"

"Something tells me when we find Lev, we'll find the girl, too."

The deal hangs heavy in the air as all three people remain silent. Each passing second has my heart racing with anticipation.

Then, Austin extends his hand, sealing the deal. "We better fucking find him."

I have to get to her.

Anger and frustration boil inside me, ripping away any thought of getting supplies and food. All I can think about is getting back to my Riley and Maddox so I can tell them everything.

My pace quickens as I resist the urge to go back and hear

more. I clutch the straps of one of the bags and hurry away from The Elders.

I can't risk them knowing I eavesdropped on their conversation. There is no doubt they'd have me hauled away, and there is too much at stake for that to happen.

My feet feel like they're on fire as they pound out a rhythm on the path behind the building.

Once I'm sure there is enough space between me and the school, I haul ass toward the trail, not stopping until I'm hitting the gravel road.

"Fuck!" I shout, hating that there are so many people searching for my girl. Maddox and I are only two people. How the hell are we supposed to hide her away from all of them?

There's only one option. We have to get the hell out of Boulder Cove. I don't care if we have to run forever. If it means she's safe, then so be it.

The cabin comes into view and I breathe a heavy sigh of relief as I jog up to it. My boots thud against the wood steps and I rip open the door. "Riley," I holler as my eyes skim the small space. "Maddox." I slam the door closed behind me and let the bags fall from my arm, hitting the floor with a gentle clap. "Where the hell are you guys?"

Rushing to the bathroom, I quickly fling it open but come face to face with disappointment when I see that it's empty.

With a quick glance into the small bedroom, I search for any sign of life. The blanket on the bed is rumpled, but the room is empty.

I walk back to the middle of the cabin and tip my head back, peering up at the loft. Light streams through the small window revealing nothing but decade-old cobwebs.

"Riley," I shout louder, but I get nothing in response. I reach into my pocket and pull out my phone, knowing it's a risk to turn it on, but I'm hopeful I'll have a message from one of them. If I see that I do, I'm tearing Maddox a new asshole for sending it in the first place. We can be traced and our phones are the easiest way to do that.

It takes a second to power on, and once it does, I swipe out of all my notifications, missed calls, and text messages, searching for two names in particular. But there's nothing. Not a single call or message from Maddox, Riley, or even Lev. I immediately shut it back down and stick it back in my pocket.

Pulling open the front door again, I step outside, leaving it open behind me. My eyes dart around the property, hoping to see a trace of them.

But, they're gone.

CHAPTER 4
MADDOX

"HOW MUCH FARTHER?" Riley asks as we continue down the trail. She ducks her head, dodging a branch, while hugging tightly to the navy blue coat that hangs off her shoulders. I found it in the closet at the cabin. It's a man's coat and based on the faint musty stench and the amount of dust on it, it's been hanging in there for years. It's keeping her warm, though, and that's all that matters.

"About another mile and we should be there."

"And you're certain no one will find us here?" she asks the dozenth question since we started our trek an hour ago.

"We'll be safe there. I promise."

Riley has no idea where we're going, but I'm certain once we arrive she'll know exactly where we are. All members who graduated from BCA know about the tunnels. They run underneath The Academy's property, with many entrances and exits. Of course, students frequent them because they're full of mystery and nostalgia, but there's a spot, in particular, no one inhabits. That's where I'm taking Riley for the foreseeable future.

Riley's foot slips out from underneath her as she steps over a half-rotten log on the trail, and my arms sweep out catching her fall. "Jesus," she gripes. "It's like a tornado ripped through these woods."

"You're not lying," I tell her. "Doesn't look like there's been much foot traffic on these trails in a while."

Her feet slow and mine do the same to keep going at her pace. "You're sure we're heading in the right direction?"

"Absolutely," I tell her, scouring the area nervously, hoping like hell I'm right.

It's been four years since I've been out here and I'm starting to think me and the guys were the last ones to take this path, considering how overgrown it is. Now that I think about it, that might actually work in our favor. The less people that know this area, the better.

A few minutes later, I see what I've been looking for. A smile grows on my face as I take Riley's hand. "This way," I tell her, pulling her with me as I pick up my pace.

It's an old cabin that's been here since before my grandparents' parents' time. Probably even before their parents, too. While it's similar to the one we were staying in that Lev owns, this one is different because of the shelter underneath. What's even more compelling is the history of The Blue Bloods that's found underground. Maps, pictures, and letters dated back to the beginning of our times as The Society.

It's also been fenced off to keep students out, and if any are caught out here, they face expulsion from BCA. It's privately owned by a member now, though I'm not quite sure who.

"It's been so long since I've been here," I tell Riley. "I can't believe this place is still standing."

Riley pushes herself up on her tiptoes to steal a glance at the old cabin sitting a few hundred yards away.

She stops moving and tugs back on my hand. "No, Maddox." Her face pales as her fingers tighten around mine. With a trembling voice, she whispers, "We have to go now."

"Baby," I say softly as I step in front of her. My hands glide to her waist. "What's wrong?"

Shaking her head, she chokes on the words as they come out of her mouth. "We can't be here."

I chuckle in response. "It's fine. The guys and I used to come here all the time. I know they've closed it off since then, but no one lives here, and no one visits."

"This," she begins, eyes darting over my shoulder toward the cabin. "This is Scar's parents' cabin. They've owned it for years."

"No shit," I wheeze. "How fucking ironic. But it still doesn't explain why you look like you've seen a ghost."

Riley gulps, still stunned for whatever reason. "Do you know what's underneath this place?"

I'm taken aback at the fact that *she* knows what's underneath this place. I shouldn't be, though, considering her best friend's parents own it.

"A bunch of old artifacts and papers," I tell her. "Some of which are interesting, others that are boring as hell."

"It's a record of us, Maddox. Of our ancestors." She shivers, as if a cold chill just ran down her spine. "It was also Governor Saint's lair when he was stalking Scar, and all of us, during our senior year at Boulder Cove Academy."

"Holy shit." I draw my fingers around my mouth as I glance over my shoulder at the cabin. "I had no fucking idea." I return my eyes to hers, understanding why she's so scared right now. "Like I said, I haven't been here in years. I heard it was fenced off and there was an order in place for students not to trespass, but I didn't know why."

"Scar's parents put up the 'no trespassing' signs and put in the order with The Academy. They made it clear that if anyone came on this property, they would be reported to The Elders."

"And the room underground?" I ask her, curious what's happened with that.

"It's been emptied. They struck a deal and agreed to hand over all the paraphernalia to The Elders so it could be sealed and kept safe, so long as they kept the rule in place that students were forbidden to enter the cabin and the east end of the tunnels. They've been closed off with a vault door."

My inquiring mind is dying to see the inside of the cabin and the room beneath it. I know teenagers, and when they are told that something is off-limits, they want to know why. There is no way in hell not a single student has jumped this fence and ransacked the cabin.

I look at Riley, though her blank stare is focused on the space behind me. "We don't have to go. If I'd known that this place was connected—"

"Actually." She pauses, her tongue darting out to wet her lips nervously as her gaze shifts to mine. "I changed my mind."

My eyebrows rise to my forehead. "You did?"

"Yeah." She nods. "First of all, you left Ridge a note to meet us here. Second, for over a year, I've struggled to come to terms with what I did, but being here right now is a reminder of why I shouldn't have regrets. I want to see that room."

She brushes past me, the fabric of the old coat grazing the sleeve of my hoodie. Her feet gently crunch on dry leaves and twigs as she zigzags around the trees, heading right for the cabin.

I jog to catch up and walk by her side. "You're sure about this? We can hide out somewhere else." I need to be sure this is going to benefit Riley and not hurt her more in the long run. There's no saying what sort of memories are going to be dredged up once she's entered that place. She went through a traumatic ordeal because of the crooked governor and I'd hate for all her progress to be for nothing.

"I *have* to do this, Maddox." Her eyes don't even meet mine as she speaks, and it's apparent she is a woman on a mission. "Can you stand guard while I go inside?"

"Not a chance in hell. If you're going in there, so am I."

"Fine." She raises her shoulders, letting them drop slowly. "But if we get caught…"

"We won't. It's not like there's a guard out here. It's the sole reason I knew it would be safe to hide here."

Riley stops abruptly and grabs the sleeve of my hoodie, jerking me around a tree. "There's a camera." She gasps. "Fuck!"

I peer around to try to get a look, and sure enough, there's a mounted black camera pointed right at us. I step out to get a better look when Riley hisses, "What the hell are you doing?"

"We're too far away from any towers. There's no way they have a Wi-Fi signal out here." I walk closer to the side of the cabin where the camera is mounted, knowing it's already recorded us. "Chances are, it's recording to a USB card." My eyes skim the ground, and when I spot a long enough stick, I pick it up.

"What are you doing?" Riley asks breathlessly.

Without responding, I swing the stick outward and bring it forward, hitting the camera hard enough to knock it down.

Once it hits the ground, I stomp the toe of my boot to it repeatedly.

"Maddox!"

"It had to be done," I tell her.

"No shit." She crouches down and picks up the remnants of the camera. "But this is what we need." Holding a small chip in the air, she smiles widely.

I lean down and press my lips to hers. "Good thinking, baby."

She stands up from her crouched position, wiping the dirt off her hands with a satisfied smirk on her face. "And now we search for more."

Ten minutes later, we've found three other cameras—one on each side of the cabin. Riley now has a stash of micro-USBs in the palm of her hand.

"Think there's more inside?" she asks me as she stuffs them into the pocket of the coat she's wearing.

"It's possible," I tell her, looking at the front door of the cabin. "We can't take any chances. We need to make sure every surface and corner is checked because if we're shown on those cameras, we're screwed."

Not wasting any time, Riley walks up the steps to the cabin. Her hand rests on the handle and I hear her audible exhale as she pushes the door open. I stay back, giving her a minute to reflect on her time at this place.

She stands frozen in the doorway, as if she's peering into her past.

"You okay?" I ask, slowly making my way toward her.

Her head twitches toward the sound of my voice, a broad

smile on her face that takes me by surprise. "Yeah. I think I am."

Three long strides bring me to her and I place a comforting hand on her hip as we step into the unknown.

"It's just how I remember it," she says, her voice nothing short of a whisper.

I follow her line of sight, taking in the abandoned space.

My first instinct is to skim the area for cameras, but I don't see any in plain sight, so I think we're out of the eye of the owner.

There's an old couch in the small living space to the left. The fabric is worn and faded and dare I say, in worse shape than the one in Lev's cabin. A tall grandfather clock with tarnished brass hands sits against a wall and isn't ticking.

In the center of the kitchen area is a round, wooden table with old newspapers on it. I walk over to them and run my fingers under one in particular from 1963.

"Damn. This is some old shit in here."

"Over here," Riley says, beckoning me to her side. I drop the paper and go to where she's standing, angling my body to follow the line of her gaze. Her eyes are fixed on a piece of wood flooring that seems to be out of place. "That's the door to the underground room."

"That's it, huh?" I draw in a sharp breath. "Then what are we waiting for?" I crouch down and drag my fingers along the edges, hoping to get a grip, to no avail.

Riley steps away as I fight with the damn floor to open, returning a moment later with a screwdriver. Without a word, she jabs it into a crack like she's stabbing her worst enemy. Then she bends the screwdriver and lifts part of the flooring.

"Damn, baby," I say in a slow breath. "Have I ever told you how sexy you are when you're determined?"

She cracks a smile and continues to lift the flooring, now using her fingers. The next thing I know, it's open and I'm staring down into a pitch-black hole.

On my hands and knees, I look over the ledge, noticing a ladder. Immediately, I fling my legs over and step onto the first plank. "Guess we're going in blind since we have no light."

Riley's eyes widen in surprise. "You brought us all the way out here and didn't bring any source of light in your trusty backpack?"

My shoulders lift and I squint in regret. "Our supplies were limited since Ridge took so long." I reach one hand toward her. "Come on. I'll be the eyes for us both. I promise I won't let anything happen to you."

Hesitantly, she takes my hand then sighs heavily. "I'm trusting you, Maddox Crane."

"As you should."

I'm forced to let go of her hand as I climb down, but she's coming right behind me. Or, above me. However it's described in a situation as such.

As I descend, I can't help but feel the weight of guilt heavy on my chest. Riley trusts me, but she shouldn't.

The truth is, I haven't been honest with her. The note I left for Ridge didn't tell him my plan. In fact, he's not coming at all because he has no idea where we are.

When I overheard her talking to Scar about leaving to find Lev on her own, I knew I couldn't let that happen.

Not only did I bring Riley here so she could hide out for a while, but I have every intention of keeping her here until I know it's safe for her to leave. Even if it means keeping her against her will.

I just hope she understands I'm doing it with her best interests at heart. Because I love her—and I won't lose her.

CHAPTER 5
RILEY

MY PLAN FAILED. After Ridge left, I was supposed to leave the cabin and go into town on foot to buy my own supplies for myself.

I need to find Lev. He is the missing link right now, and the only one who can save me by offering his own truth to The Elders.

As I was heading out the door, Maddox joined my side and said we needed to leave, fast. Now here we are, climbing down a ladder and entering the very room a monstrous man made his dark lair over a year ago.

When I first realized where we were, I was stunned. Traumatized by the events of my past, I didn't think I'd ever be able to face this place, or anything that held reminders of the governor, ever again.

But something woke inside me. A light was turned on, and suddenly, life was breathed back into my soul. Bravery washed over me unexpectedly and I suddenly had the urge to confront my fear and prove something to it.

For the first time since that bullet left the gun, it feels like

I can face all of my problems head-on and leave the past behind. Despite any inner turmoil brewing in my stomach, I know, deep down, I have to try—that somehow facing it all will lead me toward the redemption I so desperately need.

The second my feet hit solid ground, I close my eyes, taking in the familiar scent. Allowing myself to fully embrace this healing process.

Falling into a cave of madness,
Like creatures in the night.
Fretful memories fill my mind,
As we leave the last bit of light.

"You okay?" Maddox asks, his comforting hand returning to my hip. It's something he does frequently when he suspects I'm in distress, and it works. Maddox is the calm to my storm, and I'm not sure how I'd get through any of this without him—without any of them.

My mind wanders to Lev. I hope he's safe, wherever he is. As angry as I am with him for what he's done to himself and to me, I can't force myself not to care.

"Yeah," I finally say to Maddox, allowing my eyes to open. There's a glint of light coming down the ladder, so we're able to see a small area of the room, but it won't last long. "The sun is beginning to set. We need to find light."

"That we do." He squeezes my hip. "Was there any electricity running to this place last time you were here?"

"No. But there were lanterns. Do you think they may have been left behind?"

I've been here a few times, so I remember this place well. It isn't quite as traumatic for me as it would be for Scar, considering the governor was after her. He filled a small room with everything there was to know about her. Old paper clippings, reports, and pictures. Chills run down my spine at the thought. For me, it's more of a reminder of taking his life and an even bigger reminder of why I shouldn't regret what I did.

Governor Saint was pure evil in the worst form. And I can finally admit, Scar was right—I am a hero. Even if it's only in my own story.

"Jackpot." Maddox beams, holding up something I can't quite make out. I stick close to his side, still uncertain that something won't jump out around a corner at us.

With the flick of his finger, we have light.

"Hell yes!" I throw myself into his arms, shaking the lantern and flickering the flame. "I can't believe they left one down here."

Once I free him from my hold, he walks a few feet to a desk attached to the wall. "Not just one," he chirps as he picks up another lantern. "But two."

This one gives him a little more trouble, but after a couple minutes, he brings the flame to life and hands me the lantern.

I hold it up, scouring the area, and much to my surprise, the entire place is empty. "This is nothing like it was last year," I tell him. "There was so much stuff down here before. So many papers and pictures."

"I heard they cleared it out. Guess I heard right."

My eyes land on the door that leads to the tunnels. "Think anyone is out there?"

"Nah. At least, not this far down. I'm sure some rebellious students from BCA still venture this way, but they can't get past the vault door farther down, or the one we're looking at now."

Maddox returns to the ladder and looks up, before handing me his lantern. "Hold that for a sec." I take it from him and he climbs up before pulling the door down with a thud. Back at my side, I return his lantern to him. "We can't risk someone else going into the cabin and seeing the door."

"And Ridge?" I ask him. "How will he know where to find us?"

"Umm. Yeah, Ridge knows to go to the cabin. He knows about the door. Don't worry, babe. He'll be here eventually."

There's an unease in his tone that raises goosebumps on my arms. "Okay," I say because that's all I can say. I trust Maddox, and I know Ridge would cross oceans to keep me safe. "So what now?"

"Now..." he begins, holding his lantern up with his eyes on the door. "We need to get through that door. That's where we'll be safe."

"What about food and warmth? It's fucking cold down here."

Maddox pats his hand to his backpack. "I've got some stuff to last us for a couple days. As for warmth." His eyebrows waggle as he slithers up to me. "My body will offer you all the heat you need." His mouth draws lines on my neck, moving downward. Using his chin, he nudges my sweatshirt and kisses the tip of my shoulder.

I suck in the corner of my lip to mask the nervous energy bubbling in the pit of my stomach. Stuck in a dark tunnel with this sexy man, hell yes. Goes to show that looking on the bright side has its perks, even in a time like this.

"But first," he lifts his head, before pressing his mouth to mine, "we need to get through that door."

His backpack slides down his arm and he reaches inside, retrieving some sort of tool. A crowbar, perhaps.

I scoff. "That would've been handy when we were trying to get the trapdoor open."

"I would've remembered it eventually had you not been a badass with that screwdriver." He smirks as he gets to work on the door.

"You know," I tell him. "If we can get through it, that means anyone else can."

"Always a pessimist," he teases. "I told you, baby. I've got you."

Twenty minutes later, and I'm no longer worried about anyone getting through the door—because we can't get through it either.

With my back pressed against the wall and my ass planted firmly on the cement floor, I try to hide my impatience because I know Maddox is getting as frustrated as I am. The lantern beside me flickers, and I'm hoping like hell it doesn't extinguish before we get out of here.

Bringing my head back and forth, the clip holding my hair up clanks against the cement wall. Over, and over, and over again.

"Ry," Maddox says sharply.

My eyes perk up. "Yeah?"

"You're gonna bruise your head, and my ears, if you keep doing that."

"Oh," I grumble. "Is that bothering you?" I repeat the motions, this time with slower, more deliberate knocks against the wall. And while it does hurt a little, I'm too stubborn to stop.

Maddox lets out an exasperated sigh as his forearm swipes across his forehead, wiping up the sweat forming around his hairline.

His hands drop to his sides, still holding the crowbar, and he rests his head back.

Feeling the agitation inside me bubble to the surface, I

push harder for a reaction, because like Scar said, I'm my own worst enemy. "Are you planning to get us out of here, or would you like me to do it?"

His eyes slide to mine and the scowl on his face is the reaction I was hoping for because it proves I'm not alone in my misery.

"You think you can get the damn thing open?" He hands me the crowbar, and I'm a bit surprised. I didn't actually expect him to take me up on my offer. "Have at it."

I push myself off the floor and snatch it from his hand, and without a word, I begin trying in the same way he was because I have no fucking clue how to open this door.

With the end of the hook in the crack of the door, I pry with all my might, as if the thing is just going to pop open.

I grunt and groan and when I hear the sounds of chuckles behind me, I growl. "As if you were doing any better."

Not giving up, I try again. But when the next sound ringing in my ear is the constant drumming of fingers against the bottom of a flipped-over bucket, I lose it.

My hands fall to my sides and I spin around. "Are you trying to be annoying?"

"Oh. I'm sorry. Is that bothering you?"

"Don't be an ass," I snap, returning to the task at hand.

The drumming stops and I immediately feel his presence behind me. "Is this what I think it is?" Maddox asks, his breath hot against my neck.

"What are you talking about?" My words are still laced with disdain as I try to keep up this tough-girl persona.

He steps closer, his hands tracing the curves of my body through the multiple layers of clothing I've got on. Goosebumps spill down my back, responding to his touch. "This," he says softly. "You and me." In a swift motion, he spins me around with an intensity that makes me dizzy. His lips curl into a mischievous smile as his wandering eyes find my mouth. "Are we having our first argument?" Not willing to back down just yet, I fight to avoid eye contact and find myself watching the way his lips move as he speaks. "I think it's time we kiss and make up."

"Is that what you think?" I say, dropping the crowbar to the floor. It hits with a loud clunk before settling beside my foot.

"I'm sorry, babe. I don't wanna fight with you."

"Then don't," I tell him before my mouth crushes his. I press my body against him, melting into his embrace. His hands glide up my shirt, across my back, and settle on my hips.

My inner thighs pulsate, the feeling riding upward until I feel my desire for him soaking my panties.

Maddox's fingers teeter on the hem of my joggers, while his other hand still rests firmly on my hip.

"I need you," I hum into his mouth. While this might not be the optimal time to fool around, I don't foresee us doing much else anytime soon. Might as well take advantage.

In a swift motion, he shoves his hand down my pants and my insides shiver with excitement. "Like this?" he grumbles into my mouth.

"More."

Two fingers drag between my lips, stopping on my sensitive nub. "How about this?" He rubs vicious circles around my clit and a raspy moan climbs up my throat.

I lean into him, resting my face in the crease of his neck. I draw in a deep breath and inhale his woodsy scent. Everything about this—about him—has me so turned on right now.

"Getting there," I tell him. "But I need more."

It's not a want—it's a need. A manic energy pulsing through my veins. If I don't climax soon, I fear I will explode from the force of my own desperation.

When his fingers prod at my entrance, I instinctively separate my legs, granting him access. The back of his hand grates against my thigh as he pushes two fingers inside me.

Maddox grabs one of my legs and lifts it to his side, holding it in place as he walks me backward, still fingering me. I'm impressed with his ability to multitask, but even more impressed by the way his fingers work their magic inside me. My back hits the cement wall with a thud, my spine crushing against it.

He growls an anguished sound, heady and full of longing. "I need you just as bad as you need me, baby."

"Fuck me." My words come out as a strained plea mixed with a moan that rattles my chest. "Please."

"Not yet," he responds as his fingers delve deeper inside me.

My head rolls back against the wall and my eyes close. Warm lips make their way to my neck and his tongue lingers in all the right places.

He adds a third finger, spreading me wide, but it's still not enough. "Deeper," I beg.

A yelp is thrust out of me when he pushes his hand up, knuckle deep, practically punching my vagina. Again, and again, and again.

Cries of pleasure echo in the small space as my body rides up and down the wall with each plunge of his fingers.

My eyes open to find his lustful ones staring back at me. Mouth agape, it's apparent he's just as desperate for my climax as I am.

Sinking deep inside me, he works in circles, every few seconds hitting my G-spot, and each time, I wail in ecstasy.

The pressure against my hips intensifies as he thrusts harder. My back arches instinctively, and I let out a sharp cry of pleasure. His fingers dig into the flesh of my hip as he keeps me pinned in place.

"Maddox," I moan. "Oh god."

Proof of my orgasm oozes from my core and runs down my inner thigh.

"God has nothing to do with this, baby. Unless I'm your god tonight."

He drops my leg with a satisfied look on his face, and before I can inflate my lungs, he spins my body around, giving him my backside. Taking one hand, he presses my open palm to the wall, then the other.

The second he jerks my joggers down, I shiver. He removes one boot, then the next, and I step out of them with my hands remaining where he placed them.

With a jerk of my hips, he arches my back, and I bend slightly at the knees.

"Take a deep breath for me," he says with authority.

Just as I do what I'm told—inhaling slowly and deeply—Maddox forcefully shoves his cock inside me, driving the air back out of my lungs.

My head nearly hits the wall, so I press my hands to it harder, using all my strength to keep myself up.

His hands squeeze my hips with tenacity as he thrusts himself in and out of me, his pelvis ricocheting off my ass.

"Damn, baby. It's a beautiful view back here." He smacks a hand hard against my ass cheek then returns it to my hip. His words appease me, but the sting on my ass turns me the fuck on. "You gonna come for me again?"

"Yes," I whimper.

He smacks my ass again, this time harder. I yelp and smile at the same time.

"I didn't quite hear you."

"Yes," I say louder. "I'm gonna come for you again."

His hand returns to my hip once more. "That's my girl."

With his breaths growing rapid and unfulfilled, he rocks his core against mine, driving himself in and out of me.

One hand slides around to my front, settling between my wide-spread thighs. Warm, slippery fingers glide between my slick folds, stopping on my clit.

"This ought to do the trick." The pads of his fingers rub vicious circles against my throbbing clit.

Each thrust of his cock is deeper than the last, and I cry out in extreme pleasure. "Holy fuck, Maddox."

He leans forward slightly, cloaking my back with his chest as he whispers in my ear, "I love the way you say my name."

I rest my head back, desperate to feel each shallow breath he exhales as I come undone.

His body trembles on top of mine and my hands begin to slide down the wall as my soul leaves my body.

"Goddamn, baby." He growls headily. His breaths begin to come out in pants and I can feel his legs shaking behind me. With one final deep thrust, he comes undone, falling with me. I slide down the floor until I'm on my hands and knees, with his cock still inside me.

"That was amazing," he says, before pressing a chaste kiss to the back of my head. "Damn," he drags out the word.

It takes me a minute to snap out of the haze of ecstasy I'm in, but once I do, I feel his body slowly slide away from mine. I stand up, now with a clear head, and the evidence of our orgasms mingle together, dripping down my leg.

Maddox holds out my joggers from where he stands behind me. "Here you go."

"Thank you," I say as I take them from him. I pull the inside-out leg on one side, and at the same time, his chin rests on my shoulder.

His jaw grinds against the bone in my shoulder as he speaks. "I don't think we're getting out of here."

I smirk. "Is that such a bad thing?"

"Nope. It just means we need to secure that trapdoor so no one can come down."

I spin around with my pants still in my hand, eyes wide. And it's not because of the words that are about to leave my mouth. "What about Ridge?"

The truth is, it's because I need to leave. Me and me alone.

"We'll give him until midnight tonight. If he doesn't come down by then, we have to secure it. It's too much of a risk not to."

The thought of Ridge trying to get in so he can be with me, but not being able to, has my heart aching.

It won't happen, though. Because I'm getting out of here first.

I must escape,
I cannot stay.
Not because I'm weak,
But because I am brave.

CHAPTER 6
LEV

PACING the length of the apartment I share with the guys in the summers, I replay the last twenty-four hours in my head as if doing so is going to solve all my problems. I need to talk to Riley. She needs to understand I wasn't in my right mind when I started framing her for those murders. I saw her as a threat to the only relationships I have and I wanted her gone. But that was before I fell madly in love with her.

I haven't decided if I'm going to tell her it was Ridge who killed those men, because I probably shouldn't burn any more bridges with the only people who give a damn about me. But I won't lie. That, I know for sure.

No more lies.

Dammit. I need to make a move. Be it offing my uncle, or torturing the fuck out of that scumbag therapist, Dr. Edmonds. Only then will I be able to go to her safely.

I snatch up my notepad on the small round table off the kitchen. It was left on the bed in my dorm room. It's the same engraved notepad we get at the beginning of each school year with our assignment listed on the front page. The thing is, I already got mine.

Opening the page, I read the note again.

> *Find and capture, fellow Blue Blood member, Riley Cross.*
>
> *You have been sentenced, and she will be punished.*
>
> *If you fail, you will face the consequence of total banishment as a member of The Society.*
>
> *Sincerely,*
> *Austin Pemberley*

"Over my dead body." I growl as I chuck the notebook at the wall.

Not only did that son of a bitch work with my therapist to keep me on meds that made me feel fucking insane, but he's also doing it to try and claim that I am insane, so he can be named my guardian. All because he wants my damn money. Money that I don't even want. Yeah. I'm filthy fucking rich—set for life. But what good is money when you have no one to enjoy it with?

My mind is made up. I know my next move.

Austin Pemberley, aka Uncle dearest, needs to fucking die.

With the pedal to the floor of my black Bugatti Veyron, I drive as fast as I can back to Boulder Cove. Students aren't allowed to have vehicles but fuck the rules.

I know he's there. Not only did he leave the notebook on my bed, while I was caught blindsided by Riley at my cabin, but I also saw him. Walking with his shoulders drawn back and his chest puffed out like he's The President of The Society and an untouchable force. Granted, he's the leader of all The Punishers, but he's not untouchable. He's as replaceable as the cellphone I'm powering on.

I press the button on the steering wheel and wait for the beep. "Call Ridge."

I'm sure I'm the last person Ridge or Maddox want to talk to, but I need to know Riley is safe. I've also gotta fill him in on my plan. In the past, I'd work alone, not giving a damn who knew what I was up to. But that was then, and this is now. I feel more myself than I ever have, and the old me would have made sure my friends knew what I was about to do.

The phone rings through the speakers of the car and after the fifth ring, it goes to voicemail.

"It's Ridge. You know what to do."

"Hey, man. Call me as soon as possible. We need to talk."

I end the call and bite the bottom of my lip, wondering if it's even worthwhile to try Maddox. It's apparent they're ignoring me. Don't blame 'em, really. They know I'm the one who killed Zeke and assaulted Riley. Once again, it wasn't me. And it wasn't even really assault. Jesus, people are so quick to assume these days. First of all, I never drugged her. I must've just dropped the pill I stuffed in my pocket when I decided I wasn't going to take it. I didn't even know she was drunk until I got her halfway to her orgasm. She got off on my fingers inside her and never once asked me to stop, so I didn't.

If at any point in time she said 'no' that would have been the end of it.

I think.

Maybe not because I don't know who that guy was who entered her room that night. But there isn't a doubt in my mind I would've stopped now.

"Fuck!" I slam my hands to the steering wheel. When did all this shit get so fucking messy?

I'm snapped from my thoughts when my phone starts ringing. Ridge's name flashes on the screen, and I immediately hit Answer.

"Where the hell are they?" he shouts before I can even say hello.

I turn the volume down a few notches, so he's not screaming in my ear. "Where the hell is who?"

"You know exactly who I'm talking about. What did you do with Riley and Maddox?"

My hands coil around the steering wheel as my foot smashes down hard on the brakes. I skid off the road and onto the shoulder, throwing a cloud of dust in my wake. My whole body lurches forward against the seat belt as I come to a complete stop. "Riley's missing?"

"Don't play games with me, Lev."

"Shut the fuck up and tell me what the hell is going on right now, or so help me God..."

My heart hammers in my chest as a million possibilities cross my mind. *Someone took her.* What if it was my uncle? What if it was a family member of those men Ridge murdered, all because they think it was her?

"I swear on everything, Lev, if you're fucking lying to me right now, I will hunt you down." His voice rises with each word. "And I will slit your goddamn throat!"

Rage consumes me because this jackass is being impossible right now.

"Do it, asshole. I fucking dare you! Come find me and we'll see who leaves with their vocal cords intact."

"Where the hell is she?!" His screams are deafening to the point I'm forced to turn the volume down more. "Tell me!"

But I scream back just as loud because, who the fuck does this guy think he is accusing me of shit? "I don't know!"

"I don't believe you, Lev." His voice lowers to a near shout. "I don't believe a damn word you say now that I know it was you. You killed Zeke and framed Cade, then you killed Cade and you're letting her take the fucking fall for it. What a man you are." He laughs, though the sound is empty of humor. "Nah. You're just a fucking pussy."

"Is that so?" I hum. "You forgot a few people there, Ridge."

"What the fuck are you talking about?"

"The ones I framed Riley for. All those men who were murdered. Their bodies were lit on fire and evidence was left behind that connected her to them. You all think I killed them, right?"

"I don't give a fuck about those guys. This has nothing to do with them."

"Doesn't it, though? Isn't Riley being accused of murdering them, too?"

The line goes silent for a moment before Ridge finally says, "It was you. I thought it was Cade, but it was you, wasn't it?"

"If you're asking if I killed them, I think we both know the answer to that."

"Eric Mathers," he says the name, as if it's supposed to mean anything to me. "He was the last name on the list and once I crossed it off, I saw a shadow in the woods. I tried to catch the guy, but I wasn't fast enough and he got away. I thought it was Cade, but it was you." His voice rises a few octaves. "You knew this whole time it was me and you set her up! Why the hell would you do that?"

He's right. From the very first murder, I knew it was him. Ridge stalked Riley, and I stalked them both. I watched everyone. I paid attention to every calculated detail and formed my own plan for the good of my future. I had to look after myself because no one else was going to. At that time, I was doing it to protect Ridge, and even Maddox, as I saw him slowly falling for Riley, too. With her out of the picture, they were safe, and what better way to get her out of the picture than to set her up for the crimes Ridge committed? She wasn't innocent by any means—she killed our state governor. In my head, it was all justified. But my mind was in a fog and I hadn't thought clearly in years.

I just never expected to fall for her, too.

"Answer me, dammit!"

I rest my head back with my hands still gripping the steering wheel. "I did it for you! Okay. Are you happy? I did it for you and Maddox. I saw her as a threat to you, and to our friendship. I knew they suspected her of the governor's death and I thought for sure she was going to drag you both down. So I tried to get rid of her."

"Why the hell didn't you just tell us?"

"As if you'd listen to me. I was a joke to you and Maddox. I heard the whispers. Don't act like you guys didn't keep shit from me just because you were worried about how I'd react."

"Well, for fuck's sake, Lev. Do you blame us? Look at what you did?"

"Me?" I huff. "You murdered four fucking men for her. Is it so crazy that I assumed the girl had you in over your head?"

His silence is telling.

"Exactly my point," I say. "Look. We all did some seriously fucked-up shit. We've all killed with her in mind."

"We are pretty unhinged, aren't we?"

I chuckle. "We're fucking deranged. At least one of us turned out okay. There's still hope for Maddox."

"Speaking of Maddox, we need to find them. I'm not saying I believe you didn't have anything to do with their disappearance. But if I did, do you have any idea where they might have gone, or who might have taken them?"

"One hundred fucking percent. It has to be my uncle."

"I disagree."

His words take me by surprise. "You do?"

"There's a lot of shit we need to talk about. Where are you?"

"Heading back to campus as we speak." I glance at the clock on the dash. "Should be there in about forty-five minutes."

"Don't go there. Meet me at the cabin."

"Fine. But this better not be some sort of trap."

"Ditto, fucker."

The line goes dead and the only thought in my mind as I take off speeding to get to my friend is her. *I need you to be okay, Trouble.*

CHAPTER 7
MADDOX

LYING on the cold cement floor, Riley rests her head on my lap and wraps her arm around my torso. Guilt washes over me, knowing that I brought her here with nothing more than a few snacks and bottles of water. If my body could be the bed she lies on and the heat that warms her, I'd do it in a second. But she insists she's fine.

My fingers stroke her head, tangling in her messy, beautiful hair. Her eyes open and she turns slightly, cracking a smile. "Thank you for hiding away with me," she says, as if I'd be anywhere else.

"You never have to thank me, babe. I'd hide away with you forever if it meant spending forever by your side."

She squeezes my body tighter, returning to her position with her eyes closed. "I don't deserve you, Maddox Crane."

"I beg to differ. I am the one who doesn't deserve you, Riley Cross."

I don't think I've ever spoken truer words. This girl is pure gold and I am nothing but worthless common metal.

Her head snaps back around until she's staring up at me.

"You better quit being so hard on yourself. You're the type of man that little girls dream of marrying one day. You're a saint."

I shake my head slowly. "Nah. I'm no saint. I'm a sinner through and through."

"We all sin, Maddox. We're human. But please stop doubting yourself. You're a good man."

"The only good part of me is you."

She chuckles as she closes her eyes again, and I resume stroking her hair. "You're impossible is what you are. I guess I'll let you be blind to your saintliness and I'll just be the eyes that see it for you."

My lips curve into a smile as if trying to convince myself that I am the saintly man she thinks I am. But no matter how hard I try, I can't shake the feelings of guilt and regret, refusing to let me forget what I've done and what I continue to do.

A few minutes later, her audible breaths have her nostrils flaring. I watch for a moment as she sleeps peacefully before resting my head back on the wall and trying to get some shut-eye myself.

―――

I'm startled awake at the repetitive sound of a gentle thrash. My eyes snap open and I squint at the darkness around me. Then, I realize Riley is no longer on my lap. I jump up, a twist of fear in my stomach. "Riley," I call out.

The sounds stop.

I reach down beside the wall and grab my lantern, quickly bringing the flame to life. I hold it up, and I see her standing as still as can be at the top of the ladder.

"What the hell are you doing?" I hurry over to the ladder and peer up, breathing a sigh of relief when I see that the trapdoor is still closed.

"I have to get out of here, Maddox. I'm sorry. But I can't stay any longer."

"We have no choice, babe. Please just come back down. You need to rest. We can figure something out in the morning."

"But it is morning, Maddox. I can see a crack of light coming through the boards."

Damn. I must've been really fucking tired to have slept all night. Then again, I have no idea what time it was when I dozed off.

"How about if we try and get through the door again? We'll be safe on the other side."

"No!" she snaps. "I'm not staying here another night, or another day. I'm leaving, and you can come with me, or you can stay behind."

I set the lantern on the floor beside the ladder and take a step up, willing to carry her down if need be. No matter what, I am not letting her get out that door.

"Baby, please. Just come down so we can talk about this."

Ignoring my plea, she begins pushing on the trapdoor again. "This thing is fucking stuck!"

"As it should be. We can't leave, and no one can get it in."

"Maddox, please," she cries. "I'm suffocating down here. I need to get out."

I take another step up. "Just calm down. Everything is fine."

"Don't tell me to calm down!" Her voice cracks with

frustration. "This is not a calm situation. I'm worried about Ridge. He should have been here by now."

"Baby..." I say softy as I keep moving upward. "I'm going to help you back down."

"Stop!" she shouts. "Don't take another step. I love you Maddox, but I'm not coming down. Something had to have happened to Ridge."

"Is this really about Ridge? Or is this about your desperate attempt to escape and find Lev?"

Her face twists in confusion. "What makes you think I want to find Lev?"

She's within arm's reach now, but I think I can coerce her down without physical force. "I know what you were planning, babe. You were going to sneak off and try to find Lev because you think he's the only person who can end this madness."

"You were eavesdropping on my conversation with Scar, weren't you?"

"I may have overheard."

"So what? You brought me here to stop me from going to find him?"

My silence is telling and she scoffs. "You fucking tricked me, didn't you? And Ridge?"

I bite the corner of my lip, realizing I fucked up again. But, I'd do it over and over again to keep her safe. "Just come back down."

"No! You lied to me, Maddox. Ridge isn't coming, is he? Does he ever know we're here?"

I give nothing but more silence and it only pisses her off more.

"Oh my god! I can't believe you did this. He is probably worried sick right now."

"Ridge is resourceful and I'm sure he knows you're safe since you're with me."

"Does he, though? Does he know that? For all you know, he could think we were both taken in by The Elders."

"No. He would have caught wind of your capture by now. If anything, he's out there trying to clear your name. So let him. Let him do all the work, while I keep you safe...here."

"Is anyone out there?" Riley begins screaming as she pounds on the trapdoor. "Someone, please let me out!"

I move quickly up the ladder until I'm on the same step as her. Grabbing her hands, I hold them at her sides as she fights me, and I fight not to send us both falling down. "Stop!" I demand. "You're wasting your energy and doing yourself no good. No one is out there, and no one is coming."

"You fucking tricked me, Maddox! You lied to me!" Tears stream down her face and my heart splinters.

"I'm so sorry. I just couldn't let you run off and risk getting caught. Once they have you, they won't hear anything you have to say. We'd never see you again."

"It's still my choice to make. Not yours!"

In a swift motion, I grab her by the waist and squeeze her body tightly to mine, holding her up with one arm. She wails and screams, but I hold tightly to the edge of the ladder and turn around to descend backward.

"Let me go! I'm so fucking mad at you, Maddox!"

"I know you are, but you'll forgive me eventually."

"Oh no, I won't. I will not forgive and I won't forget."

Her words hurt, but not as much as losing her would. My world would crumble without her. She can hate me now, and I'll endure her wrath as long as it means she's safe.

I set her down and take a quick step back, knowing

what's coming. As suspected, her fists fly into my chest and she pounds repeatedly, as if she's trying to break through a door. "I can't believe you did this! You tricked me into coming down here and you told me Ridge was coming!"

Ridge. Ridge. Ridge. It's always about Ridge.

Words keep flying out of her mouth about how he's probably worried sick, and I lose it. "God damn it!" I shout. "Would you stop talking about fucking Ridge? He's not here! I am! Why isn't that enough?" My hands rake through my hair and I spin around with my eyes downcast. "I get it, you love him, too. Great. I'm glad. But for once can you not think about him when you're here with me?"

"This isn't about me thinking about him. This is me worried about the other man I love. Ridge is crazy. Who knows what he's out there doing to try and find me. He could be slashing bodies left and right."

"So let him!" I huff. "Ridge isn't my concern right now." I drop my hands from my head and lift my eyes to meet hers. "You're my only concern."

She swipes the tears from her eyes and drops her hands to her sides. "I know you want to keep me safe, but this isn't the way to do it, Maddox."

"What other way is there?"

Her shoulders slump in defeat. "I don't know, but I know I can't stay here."

"I'm sorry," I say softly. "But I can't let you leave. Not yet."

"You don't have a choice. One way or another, I'm getting out that door."

She turns around and steps up on the ladder, but I grab her by the waist and pull her back. "No, babe. You're not going anywhere."

CHAPTER 8
RILEY

"I OFFICIALLY HATE YOU," I tell him, truly believing what I say as he hammers another nail into the board at the top of the ladder.

"You can hate me now, but I know you'll love me again later."

"Nope," I quip. "I'm going to hate you until I take my last breath on this cold floor in this dark and dirty room. Because that's what's going to happen. We're going to die down here. Be it starvation, hypothermia, or even murder. It's going to happen if you don't let me out."

"Murder, huh?" He chuckles. "You plan on killing me?"

My shoulders rise and fall slowly. "I've contemplated it."

"Guess I better sleep with one eye open then."

He hammers another nail into the board. When those idiots cleared this space out, it would've been nice if they took all their tools and shit with them. Somehow Maddox stumbled across some old two-by-fours and a box of nails. He couldn't find a hammer, but he improvised with a big flat rock. Fortunately, he's doing a poor job of getting them in all the way, which should make it easy for me to get them out.

"So," he begins. "How do you plan on taking me out?"

"Oh, I don't know. Maybe with that rock in your hand."

He laughs again as if I'm not serious. Which I'm not. I could never hurt Maddox, but I have every intention of making him realize how extremely pissed off I am right now.

I grab his backpack and reach inside to pull out an individual bag of pretzels. "Or starvation. Maybe I'll just eat all these snacks until you're so hungry, you're forced to take down the boards on that trapdoor and go out for food."

I rip the top of the bag apart and reach inside to grab one, then I pop it in my mouth, smirking at him.

"I've gone days without food before. I can do it again. Especially for you. I do suggest you eat the food sparingly, though."

My entire hand goes in the bag and I bunch every pretzel in my fist, then I stuff them all in my mouth until my cheeks are stuffed full with every last one.

I glower at him as I hastily chew on the dry pretzels out of sheer defiance. "Don't tell me what to do," I say as a powder of crumbs puffs out of my mouth.

Maddox sighs heavily and rubs his temples with a smirk on his face. "You are something else."

I swallow in one gulp, barely chewing them all. Suddenly, I feel the prickle of a jagged piece scratch against my throat. I try to cough, but a small piece gets lodged. When it doesn't come up, I panic.

Beads of sweat form on my forehead, and my heart races as I claw at my throat, trying to dislodge the pretzel.

Oh my god. I'm choking.

This is how I die.

Death by pride—in the form of a pretzel.

"Jesus Christ, Riley." Maddox hurries down the ladder as I push myself up on my knees, choking on a fucking pretzel. "You'd literally choke yourself to death just to prove a point."

He runs to my side, but before his assistance is needed, the pretzel dislodges. I cough and sputter then swallow the rest of the food in my mouth. "Water," I tell him, fingers snapping in the air. "Hurry."

Maddox retrieves a bottle of water from the bag, swiftly takes the top off, then shoves it toward me.

I grab it, spilling some of the liquid sitting at the top of the rim. I tip it back and chug half the bottle.

Once I've caught my breath and I'm certain I'm not dying, I pound my fist to my chest. "Don't you dare tell me to drink this water sparingly."

Maddox throws his hands up in surrender. "Wouldn't dream of it because knowing you, you'd drown yourself in it just to prove you can."

I bite back a smile, not willing to give him the satisfaction. He's also right and I refuse to agree with him.

His hand grazes my back softly, and even though it's on top of many layers, I still feel the heat of his touch. It's comforting. Even when I'm pissed. Then again, I'm not sure who I'm more pissed at right now—him or myself.

"Maddox," I say softly, feeling a bit emotional after my near-death experience. "Can we please leave?"

He exhales a shuddering sigh and his shoulders droop. With his gaze fixed on the area between his feet, he leans into me. In a low, desperate voice, he says, "I can't bear the thought of losing you, Riley."

"Hey," I turn to face him, while taking both his hands in

mine, "you're not going to lose me. You want to know how I can be so sure?"

He quirks a brow. "How?"

"Because I can't bear the thought of losing you either. Therefore, I would never put myself in a position where it's a possibility. We're in this together—whether we're down here," my eyes lift to the partially boarded up trapdoor, "or up there."

"I hear what you're saying." His voice is barely a whisper, as if speaking these words pains him. "I really do. But it's not a risk I'm willing to take."

I tip his chin with my forefinger. "I didn't do what they're accusing me of. *If*—and that's a big *if*—I do get myself caught, I'll get myself out of it."

"You don't know how serious these people are, babe."

"What people, Maddox? The Elders?" I chuckle. "As in, my mom and my dad and all the other parents of the students here?"

"No!" he stammers as he gets to his feet. Pacing back and forth, he acts as if he's sorting through a million different thoughts. He stops, a look of shame on his face. "Not just any Elder, or any parent. *My* dad. *My* parent."

I push myself off the floor and walk over to where he's standing near the ladder. Softly touching his arm, I ask, "What the hell does that even mean?"

"You say you didn't do what they're accusing you of, but babe, you did." There's a fearful look on his face that has me wondering if he truly is worried for my life.

It doesn't make sense, though, because he's wrong. I didn't do the things I'm being accused of.

"I didn't kill Cade, or Zeke, or those other guys. That's why they want me. That's why everyone is on lockdown."

"Everyone has their own motive, Riley. Even The Elders. Cade's dad wants vengeance for his son's death. Zeke's parents want the same for their son. And those other men have a connection to the governor, which raises suspicion and has everyone thinking they were killed by the same person who killed the governor."

"Everyone? Or your dad?"

"Let's just say, some people, but mostly my dad."

"Why, though? The governor committed suicide. Why isn't that enough for him? It was enough for his kids, and his fellow members. Why does he even care?"

Maddox shrugs his shoulders and I can tell he's as confused as I am. "I really have no idea. But I know he's got some sort of connection to him. I just haven't had a chance to figure out what that connection is."

"Well, maybe they were just friends. I mean, it could be something as simple as that."

"Doubtful. No, my dad is definitely hiding something and I get the feeling he has an agenda of his own in finding out who killed the governor and punishing them."

I slap my hands to my thighs and exhale profoundly. "Which was me. I killed him, and now he wants me punished."

"I truly believe he's the one who is in every Elder's ear trying to blame this all on you, because he has some sort of proof that it was you who killed the governor."

I shake my head in disbelief. "This is all too much. How the fuck do I get myself out of this, Maddox?"

"You hide. Just like we're doing right now. You keep a low profile, and when suspicion is shifted elsewhere—because it will be. Ridge will make sure of it—then you can come out of hiding as an innocent person."

My cheeks inflate with air and I blow it all out in one sharp exhale. "I had no idea your dad was so hell-bent on proving I killed the governor." My eyes lock on his. "This is fucking scary, Maddox."

"No shit. Now do you understand?"

"I...I guess so. I think I was just in defense mode and thought I needed to do everything possible to protect my reputation. Now, I just want to hide away to protect my life."

Maddox wraps his arms around me, and while normally I would break down in tears, I don't. It's proof that I'm stronger than I imagined. It gives me hope that I will make it out of all this alive. Until then, I suppose I'll just hide.

There's just one thing I have to do before I get too comfortable down here.

CHAPTER 9
RIDGE

BY THE TIME Lev got to the cabin last night, I was passed out. I didn't realize how tired I was until I sat on the couch to wait for him.

It's morning now, and I've been filling him in on everything I heard yesterday.

"No." Lev sighs. His hands are pressed to the kitchen counter in the cabin, his head hung low. "Just fucking no. There isn't a chance in hell my dad would ever hurt your mom. They have to be wrong."

"Heard it with my own ears, man. Why would all three of them make this shit up when they didn't even know anyone was listening."

His head shoots up. "Hell if I know, but there has to be a reason. Sure, my dad was a Punisher, but I just can't imagine him hurting anyone, let alone killing someone."

"There's a lot our parents did when we were kids before we knew about the roles of The Society. They hid that part of themselves. It was a job and he had an assignment. Believe it or not, but according to your uncle and Maddox's father, he killed my mom."

I'm not surprised Lev is having such a hard time wrapping his head around this. No one wants to think their parents committed heinous acts of violence, let alone murder. Since we were kids, we knew there was a dark side of The Society, but it doesn't make it any easier for us to accept that now. I remember us eavesdropping to find out some of the secrets, but we never heard anything too incriminating. Still to this day, there is likely so much we don't know.

"We can't be like them," Lev quips. "You're still in this fight, right?"

"Of course I am! That's exactly why we've been fighting since we were fucking teenagers. That's the whole point of everything we've done. The only way we can take these fuckers down is from the inside, and in order to do that, we have to play their game for a while. We get our assignments and we fulfill them. We become Elders and we move the chess pieces around so that, in time, we can destroy those fuckers."

Lev drags a chair across the dingy floor, then lowers himself into it. Leaning forward, his elbows rest on the splintered tabletop and he drops his face in his hands as he speaks. "You took an assignment at the start of the school year to find out who killed the governor, but you never had any intention of completing that assignment, did you?"

"At first I did...until I saw her. The second I laid eyes on Riley, I knew I would not only fail, but I would do everything in my power to keep her secret from The Elders."

"But they know now. It was all for nothing."

"Nah." I sweep the air with my hand. "They've got nothing. The only evidence is the stuff you stacked against her and any good Sleuth or Elder would be able to recognize planted evidence. The only reason they're pushing this is because one of The Elders wants it to be pushed. I'm certain I know who that person is. I just can't figure out why."

"Who do you think it is?"

I'm still pissed the fuck off. He's the last person I ever would have suspected until today.

"Stanley Crane," I stammer.

Lev's eyes shoot up. "Maddox's dad? No fucking way."

"I don't make jokes about this shit, Lev."

He chuckles. "You're telling me the same guy who drove three hours to rescue a box of puppies is the one who wants a sweet girl like Riley to be punished? I'm not buying it. It's my uncle Austin. I can promise you that."

"Nope." I shake my head. "Your uncle wants *you*." Pointing a stern finger at him, I make it clear. "Stanley wants Riley. I'm telling you, man. I heard it all."

A heady growl escapes him. "What the fuck did he say about me?"

"Well, he's determined to find you, so he must need that money for something big. He must not think you're guilty of anything extreme or else he would be using it against you in order to take your family's money, but he does seem desperate."

"I say we just kill 'em both and solve everyone's problems."

"Your uncle, hell yes. But Maddox's dad?" I shake my head. "Not sure he'd ever forgive us for that one."

Lev smacks his thighs then jumps up. "Your car or mine?"

I don't even have a car here, so it's a stupid question, but that point is moot. "You're serious? You think we're just gonna walk out there in the light of day and kill the fucker?"

"Why the hell not? Not like you haven't done it before." He shrugs as he grabs his keys and heads toward the door.

"Everything I do is well thought out and never spontaneous," I say as I get up to follow him, apparently going along with his insane plan.

"First time for everything. Grab your shit and leave no trace you were here. I'll meet you in the car."

Killing Lev's uncle was the last thing on my to-do list for today, and it pisses me off that even ending him will in no way bring us closer to finding Riley and Maddox. Unless, he and his wife know more than they were letting on during their conversation with Stanley.

―――

"I've missed this girl." I pat the dash of Lev's fucking awesome ride. "One day I'm gonna have one of these."

It's a dream that will never come true, but one can wish. I'll never have the money Lev does, or even Maddox, but at least I get to relish in all their goods when I'm with them. Such as now—the window down, my hand hanging out, and the breeze in my hair. The rumble of the car vibrates through my body and I'm so fucking tired, I wouldn't be surprised if it lulled me to sleep.

"It's just a car." Lev shrugs.

I mock him. "'Just a car,' he says. You know the things I'd do for a car like this?"

"Lose your whole family so you inherit all their money. Ten out of ten do not recommend."

I tsk. "In case you've forgotten, my family is gone, too."

"Shit." Lev sighs. "Sorry, man. It's just, you know how much I hate materialistic stuff."

"Why'd you buy it then?"

He's quiet for a minute before he glances quickly at me. "You really wanna know?"

"I'm just asking because it's a nice fucking car for someone who hates materialistic shit."

"I got it for Emery," he says softly, and it's a tone I don't hear often from Lev. It's also the first time he's said his little sister's name since she died. I don't say anything because I'm sure he's not done talking, and because I don't know what the hell *to* say. A smile creeps across his face. "She fucking loved these cars. I remember her coming into my room and flipping through my car magazines just so she could circle all the Bugattis she wanted. I told her one day I was going to buy her one."

A minute or two passes of complete silence before I finally say, "I bet she'd love it."

"Yeah." He nods with a smile, eyes on the road ahead of us. "I like to think so."

"Lev?" I say with a gentleness to my tone. His eyes widen in question, so I continue, "Who do you think did it?"

I don't even have to explain what I'm talking about. He knows.

He rolls his neck and takes a deep breath. "That question has been heavy on my mind every day for years, and to this day, I still don't fucking know who to suspect."

The weight of the guilt on my chest is so heavy that I fear I'm going to burst at the seams if I don't say what I'm thinking—or what I know to be true.

"It was my fault," I blurt out.

Lev's eyes snap to mine and his eyebrows pinch together. "Why would you say that?"

We come to a stop about thirty yards from the closed gate on campus and Lev shifts the car into park.

He turns to face me, still wearing a look of confusion.

I can't even face him as I say what I need to say, so I look out the window to my right. "I didn't realize it until yesterday, but your dad killed my mom because he was sentenced to punish her. It was an order, and I know that. Nothing personal, and I'm not taking it that way. I don't blame him. I blame them, and they will all fucking fall for what happened to all our family members."

"Don't beat about the damn bush, Ridge. Just tell me why the hell you think it was your fault that my family was killed."

I nod repeatedly. "Right. Well, from what I heard yesterday, everyone assumes your dad was murdered for what he did to my mom. And he was only sent on that assignment because of what I did."

"You're not making any fucking sense."

"Remember when I was eleven and I killed that man who was beating on my mom?"

"Yeah. So what about it?"

It's not normal how either of us can talk about murder and death so casually. As if it's an everyday occurrence in our lives. We are clearly beyond fucked up.

Lev snaps his fingers, pulling me out of my thoughts, and back into the memories of what I heard. "Out with it!"

"My mom was punished because she took the blame for what I did. In the eyes of The Society, she killed an innocent member. So if your dad was murdered out of revenge for taking my mom's life, then it was my fault."

There. I said it. It's out in the open. He can fucking hate me if he wants to.

There's a moment of silence before Lev surprises me by bursting into laughter. "You have way too much time on your fucking hands, Ridge. Quit thinking so damn much." He shifts the car back into drive and presses a button on his steering wheel. "Call Asshole Austin."

"Calling Asshole Austin," comes through the speakers and I laugh.

"Where the hell are you?" is the first thing his uncle says when he accepts the call.

"Question is, Uncle, where the hell are you?"

"You better be calling to tell me you have an update on your new assignment, Lev, because so help me God, if you fuck this up and don't bring that girl in, you'll be the biggest disgrace ever born into our family." His voice booms with rage. "You'll be finished! Done for! You hear me?"

"What assignment?" I whisper, but he shushes me with a finger over his mouth.

"Oh, I hear you." Lev leans his head back and looks at me with a shit-eating grin on his face. "But not loud enough. Meet me out front of the main building on campus in, say, five minutes?"

"You best have some news for me, boy."

The call drops and Lev stretches his legs out beneath the steering wheel. "Hold the fuck on."

The next thing I know, he's gunning it and we're driving eighty miles an hour straight at the wrought-iron gate.

I grab the 'oh shit' handle on the door and flatten my arm on the center console, bracing myself for impact. "You're gonna fucking kill us, Lev!"

"Since when are you scared of anything?" he shouts over the roar of the engine.

With a loud crash, the metal barred doors fly open. Shards of rusted metal rain down as we barrel through, leaving a trail of destruction in our wake. Lev pushes down harder on the gas pedal as he drives full speed toward the center of campus, while choosing to ignore the five-miles-per-hour speed limit.

"Holy fuck," I roar. "That was insane."

"It ain't over yet." He howls in excitement, the most emotion I've seen on his face since his family died, and it brings a smile to my face.

We fly past some of the student housing, and Lev shows no signs of slowing down.

"Dude." I drag out the word. "What the fuck are you doing?"

Up ahead is Austin, standing outside the building. He glances back and forth at his watch until he finally sees us. He freezes, eyes wide with fear. Stumbling back in a desperate attempt to get away, he trips over the cement slabs of the staircase before awkwardly getting back to his feet.

One look at Lev and I can see victory in his eyes. A broad smile is plastered on his face as if he's entering his own redemption story.

The next thing I know, Austin is smashed against the bumper of the car and thrown onto the hood. It all happens so fast as Lev maintains his speed, ripping through campus as if it's his own personal playground. He drives straight over a few bushes at lightning speed, sending his uncle sliding up the windshield and over the car.

My head whips around and I see Lev's uncle's body hit the pavement with a thunderous clap.

"That's my fucking boy." I slap a hand to Lev's shoulder, grinning like a schoolboy.

"Take that, you fucking asshole! That's what you get for drugging me and destroying all those years of my life. Try and take my money now, you little bitch!"

I sink back in my seat and watch Lev as an array of emotions passes over him in waves. From sheer joy, to pain, back to happiness. Maybe a little regret. He licks his lips, swallows hard, eyes darting from his trembling hands, back to the road, then finally when the car slows, he just smiles, pleased with himself for ending the madness that threatened his future.

"Where to now?" I ask him, certain that the reality of what he just did is front and center in his mind.

"Now we get the fuck out of here and find our girl."

Our girl. Is that what she is? I know she's mine. I'm positive she's Maddox's too. Can I really trust Lev enough to allow him to have a place in her life? Assuming she'd even want him.

I still don't know, but I can't find it in me to burst his bubble right now. I guess only time will tell.

CHAPTER 10
MADDOX

RILEY GRUMBLES from where she's lying flat on the floor, making dust angels. She stops, sits up, and looks at me. "I'm hungry."

"I told—"

"Nope. Don't even say it."

"I'm just saying—"

"No, you're not. Don't finish that sentence because I refuse to call you Daddy and that's who you'd be acting like."

I smirk. "I wouldn't mind if you called me Daddy."

"Gross." She scoffs. "I hate to sink your boat, but if you're into that sort of thing, you're with the wrong girl."

"We'll see about that."

"You're twenty years old, Maddox. You're not some silver fox in one of those romance novels where she calls him Daddy and the readers' panties melt."

"I bet if you said it, your panties would melt."

Riley gets on her hands and knees and crawls toward me

all seductively. There's a prominent arch in her back and her eyes are full of lust and want. "You really want me to call you Daddy?"

I chuckle. "I'm not so sure I do now."

She makes her way to where I'm sitting on the floor with my back to the wall and inches between my legs. "You either do or you don't."

"I just want you." I grab her by the ass and jerk her onto my lap so she can feel my erection as I grind into her.

Her mouth ghosts over my ear as she whispers, "How about a deal? You can have me, and I'll call you Daddy, but you have to fulfill a fantasy of mine."

My fingers run down her arms, peeling back the dirty coat she's got on. "I'll gladly fulfill all your fantasies."

She kisses her way down my neck. "You mean that?"

"Every word." My fingers delve into her plush curves, and I thrust upward, showing her what she does to me. "Show me how good you can ride my cock, baby, and I'll do whatever you want me to do."

Her back straightens and she presses her lips to mine. "Hold that thought." She climbs off my lap and waggles her brows as she walks backward with a slow swag. Her shoulders roll and she puffs out her chest...

"Watch out!" I shout, but I'm too late.

She trips over a cardboard box and falls backward, immediately jumping back up and dusting herself off. "I'm okay," she blurts out.

My face falls into my hands and I massage my temples. "Girl, you are a walking disaster." When I lift my eyes, she's walking back toward me with a rope—swinging it in the air like it's a lasso.

"Wanna know what my favorite type of romance book is?" she asks, and I'm afraid to guess. "Small town cowboy. There's something about a strong cowboy wrangling his girl."

My eyebrows cave in, in wonder. "You wanna wrangle me?"

"Mmhmm." She hums as she stands in front of me and pushes down her pants. She steps out of them, my eyes fixated on the space between her legs.

My gaze slides up to her chest when she drops her bra. "Fuck." I growl. "Get that cute ass back over here." I reach out and grab her, pulling her down to the floor with me.

I'm not sure I've ever seen Riley exude so much confidence. Now that I think about it, I haven't seen her this happy in a while. She speaks so often about the girl she was before she shot the governor. How she was carefree and always smiling—the life of the party. I can see that now. It's as if coming to this place allowed her to step out of the cage she put herself in. And all it took was facing her demons head-on.

On my knees, I pop the button on my jeans, and Riley careens into me until I'm on my back on the floor. "Let me," she says insistently. She moves my hand out of the way and pulls my zipper down. Her eyes remain on mine, while she takes off my jeans and boxers.

My eyebrows rise and I bite the corner of my lip. "I like this side of you."

"Oh yeah? What side is that?"

"You. Taking control like this. It's sexy as hell."

With her legs on either side of me, she leans down until her breath is a whisper in my ear. "Is that so...Daddy?"

I can't help the smile that grows on my face. I wanna

laugh, because it's almost humorous hearing her speak that way, especially after we had an entire conversation about it. Her head lifts and I immediately notice the pink tinge to her cheeks as she rolls her lips together. "Wrong time?"

"Nah," I tell her. "It was perfect."

"Good. Now it's my turn to fulfill my fantasy." She reaches over and grabs the rope and her eyebrows do a little dance. She takes one of my hands and begins tying the rope around it.

"Baby? What are you doing?"

Her response is just a flirtatious grin, as she takes the other hand and brings both over my head, tying them together.

"I...don't know about this," I say, feeling a little unsure about the whole situation.

"A deal is a deal."

"All right," I drawl, "do what you gotta do. As long as you promise to sit that ass down on my cock."

"I promise." She messes with the rope a little more, and when I lift my wrists, I realize I'm bound to something. I lift my head and twist my neck to see that I'm tied to a metal pipe against the wall.

Riley slides back down until her entrance is lined up with my cock, then she sits down, just like she promised she would.

I inhale deeply, relishing how good it feels to be buried inside her tight pussy. "God, baby. You feel so good."

"Uh-uh," she tsks. "God has nothing to do with it, remember?" Then she cloaks her body with mine. "Unless you want me to be your goddess tonight?"

"Touché."

Her hips roll as she rocks against me, taking the full

length of my cock. Back arched, she presses two hands to my chest and her mouth falls open.

My wrists wriggle, trying to break free, because I need to touch her so badly. I try to lift my back off the floor so I can suck on her breasts, but I'm bound too tightly. "Fuck, baby. Untie me. I need to touch you, taste you, hold you."

She shakes her head slowly as she increases the speed of her hips, pushing them back and forth on my rock-hard cock. Her eyes close, and her lips part as she drops her head back.

"You *are* a fucking goddess." I growl headily.

Digging her nails into the skin of my chest, she drags them down and the pain arouses me even further.

I plunge upward, finding friction—desperate for more.

I take in every inch of her body as I meet her thrust for thrust. The small freckle above her left breast. Her rose-colored areolas. Every bend, every curve.

Her face is a picture of perfect beauty with a cute little dimple on her chin that I want to kiss. The crook of her neck tilts slightly and all I can think about is how desperately I want to nuzzle my face in it as I inhale her sweet scent. "You are sheer perfection, Riley."

As much as I love seeing her face and her front side, I need to memorize her backside as well. "Turn around and keep riding me."

Her eyes open and she lifts up as she nibbles on her bottom lip. Flinging one leg over, she positions herself backward. Her perfectly round ass sits back down and I groan as she moans in pleasure at the same time.

"Fuck," she whimpers.

This angle allows me to go deeper inside her. Instead of rolling her hips this time, she lifts up and drops back down repeatedly. I watch the way my cock slides in and out of her slick pussy. It's like she was molded just for me.

God damn, I want to touch her so badly. Get a fistful of her ass and guide her movements, even though she's doing perfectly fine without my help.

Her pace quickens more and more with each passing second until she's crying out in ecstasy, pounding herself into me.

My entire body fills with an insatiable heat, my cock pulsing inside her. Breathless, I let out a deep, guttural groan as I release and fill her up.

She keeps moving, riding out her own orgasm. Her walls clench around my cock, milking me of every last drop.

As her movements slow, I feel a tightness in my chest, knowing we have to leave this room eventually. I might be hungry, tired, and in desperate need of a shower, but I've never been more satisfied in my life.

Riley gradually lifts up and proof of our orgasms spills out of her, pooling around my shaft and dripping down my balls.

She gets to her feet and turns around to face me with a crooked grin. "Thanks for letting me tie you up."

"You never have to thank me. I'm always here to fulfill all your desires." My body feels sated, but the tension in my wrists isn't my favorite thing.

She bends at the waist and snatches up her clothes. I watch her as she gets dressed. Riley is like no other girl I've ever met before. She's so uncoordinated, yet graceful at the same time. She puts her foot in her mouth a lot, but she seems to always know exactly what to say to make me feel better. She's stubborn as hell, but as sweet as can be.

She's everything I never knew I wanted, and the one I refuse to ever let get away.

Once she's dressed, I wiggle my hands. "My turn."

She stands in front of me, a look of sorrow now on her face. I watch as her throat bobs when she swallows and alarms go off in my head.

Walking over to the far wall on the other side of the room, she picks something up. I lift my head to try and get a better look, but it's not until she steps back in the glow of the lantern that I see what she's holding.

A copper pipe.

"Riley? Baby?"

"I'm so sorry, Maddox. I can't stay here any longer. If you'd agreed to leave with me, it wouldn't have come to this. But you won't. I have to find Lev and clear my name."

My face twists in disbelief and I pin her with a scathing glare. "Dammit, Riley," I say, attempting a weak laugh. "You better be fucking with me right now."

She moves toward the ladder then gives me one last glance before going up. "Please don't take this personally."

At the top of the ladder, she beats the fuck out of the boards I loosely put in place. My options were limited and it was really just a weak attempt at making her feel stuck so she wouldn't do exactly what she's doing now. I guess I underestimated her.

"Riley!" I shout. "Get your ass back down here. You're not going anywhere." My words are futile because she keeps going until one board is off, then another.

"I'm going to send someone down for you. I promise." She pushes open the trapdoor but stops before climbing out. Although I can't see her face, I'm hopeful she's having second thoughts.

"I love you," she says, before her entire body disappears through the hole.

The sound of the trapdoor closing is what I assume nails in a coffin would be like.

"Riley!!! Riley!!!"

I twist my wrists, not caring if they break, because I would lose limbs to save that girl. She just walked into an inferno and has no idea she's about to be burned.

CHAPTER 11
RILEY

AS SOON AS the sun kisses my skin, guilt hits me like a tidal wave. I meant what I said to Maddox, I do love him. If there was any other way, I wouldn't be out here alone right now. Lord knows, I don't want to be alone. In fact, I'm downright petrified.

Dry leaves coated in flakes of snow crunch beneath my boots. Fortunately, it's nothing but a light dusting, although the scenery is deceiving. I have no doubt the temperature is below freezing. My footprints trail behind me as I walk, making my anxiety skyrocket as I try to think up a plan. Thankfully, when I look up at the mountains, a thick haze covers the peak, a sure sign more snow is coming. Soon my tracks will be covered. I just need to get word out so someone will come for Maddox, while I put space between us.

Reaching into the inside pocket of the coat I'm wearing, I retrieve the phone Scar gave me. My feet don't stop moving as I power it on.

No service is centered across the screen and I sigh heavily. I should've known I wouldn't have a signal out here.

It's okay. Everything is fine. I just need to get within reach of a tower.

And I know just where to go.

There's strength deep inside me,
Though it hides itself well.
Refusing to be conquered,
I'll give them all hell.

It's been a while since I've walked the path I'm on, but if memory serves me right, it should take me straight to Boulder Cove Academy—the place where it all began.

Chills skate down my spine, and it's not due to the chill in the air. Memories of when Scar's guys had Jude—who actually turned out to be Scar's brother—tied up in the same room I just escaped from. During his short stay down there, I'd bring him food and water, and just keep him company. I was convinced he was innocent, and I was correct.

Turns out, Jude wasn't the one terrorizing the students at BCA. It was the governor all along. The day he died plays in my head like a movie set in slow motion. Not as much as it used to, but every now and then, it rewinds and plays again.

I thought those were the worst days of my life, but I was wrong. I'm currently living my worst days and I have an awful feeling there is still more room to fall before it starts to get better.

As I trek farther into the deep forest, I can't shake the sense that someone is watching me. Every few seconds, a branch snaps, a leaf crunches, or an animal scurries away, but the looming presence never seems to fade.

Suddenly, the air is chillingly still. Goosebumps prick at the back of my neck, and I move slower, straining to hear any sound that's not my own.

The unexpected pop of a branch, or something like it,

has my movements freezing. I hold my breath, until I can't hold it any longer, and I'm forced to exhale. My heart gallops in my chest and I fear the sound of it rattling against my rib cage is going to draw attention to me.

When silence engulfs me, I stretch my neck out, peering around the tree I'm standing behind.

My entire body jolts and I press my back firmly to the bark, while locking all of my limbs in fear.

I should've just stayed with Maddox. Why the hell am I so damn stubborn all the time? I'm not built for this shit. I'm afraid of my own damn shadow, yet I embark on a journey through the woods when I know the sun will likely set before I even make it to my destination.

The phone!

I've only made it about a hundred and twenty yards, but it's closer than I was when I last checked.

A quick glance at the phone shows that I'm still too far out. I stick it back in my pocket and take a deep breath before walking again, very slowly. Practically tiptoeing.

If I want to get out of these woods before the sun sets, I need to move faster.

I'm fine. No one is out here. It was probably just a squirrel.

Yeah. That's what it was. No one even knows I'm out here, so there's no reason for anyone to come looking.

A few minutes later, I'm feeling hopeful. I'm already a quarter of the way there. I take the phone back out and squeal when I see that I've got one bar. But more than that, a swarm of messages flood through. All from the same person...

> Your Bestie: Girl! Where the hell are you?

> Your Bestie: I'm literally freaking out, Ry. This shit is getting scary. You better call me as soon as you can. If you can and you're not, then I hate you.
>
> Your Bestie: I don't really hate you. I could never hate you. But I really am freaking out.
>
> Your Bestie: OMG! Cade's dad is DEAD!

I stop there. My feet. My thoughts. My movements. Possibly even my heart.

Cade's dad is dead?

It's probably safe to assume he didn't die of natural causes. And if I had to think of one person who would want Cade dead, it would be his nephew, Lev.

My heart splinters at the thought of Lev, not only doing such a heinous thing, but more so getting caught.

I'm mad at him. Beyond livid. But there's still that small part of me holding on to hope that there's an explanation for every cruel thing he's done.

Who am I kidding? He killed Zeke. He killed Cade. He killed three strangers. And he framed me for all of it. Never once attempting to clean up his mess and clear my name. Nope. He just took off and ran to save his own ass, while leaving me to burn.

Karma is a fucking bitch and she's gunning for him.

I just hope she isn't too cruel.

Stop it, Riley! Stop empathizing with that asshole!

Okay. I'm getting delirious. I need food and water and sleep because I'm literally having a conversation with myself in my head.

I close my eyes and shake away the thoughts then I keep reading Scar's messages.

> Your Bestie: I'm scared for you. This is bad. Very bad. The President of The Society is on his way here. Not one of the Chapter Presidents. THE PRESIDENT of the whole thing. Please be safe.

> Your Bestie: He's here. Neo snuck out and listened to a couple of The Elders gossip and they have no suspects.

One final message...

> Your Bestie: Seems no one really gives a damn about Cade's dad. They are still too concerned with finding you. I'm deleting all these messages. Please respond when you can.

My heart sinks into my stomach. What if they think it was me who killed Cade's dad? They already think I killed Cade. Why wouldn't they assume I would just keep going?

I quickly type her a response before continuing on my way to BCA.

> Me: I'm safe! I'll tell you where I'm at soon. But please send one of the guys to your parents' cabin. Maddox is tied up in the basement. I suggest Crew or Jagger. Neo would probably just leave him there. I promise I'll explain later.

I hit Send. We're only about thirty minutes from the university, so they shouldn't take long.

I glance back at the phone to make sure it sent, but it's going too slow.

A minute later, still sending.

"Dammit!" I blurt out, and at the same time, I hear footsteps.

Not animal steps. Actual human footsteps heading straight for me.

I hurry over to a nearby bush and crouch down, remaining as still as possible.

"I think it was this way," I hear someone say. A man's voice, one I don't recognize.

"Probably just that fucking freak girl who comes out here and takes pictures of birds," another guy says.

"One can only hope," another says. "I wouldn't mind getting a piece from her again."

My jaw drops open, while my heart pounds like a jackhammer. So far, I know there are three of them. I have no idea who these guys are, but they don't sound like anyone I want to cross paths with.

"A piece of what?" One of the guys laughs. "The girl practically dismembered your dick."

"Fuck that. She wanted it. Just got cold feet. Besides, she barely skimmed the surface. Three weeks of healing and I was good to go. She owes me a blow job, actually."

The footsteps come closer, and closer, and...

"Found her."

I pinch my eyes shut and tuck my head between my knees, pretending that if I don't see him, he won't see me.

"Who the fuck is she?"

One of them kicks at my boot. "Hey. Show us your fucking face, or we'll have to make you show us." One of the guys growls the demand.

Slowly, I lift my head with a fake smile plastered on my face. "Heyyyy," I drag out the word as I lift my hand to wave. I stand up nonchalantly and point at the space between two of the guys. "I was just...passing through. So if you don't mind." I attempt to squeeze through them, but I'm halted by an arm around my waist.

"Not so fast," a guy with sleek black hair says. I lift my head to look at him and I'm dumbstruck by his piercing blue eyes. They are literally the bluest eyes I've ever seen. What's even more unique is the tattoo underneath his eye. Written in cursive, is the word *Savage*.

I point at his eye, hoping small talk will ease the tension. "I like your tattoo. Did it hurt?"

His lip curls up in a mischievous grin. "Probably about as much as it did for you when you fell from heaven."

"Smooth." I chuckle. "No. Really. Did it hurt?"

"Who the hell are you, and why are you in our woods?" another guy barks, and I spin around to face him. He's more cowardly than the other because his face isn't sporting ink. But on his neck in big letters, is the word *Vicious*. This one has longer hair with waves and natural blond highlights—sort of a sexy surfer appeal—and his eyes are as dark as I imagine his soul is.

"Umm. I can't tell you that. You see, I'm wanted for multiple murders, and if I tell you my name, well, I'll have to kill you."

Vicious's eyebrows cave in. "Are you fucking high?"

I look at the last guy. The quiet one. There's a cigarette perched on his ear and a lighter in his hand that he flicks open and closed over and over again. Bringing the flame back to life, he holds it up to his mouth and I watch him intently, curious what he's going to do. He looks like he's going to eat the flame, but he can't be that fucking dumb.

Suddenly, he blows the flame out in one forceful breath, making it dance toward me. I startle back and he bursts out in laughter before he reaches to grab the cigarette from his ear. That's when I notice the tattoo on his wrist. It's in the same cursive writing as the others', but this one has the word *Twisted*.

My fingers snap as my eyes dance from one face to the next. "I know you guys. Not personally, or at all really. But I know your type. You're Crew, Jagger, and Neo. You're also Ridge, Maddox, and Lev." I laugh under my breath at the realization and say more to myself than them, "I've survived them all. I'm not scared of you." I shove my way through them and continue on my path, fully aware that they are following closely behind me.

"She's cute," I hear Vicious say.

"Even cuter that she thinks she's getting away from us that easily." Savage snarls.

My eyes nearly pop out of my sockets and my heart jumps back into a frenzy of rapid beats.

I pick up my pace, and immediately notice them doing the same.

Before I know it, I'm full-on sprinting through the woods. I dodge branches and jump over logs, and a quick glance over my shoulder shows them doing the same.

The next thing I know, my chest is crashing into the ground and the wind is knocked out of me. Once I refill my lungs, I'm able to get a roaring scream out before a hand is slapped over my mouth. I squirm and kick and try to break free, but I'm no match for one of them, much less three.

My defensive instincts kick into gear and I square my jaw, then sink my teeth into the meaty flesh of the hand silencing me. The metallic taste of iron seeps onto my tongue, but I ignore it, knowing I have two more guys to fend off.

"She fucking bit me!" Savage howls as he cradles his injured hand. "The whore fucking bit me!"

Suddenly, I'm flipped over onto my back, face to face with Twisted. "You know what we do to whores who don't know how to behave?"

"No," I answer, lifting an eyebrow at him because I'm a glutton for punishment. My own worst enemy, as Scar would say.

"We treat them like dirty whores," Twisted grits out, and each word will now be permanently etched in my memory. But what's worse, what will really stick with me, is the sound of my shoes thrashing against the tree, one after the other because the wrenching of my gut tells me my pants are next.

I press my legs together so tightly, it would take all three of these guys to pry them apart.

"Hold her hands," Twisted barks to Vicious.

My fearful eyes land on Vicious and I mouth the word, "Please."

He's hesitant. It's possible he has half a heart and isn't as cruel as the other two. He's the one I need to get through to.

His shoulders shrug and when he kneels at my head and pins my wrists to the ground, I know exactly who I'm peering up at. It's the Maddox of the group, the softy. The one who does what everyone says because he wants to be liked. Yet, even Maddox broke free from the chains that bound him. He's different now, I can see it. I have to pray that there's hope for this vicious guy hovering over me, too.

"This is a big mistake," I tell him, ignoring the other two because anything I say to them is a waste of air. "I wasn't kidding when I said there's a manhunt for me. I'm wanted for the murder of, like...five people." I had to think about it because I'm not really sure how many guys were murdered in total. Obviously, seeing as I didn't do it.

"Yeah, fucking right," Vicious says with an airy chuckle. "You? Murder someone?"

"You have no idea who I am, do you?"

"Shut the fuck up," Twisted snaps. "We don't know, and don't care."

One of them fights to pry my legs apart, but I don't make it easy on them.

I clench every muscle in my body, making it clear I'm not going down without a fight. My eyes pinch together tightly and I search for my own inner strength.

All of a sudden, my wrists are freed and the guys around me begin cursing. "You fucking bitch!"

"Get the hell outta here." This voice is a new one. One I haven't heard before. A girl's voice. "Now!" she snaps. "Or I'll call the headmaster and tell them exactly what you guys are up to!"

The sound of footsteps scurrying away has my eyes popping open and I immediately see continuous flashes of light that are nearly blinding.

The girl comes behind me and helps me sit up. "Are you okay?" she asks, now crouched at my side. "Did they hurt you?"

I shake my head. "No. They tried, but they didn't, thanks to you."

I look down at her hand and see a large camera. One of those fancy ones with a long lens. She reaches her hand out and a smile creeps across her face. "I'm Temper."

My shaky hand rests on hers and my voice cracks as I say, "Riley."

I can't believe I just said my name, but for some reason, I'm not worried. Something tells me Temper is on my side.

"It's nice to meet you, Riley."

I watch her as she stands up and wanders through the nearby woods, collecting my shoes.

She's a tiny little thing. Probably only five-two at best. Jet-black hair, and eyes that match. Her skin is as pale as the snow falling around us. She's dressed head to toe in black and in a way, she reminds me of Scar, but more gothic-like.

"Here you go." She hands me my shoes. "I take it you're not a student here?"

"Umm. No." It's all I say; I don't have the emotional capability to explain myself at all right now. I'm still too shaken up and working on accepting the reality that I'm no longer under the hands of those men.

"Thank you for helping me. I have no idea what those guys would have done if you hadn't."

"I do," she says. "They're notorious for doing whatever the fuck they want, to whomever they want. Tonight, they must have decided they wanted you."

I lace one boot up then shift to the other. "You know them well?"

"Everyone knows them. They're The Lawless. But, you probably have no idea what that means."

"I do." Feeling a bit more levelheaded, I say, "I'm a former student here, and a Blue Blood."

"Oh, so you know that those guys can practically do whatever the hell they want and get away with it?"

"I guess so, but our Lawless were never that cruel. I mean, they were bad. Just not *that* bad."

"Guess some get it bad, and some get it really bad."

I gulp, a question weighing heavily on my mind. "Did they...did they ever—"

Her eyebrows flex. "Assault me? Hurt me? Fuck no! Tried once." She tilts her head slightly to the left. "But I practically chewed off one of Arlo's nuts. They've left me alone ever since."

"Which one is Arlo?"

"Ugly-ass eye tattoo. Walks with a limp."

I smile. "I take it the limp is your doing?"

"I mean, I like to think so." She waves her hand through the air as she starts walking. "Walk with me. I'll take you back to campus so you can call your friends, or whoever the hell you're out here with."

"Actually," I say, "I'm all alone."

It's a partial truth. Technically, I wasn't alone, but the minute I left Maddox, I was on this venture by myself.

My body jolts when the phone in my pocket buzzes. Quickly, I reach inside and pull it out.

Temper leans in and glances at the phone in my hand. "Please tell me that you time traveled here from the nineties and plan to return to your time with the news of our technological advancements."

"Oh," I laugh, holding up the old flip phone, "it's not mine."

"Annnnd, you have it, why?"

I laugh under my breath at her questions, loving how bold she is with someone she doesn't know from Adam. "So I can't be traced."

"Right. Right. Because you're on the run as a serial killer and all?"

My eyes widen in surprise. "You heard that?"

"The ass end of the conversation. But, yeah. So is it true?"

My lips roll together and I steal a quick glance at her to read her expression. She's so calm about the situation that I doubt she'd believe me even if I told her. "Maybe."

"That's cool as hell." She stares blankly ahead of her, moving her hands through the air as if she's framing a picture. "A life on the run as a wanted killer. Sounds like an adventure I want to go on."

"It's...definitely an adventure. But, I didn't do what I'm being accused of."

"Don't burst my bubble, college girl. Let me dream that I'm walking with a real Thelma."

"Thelma?"

"Thelma and Louise?" She huffs. "You are definitely *not* from the nineties. Quite possibly, not this world at all, for that matter. Can I be your Louise?" She folds her hands in prayer. "Please say yes."

"No idea what you're talking about."

"Eh, that's probably for the best. They die in the end."

Side-eyeing Temper, I quickly read the text from Scar, while trying to keep my new friend from seeing it.

> Your Bestie: Where the hell are you!? And if it's away from BCU, stay there, because this place is swimming with The Elders. Please text me again so I know you're safe.
>
> Your Bestie: PS. We're all going to get Maddox.

Thank God, they're getting him.

A smile spreads across my face, and Temper takes notice. "Boyfriend?"

"Uh. No," I say. "My best friend."

"Of course. Your Louise. Should've known you had one." She flips her hair and keeps walking, making me smile.

"Actually," I inhale deeply as I contemplate how to say this without sounding like I'm guilty of murder. "How would you feel about being an accomplice, just for a little bit?"

"Accomplice to murder?"

"No." I chuckle. "An accomplice to possibly hiding me out in your dorm, while feeding me food and giving me warmth." My mouth draws back, teeth bared in a wide smile. "Just until I figure out my next move."

She stops walking to face me, so I do the same. "On one condition."

"You name it."

"If you ever write a book about your adventure on the run as a wanted woman, you mention that I saved you from three big bad wolves and kept you from starving to death."

"*That's* your condition?"

"Too much?"

"No." I begin walking again. "Not too much at all. It's a deal."

She claps her hands together gleefully and I follow her lead as we take a sharp left, straight toward the Falcons' Nest—the same dormitory Scar and I stayed in during our attendance at BCA.

"Oh," I blurt. "No one can know about this. So your roommate—"

"Don't have one," she says.

"You don't have a roommate?"

"Nope. Loner through and through, until now, I guess." Her eyebrows waggle.

"Doesn't that get...lonely?"

"I love being alone. I'm your typical bookworm, tree-hugging, nature-loving introvert."

Yep. She's Scar in a different body.

"So where are you from?" I ask her, hoping to get to know the girl who's helping me a little better.

"Annex. About six hours away from Boulder Cove."

"Never heard of it."

"Not many people have. Our town is so small, we have to travel two hours for our Chapter meetings."

"Small towns are nice. Have you lived there your whole life?"

"Pretty much. I almost didn't come here at all. My mom was insistent, but I snuck behind her back and got approval from our Chapter President. To say she was pissed is an understatement. I wanted the full experience as a member and *had* to get out of that one-street town. Plan to go to BCU when I graduate, too."

"My best advice to you, stay in your lane and don't piss off the wrong people. But if you do, you seem like a girl who can take care of herself. You must have brothers."

"Actually, no. I'm an only child."

"Me, too. It has its perks, but it does get lonely sometimes." I smile at her. "But you like being alone, so I guess it's great for you."

Before I know it, the dorm comes into view. I flip the hood of my coat up in an attempt to be as inconspicuous as possible, though I doubt anyone here is looking for me.

"This way," Temper says, as if I may have forgotten where to go.

Nope. This place is just as I remember it. Dark and gloomy. It seems no one took my advice on planting some pretty pink flowers around the girls' dorms. I'm not the least bit surprised.

We step through the front doors and the smell alone has dozens of memories swimming through my mind. It was just last year, but it feels like it was ages ago. I can't believe how much has happened since my stay here. I can't believe how much *I* have changed.

"Second floor," Temper says as she begins up the stairs. I follow behind her, my palms skimming along the rail, while taking it all in. This place holds a lot of awful memories, but it also has so many good ones.

Scar and I were in the double rooms on the top floor and it wasn't often we visited the second floor, if at all.

We take the turn off and walk down the long stretch of hallway. One of the lights on the wall flickers in an almost mocking pattern. It casts an eerie glare over the area and my chest suddenly feels heavy again.

I'm taken aback when Temper stops in front of a door with three different locks on it. I look beside us at the neighboring door and notice it only has one.

Using three different keys on a ring full of them, she unlocks one at a time.

"Um. What's up with all the locks? A little cautious, are we?" My words come out in a joking manner, but I'm not really joking at all. This feels weird and for a moment, I wonder if trusting the strange girl dressed in black in the middle of the woods was the right thing to do.

Once they are all unlocked, she turns the handle and pushes the door open. "Let's just say the girls, and boys, here don't make it easy on me."

My heart pangs with remorse for her. "You poor thing," I say, immediately regretting my words. I'm sure the last thing she wants is pity.

"Trust me." She grins. "I don't make it easy for them either."

Walking into Temper's room is much like crossing over into an alternate universe. Though, it's pretty much what I expected. There's a skull on an oak desk with green and purple worms coming out of the mouth, and a stack of tarot cards piled beside it. It's cringeworthy, to say the least, but nothing I'm not used to. Scar's side of the dorm we shared here was a similar style—aside from the tarot cards, and yeah, okay, she definitely didn't have any decaying body parts as decor.

I walk over to the tarot cards and pick one up, curious to know what it says. I've never had a tarot reading done, or even seen the cards in real life for that matter.

"It's just something I do for fun," Temper says, joining my side.

I shake the card in my hand. "Death. That's a little freaky."

She chuckles. "Good thing it wasn't meant for you."

My eyes catch a math worksheet on the other side of the skull with her name on it.

"Temper Rose," I say. "That's a pretty last name."

"Yeah, it is. Even though it's not my real last name."

"Oh yeah?"

"Yup. It's my mom's maiden name. I've had it since birth, but my real last name—my father's last name—is Foster."

I gasp, feeling as if all the air has been vacuumed out of my lungs. "Did you say...Foster?"

Her eyes widen in surprise. "Yes. Why? Do you know

any Fosters? Please tell me you do. Ever since I learned of my father two years ago, I've searched high and low for any information on him, but they seal everything so damn tight in The Society. I've found nothing. All I know is that he was once a member, and now he's not, and his last name is Foster."

The idea of Ridge having a living family member would be amazing. And a sister! He'd be ecstatic. For years, he's been alone. *No. It can't be.* That would be far too much of a coincidence.

"I know a Foster who is a member." I shake my head, feeling silly for even thinking it's possible. "But his dad left him and The Society when he was very young."

Her eyes soften, and a gentle smile spreads across her lips. "Who?"

"My boyfriend. Ridge Foster."

CHAPTER 12
MADDOX

"UN-FUCKIN-BELIEVABLE!" I grit out as Crew begins to untie me from the fucking pole. And yeah, I'm still butt-ass naked, so naturally Scar and Jagger have their backs to me while they crack jokes. "I can't believe she left me here."

"What can I say, my girl's got some balls," Scar says before a giggle sputters out of her mouth.

"I'm gonna need you to be more specific," Jagger retorts. "Are we talking big balls, small balls, or Maddox-sized balls?"

All three of them burst out in laughter, including the jackass untying me.

I shake my head in a mixture of annoyance and humiliation. "Real funny, guys. Glad we can all be mature about this."

"You're right," Scar says. "It was a little premature of us to make you the butt of our jokes."

They all laugh again, and I've had enough. I pull back as hard as I can, slipping my fist out of the rope Crew was in the process of loosening. "I've got it from here." I growl as I twist around and untie my other hand. "I'm glad I could make you all laugh today." I straighten my back, feeling a little light-headed as I get to my feet. "Now, if you don't mind, I'd like to go find my fucking girlfriend."

"Dude," Crew says, and I pin him with a hard glare, "might wanna put some pants on first."

Fuck. I sigh heavily as I go over to my pants and boxers and sweep them off the floor angrily. My eyes roll as I stomp one foot in, then the other. I glower in their direction the entire time, until I'm fully dressed. Then, I pay them no attention at all and head for the ladder.

"Whoa. Whoa. Whoa," Crew sings. "Do you even know where the hell you're going, or what's been going on out there while you've been playing king of kink underground?"

I stop halfway up, the scowl on my face even more prominent. "I'm going to find my fucking girlfriend."

Scar scoffs and heads to the ladder. "Not without me."

"Not so fast, baby." Jagger pulls her back. "We came and let him go like you asked, but you're not getting yourself mixed up in this mess."

"I'm doing this alone," I say as I grab the ladder. "I appreciate your help, but Jagger is right, you guys need to stay out of this. All of you." I've got no problems with Scar. In fact, she's a good friend to Riley and she can be fun when it doesn't involve me being tied up naked. But the last thing I want is anyone holding me back or chirping in my ear. I need to have a clear head so I can think strategically.

I continue up the ladder and just as my head pops out of the opening, Scar shouts, "There's been another murder."

I gulp, eyes wide in surprise as I stoop down. "Who?"

"Cade's dad," she says. "Hit-and-run on campus."

"Damn." My fingers graze my chin.

There's only one person I can think of who would take out Cade's dad, and that's his deranged nephew, Lev.

"Any suspects?" I ask. None of these three know about Lev's fucked-up history with his uncle, so I don't bother sharing my suspicions.

"Honestly," Crew says, "I don't think anyone even cares. Pretty messed up, but everyone is so hell-bent on finding Riley that there hasn't been much said about Austin Pemberley."

That's both good *and* bad news. Good for Lev because he's likely out there living his best life, thinking he gets away with everything. Not that I should judge—after all, my friends think he killed Cade when I'm the guilty party there.

This is bad for Riley, though. I imagine the search has expanded for her and it won't be long until she's caught. I have to find her and I have to take her far away from this town—hell, maybe even this state. If it comes to it, I'd flee the damn country with her. We'll live under assumed names and start a new life together. I'd do anything for her.

"All right then," I grumble. "All the more reason for me to get the hell out of here and find Riley."

"Please," I hear Scar say as my feet leave the ladder, "we have to help."

Keep her back, guys. She'll only be in the way.

I don't say it. Instead, I bolt out the front door of the cabin as fast as I can before any of them can catch up to me. As I'm jogging down the trail, I pull out my phone and power it on.

My feet don't stop moving while I bypass all the unread messages and missed call notifications. I tap my dad's name and hold the phone to my ear.

It only rings twice before he picks up. "Maddox Crane,

where the hell are you?" His tone is laced with anger. "I've been calling every fucking hour for the last twenty-four!"

"I'm fine, Dad. Thanks for asking." My sarcasm is apparent and I hope he caught on to it.

"Obviously, or you wouldn't be calling me. Now, where the hell is that Cross girl? I know you and your friends are hiding her, and the punishment of your involvement is already up for debate by The Elders. No son of mine will be banished as a member. You hear me?"

"Loud and clear, Dad. As for *the Cross girl,* I can honestly say I have no idea where she's at. That's not why I'm calling, though. I need your help."

"You need my help?" He barks out a laugh. "I've been asking for your help since the school year started and all you've been doing is going against me, your assignment, and your role as a Guardian."

"Yeah, Dad. I'm a fuckup. We all know it. Are you gonna help me or not?"

"Where are you?" he deadpans.

"Boulder Cove Academy."

"Boulder Cove Academy?" he shouts. "What in God's name are you doing there?"

"It's a long story. But I need you to come pick me up and we need to have a nice, long chat on the way back. Meet me at the gate as soon as possible." I end the call before he can ask any more questions. If he wants answers, he'll come.

CHAPTER 13
RILEY

"THIS IS ALL TOO COINCIDENTAL. Don't you think?" Temper asks with a mix of anticipation and worry.

"I really can't say," I tell her honestly. "I've probably said too much already. I think the best person to ask is Ridge."

She jumps up from where she's sitting beside me on the edge of her bed. "Then let's go. What are we waiting for?"

"Not so fast." I pull her back down. "In case you've forgotten, I'm a wanted woman. I can't go anywhere."

"How long is the hideout supposed to last?" she asks, disappointment lacing her tone.

"I'll be out of your hair by morning."

"What if you get caught?"

"I won't, but there is someone I have to find. He's the only person who can clear my name."

"Is this person a member?"

"Yeah." I nod. "It's actually Ridge's best friend, Lev."

I'm not sure why I'm divulging so much information to a stranger. I guess it's because she doesn't feel like one. And because she helped me get away from those creepy bastards in the woods."

"Is he cute?" Her eyebrows waggle. "The friend, I mean?"

"He is."

"Brother's best friend. I could dig that."

"Please don't get your hopes up with Ridge. This really could all just be a coincidence."

I stop myself from going into more detail about Lev because then I'll be forced to tell her about Maddox, and this girl will question all my life choices if she knows I'm in a relationship with multiple men. We're not quite there yet.

"I'm not. I'm just daydreaming about a life with a brother as you talk. So, tell me more about Ridge. I need to know everything."

I bite the corner of my lip, contemplating how to best describe Ridge. "Well," I begin, a smile tugging at my lips as I stare off. "Ridge is mysterious to outsiders, but an open book when it comes to me. He loves hard and he fights even harder when it comes to the people he loves. He's dangerous—maybe even deadly. But he's also gentle and kind."

Excitement lights up her eyes. "Deadly?"

My eyebrows pinch together at her depravity. "Is that a good thing?"

"Depends. You said yourself, he fights hard for the people he loves. I believe when it comes to matters of the heart, there are no limits."

"Yeah," I quip. "Ridge is your brother."

She laughs. "You don't agree?"

"Are you really asking me if I think it's okay to take someone's life if they are a threat to someone you love?"

Now that I've said it out loud, I guess I shouldn't be so quick to judge. That's exactly what I did.

"I guess I am." Her shoulders rise.

"Like you said, it depends. We all have our own reasons for doing the things we do. Doesn't mean they're always right. But it also doesn't mean they didn't feel right at the time."

"Are you hungry?" she asks out of nowhere. "I'm fucking starving."

The familiarity between Ridge and Temper is astounding. They are both batshit crazy. But I love Ridge's crazy, and something tells me Temper is going to grow on me just as fast. If she is Ridge's sister, we will both have our work cut out when it comes to protecting this girl. She's a fucking tornado.

"I suppose since we're done with that conversation, I could eat." I slap my hands to my legs. "Maybe a shower, too."

"Perf," she says as she springs to her feet. "I'll show you to the showers and give you some fresh clothes, and while you're cleaning up, I'll go fetch us some food."

"Just one problem. I can't be seen, remember?"

"As if anyone will have any clue who you are. You're fine."

"Even if there wasn't any word of the manhunt for me here at The Academy, I was a senior here last year. Someone will recognize me and people will talk."

Her eyes widen as her face lights up with realization. Slowly, she raises a finger. "I think I've got an idea." She scurries to her dresser and pulls open the top drawer, retrieving a pair of sunglasses and a black baseball cap.

My face contorts in amusement. "You want me to take a shower wearing a hat and sunglasses?"

"Not *in* the shower. Just until you have privacy. It'll be fine. You won't look weird at all."

I chuckle. "Sure, I won't. Everyone wears sunglasses and baseball caps to the bathroom when it's snowing outside."

She throws them at me and I catch both against my chest. "Exactly."

Is she even listening to a word I say?

I'm not even going to argue this because I feel absolutely disgusting, and a disguise is necessary if I'm going out in public. Once I'm done, I'll eat and make a call to Ridge to see if he's got any updates. I'm hoping Scar has already untied Maddox and they are all together now. Once I'm sure all my friends are safe, I'll leave on foot to find Lev.

"Here." She shoves a black bag to my chest, then some clothes. "Shampoo, conditioner, body wash, and a used razor."

"Wow. Thanks. I'll hold off on shaving. Really, though. I appreciate this."

"It's the least I can do for my potential brother's girlfriend."

My lips purse and my eyebrows arch. "Right."

If Temper does end up being Ridge's sister, it's safe to assume they get their weirdness from their father. The thought makes me smile. Ridge is so beautifully weird, and man, do I miss him.

"Out you go," Temper orders as she shoves me through the open door. "End of the hall on the right."

I hesitate, feeling like I'm forgetting something, but when she sets the hat on my head and slips the sunglasses over my ears, I think I'm all set.

"Oh," I begin, spinning around to face her, but before I can finish my sentence, she closes the door. "What kind of food are you going out for?" I mumble to myself sarcastically.

Guess it'll be a surprise. I'm so hungry, I'd eat damn near anything at this point.

My walk down the hall is a quick one, and fortunately, I didn't cross paths with any students. I push open the door to the girls' showers and poke my head in. "Hello?" I call out.

"Hello," someone shouts back over the sound of running water.

"Just seeing if anyone is in here."

"Someone is. Just me."

Not saying anything else, I hurry past the sinks, down to the row of showers, and slip into the first one, yanking the curtain closed before I undress.

The minute the hot water kisses my skin, I feel the tension unravel in my knotted muscles. I'm not sure if it was wrestling around with those guys in the woods, beating the hell out of the trapdoor, or screwing Maddox—twice—on the cement floor, but my body fucking hurts.

My fingers run through my knotted hair and I lean my head back, closing my eyes.

This will all be over soon.

Even if I do get taken in due to my involvement in the governor's murder, I'll plead my case and I have a good shot at winning. It's easy to prove what a psycho the man was. Especially when I know Neo and his sister, Maddie, will vouch for me.

As for the other murders—I didn't kill anyone else. I shouldn't be scared because I had absolutely nothing to do with the deaths of those other guys. I'm innocent and I'll do everything in my power to prove that.

As I try to relax in the shower, I start to realize just how much I miss my guys. Maddox, Ridge, and even though I don't want to admit it to myself, Lev.

Lev might not be mine, but it still feels like there is a string attached between us, pulling us together like a moth to a flame. I can feel it in my gut. There has to be a reason he did what he did. I'm still angry, but I have a feeling once I hear his side of the story that anger will subside.

Once I finish my shower, I reach outside to where the towel hook is. "Son of a bitch," I grumble. I forgot a towel.

With no other option, I use my dirty shirt to pat myself dry then hold up the clothes Temper gave me.

Black leggings that look two sizes too small. Fortunately they're stretchy so I manage to squeeze into them. And a solid black crew-neck sweatshirt that hugs the hell out of my tits.

Once I'm dressed, I slide the old flip phone from Scar in my bra for safe keeping, then I slip on the hat and glasses and sneak out of the bathroom. My bare feet pad against the worn carpet in the hall as I walk briskly back to Temper's room, carrying my dirty laundry and the ugly old coat I hope I never have to wear again.

Stopping at her door, I look both ways, making sure no one is coming as I knock my knuckles to it. To my surprise, it pops right open.

"I'm back," I say, eyes skimming the small space. "Temper?"

I close the door all the way and go inside. She must not be back from getting food yet.

I decide to make myself comfortable on her bed, but not too comfortable. As tired as I am, it feels weird lying down in a stranger's bed. It's crazy how we just met an hour ago and I already feel so comfortable with her. Like she's an old friend who has my trust.

Twenty minutes later, she's still not back, so I lean to the left, allowing my body to drop into the plush mattress.

Before I know it, my eyes are closing.

"Shit!" I jump up from a dead sleep. My heart races, and my chest tightens as a wave of panic washes over me. It's an awful feeling, as if I missed something really important. But all I've missed is time. Time that I should be using to search for Lev.

I take a deep breath and try to shake off the feeling, but its hold is strong.

One glance at the clock on Temper's nightstand sends me into a full-blown panic attack. She should have been back by now. Every place on BCA grounds is within walking distance of only ten minutes tops.

It's been over an hour since I returned from the showers. My air supply feels restricted, like a tight hand is around my throat. There's an immense fear inside me that something happened to her. That somehow I dragged her into my mess.

Where the hell is she?

Maybe she ran into some friends. Then again, she said she's a loner. I can't imagine she's hanging out with anyone, especially when she knows I'm here waiting for her to return.

A thunderous knock at the door has me jumping up from the bed. Light-headedness ensues and I clutch the nearest wall for support until the feeling passes. It's a telltale sign that my body needs food. The last thing I ate was a pack of pretzels this morning that nearly killed me.

"Coming," I say loud enough for Temper to hear. At least, I assume it's Temper. Now, I'm not sure. Once I reach the door, I press my ear to it. "Who is it?"

There's no response. Not a single sound can be heard.

I try again, hoping for a sign that it's Temper. "Is someone there?"

Still nothing.

I can only assume it was a delivery and the sender left. I pull open the door just to be sure, but just as it comes open, I'm shoved back and someone else comes in.

Only, it's not Temper.

Before a scream can even leave my mouth, a hand holding a cloth is smacked over it. I gasp and sputter, trying to get words out as my body tries to fight, but it's no use.

Help me, I silently beg as everything goes black.

My eyes flutter open, and in a disoriented panic, I take in the scene. Shiny leather seats with tinted windows. Outside is nothing but endless fields. The second I try to move the hair from my face, I gasp at the realization that my wrists are bound together with a scratchy rope.

"Did you have a nice nap, Riley?"

My blurry eyes catch a pair of bluish gray ones in the rearview mirror. I blink a few times until more of his face comes into view.

"Who are you?" I ask through dry vocal cords while the scent of a cigar fills my nostrils.

He dubs out his cigar into an ashtray between the two front seats. "Don't worry, I'm not going to hurt you. I have to say, it's a pleasure to finally meet you."

My throat tightens as I hear my own voice echo in the enclosed space. "What do you plan to do with me?"

"I'd just like to talk. That's all."

"Are you..." I choke out. "Are you a Blue Blood?"

"I am." His eyes soften as if he senses my disdain. "Don't worry, dear. You're in good hands. I've come to help you."

It's hard to believe I'm in good hands when mine are literally tied. I suppose it's possible he's just worried I'll try to escape like I did with Maddox.

"Do you know where my friends are?"

"The girl you were with? Temper, I believe, is her name?"

How does he know Temper?

"Her. And the others." I'm not sure if he knows who I'm talking about, but I'm not sure how else to ask him who sent him.

"If you're referring to Lev, I was hoping you could tell me that."

"I...I have no idea. I haven't seen Lev in a couple days."

The car takes a sharp turn to the right, then the mysterious driver presses his foot firmly to the gas pedal, picking up speed.

Fear grips my chest. "Sir," I say softly, but he ignores me and accelerates even faster. "Sir!" I shout over the roar of the engine.

"Did you kill Governor Saint?" He howls like a madman as he drives at full speed down the desolate road we're on. Bumps in the road cause my body to jolt back and forth until my head is spinning.

"Excuse me?" Just as the words leave my mouth, I tip over. My head collides with the side of the door handle and the dull thud of my bone hitting the metal rattles my brain.

My wrists throb in agony as the rope digs deeper into my skin.

"Answer the damn question!"

"I..." I sputter, immense fear monopolizing my tongue, as it tries to prevent me from speaking. "No," I lie on impulse. "I didn't do it. Governor Saint took his own life."

This must be The Punisher assigned to me. He wants a confession so he can end me.

"Don't lie to me, little girl." He whips the car to the left, before slamming on the brakes and bringing it to a screeching halt.

"Why are you doing this?" I cry out.

He aggressively rips off his seat belt, then twists in his place to turn and face me. It's the first time I see his whole face and the familiarity in his features is uncanny. It's like I've seen this man before, but I don't think I have. If he wasn't acting like an insane psycho right now, I might even be able to say he was attractive, in an older man sort of way.

"You've made a big mess, Riley, and unless you want your future to go up in flames, you better tell me the damn truth." His tone is forthright and domineering, and the level of intimidation I feel is making it really hard for me not to break down and tell him everything about the governor. "The truth!" he stammers. "Now!"

My entire body is shaking. My thoughts elude me. I can't focus. I can't think. "I didn't do it," I manage to spit out. "He killed himself!"

His jaw tics, teeth grinding as he speaks. "In three days, they are closing Governor Saint's case. Once that happens, the sealed files from his office will be handed over to The President of The Blue Bloods. Do you know what that means, Riley?" My head shakes no rapidly. "That means anyone the governor was protecting, any secrets he was keeping, will all be exposed."

I gulp. "I don't know what that has to do with me? I'm sorry. I—"

"Shut up!" he roars. "You're lying." Dropping his tone a few octaves, he continues, giving me no choice but to listen while shock and fear consume me. "We need a confession. Proof that he did not end his life on his terms. Only then will his confidentiality rights continue after death. This isn't the real world, Riley. Do you understand that? There are rules in place and steps that are taken." He pulls out some sort of handheld device. "I'm going to need that confession, Riley."

I crane my neck to get a better look at the object and see it's a voice recorder. His finger presses a button on the side as he says, "State your name for the record?"

Is this even admissible? I could be anyone pretending to be someone else. At this point, I have every reason to believe this man is desperate. Governor Saint had something on him that he desperately doesn't want exposed.

Right now, I need to distract him, while getting more information that will help me in the long run.

"Fine," I say, leaning my shoulder into the door with my bound hands only inches from the handle. "I'll give you what you want. But first, can you tell me how you found me?"

He scoffs a laugh, as if I'm a child playing silly games in his world and not attempting to run for my life. "You were practically hiding in plain sight." He waves a hand dismissively, and again, I feel like I'm being judged by a parent. "Any fool could have found you. The Academy was a terrible choice, I might add."

"But I was in a room and you knew exactly what room to go in."

There's only one person who knew I was there, and that person seems to have just disappeared. I thought I could trust Temper, but I was obviously wrong. I must have just been so desperate and her similarity to Scar clouded my judgment.

"If I tell you, will you answer my questions honestly while speaking clearly into the recorder?"

I nod.

"I saw the girl, Temper, at The Academy. She seemed to be in a hurry, as if she was trying to escape something or get somewhere fast. So, I got out of my car and caught up with her. After a few minutes, we realized we could help one another. I got her a ride to where she wanted to go, and here I am."

That fucking bitch! She ratted me out.

"Did she say where she wanted to go?"

"Boulder Cove University."

She's going to find Ridge.

Different thoughts and plans race through my mind as I try to get the upper hand. My heart is pounding fiercely; I fear it's going to flee from my body. My only hope is that she can get to Ridge and maybe tell him who has me or what's happened to me.

"I have to pee."

For fuck's sake, Riley. This man kidnapped you, tied you up, and drove like a madman to this point and you really think he's going to let you out to go pee?

"Piss your fucking pants then. We had a deal."

I swallow hard and before my mind can catch up, my body takes control. My foot lifts and the next thing I know, it's colliding with the soft flesh of his face. He groans and reels backward, and I react instinctively by clawing at the door in an attempt to find the handle. The second my hand wraps around it, I yank the handle downward. In an instant, I'm tumbling out onto the gravel road in the dim light of the full moon.

The driver's door comes open and I watch in slow motion as one boot thunderously hits the gravel.

I roll a couple times before reality slaps me in the face. If I don't get up and run as fast as I can, this man might kill me.

Grit and dust fill my mouth as I desperately search for enough leverage to lift me from the ground. With my hands still bound, I push against the sharp gravel road, giving me enough strength to get to my feet. My eyes flick to the left and I see his face, distorted with rage. Adrenaline courses through my veins, and without a second thought, I sprint down the road barefoot.

I don't dare look back because If I see him chasing me, I'll panic. In which case, I'll likely fall and it will be the equivalent of falling into my own grave.

After about a minute has passed and I'm still on my feet, I do it. I look over my shoulder.

Only, he's not there. The brake lights of the car come on in the distance and I slow my steps. Staring straight at the car, I gasp when I see it whip around, heading straight for me.

I cry out as I take off running again. Rocks and gravel dig into my feet, but the pain is no match for the ache in my wrists. I force my focus on where it needs to be, which is surviving.

I have to get off this long stretch of road.

With one giant leap, I clear a small ditch and sprint straight for the woods.

The bouncing of the phone inside my bra reminds me that it's there, and suddenly, I feel a fleeting moment of hope. The realization that I might not have service is heavy on my mind, but I won't let it bring me down.

That is, until I glance back and see the headlights of the car stopped on the side of the road. My heart is pounding and my breath is ragged, but I don't slow down.

I stumble blindly into the dense woods, pushing past branches and moving around trees, so I can find a safe spot to stop and call for help.

The crunching of twigs in the distance is deafening. It's a sign my captor hasn't given up the chase. I move faster, going in all directions to try and lose him. Left, then right, then straight and turning left again.

I have to get this rope off my hands or I'll never survive this.

Spotting a branch with a jagged edge, wedged between two logs, I creep over to it and turn around so my back is to it. I wince at the sudden tugs on my wrists as I move them back and forth, forcing the rope against the stick's spine. Finally, it snaps off, and my hands are free.

I exhale a sigh of relief as I tuck myself behind a tree and curl over with my palms pressed to my knees.

I hear footsteps crunching in the distance. Only, they are no longer coming closer. They're moving farther away.

Next, I hear the sound of a car door closing. At least, I think that's what it was. It's so far away I can't tell.

My heavy breaths are the only sound as I listen carefully for any clues that this crazed man is still out here.

A few long minutes pass, and I'm almost positive he left, I reach into my bra and pull out the phone.

I'm shocked to see that I actually have a signal out here. With a shaky hand, I tap the button to call Scar. My eyes dance back and forth, all around me as I tremble, waiting for this monstrous man to emerge out of nowhere.

The first ring has my heart fighting to flee from my chest.

The second has it sinking into my stomach.

"Oh my god! Riley!" Her voice is like music to my ears. "Where the hell are you?"

"I need help," I say with a breathless whisper as my eyes peer around the tree. "Someone kidnapped me. He's coming, Scar. Please send help!"

"Who?!" she says in a panic that mirrors my own. "Where are you?"

"In the woods. I don't know where. I was unconscious and woke up in the back of his car. I don't know who he is or where he was taking me. Can you track this phone?"

"It's a burner phone, babe. It can't be traced. Can you get out of the woods and go to a road so you can find a street name?"

"I...I don't think I can. I'm scared, Scar." Tears stream down my face at the realization that my life is on the line here. "I don't even have shoes on."

There's some muffled words and I'm sure she's covered the speaker to tell one of her guys what's going on. A new voice comes on the line and relief floods me, knowing these guys would do anything to come to my rescue just like Scar would. "Are you there?"

"I'm here," I say to Crew. "Please come find me. I don't know what else to do."

"Just stay calm, Riley. We're going to get you out of there."

"Easy for you to say." I scoff as my back slides down the tree. The fabric of the sweatshirt I'm wearing gets caught on some bark, but I keep going down until my ass is planted firmly on the ground. The air around me is freezing, and with no shoes and only a thin shirt, I feel like my life is hanging in the balance, even without this madman chasing me.

I listen intently for any sound around me. There's some leaves crunching in the distance, but nothing that alerts me to a person being nearby.

"Hello?" I say, getting impatient and even more worried with each passing second. "Crew?"

"I'm here. We're just trying to come up with a plan."

Seconds turn to a minute and my stomach begins growling as I wait. I haven't eaten all day. The sun is now completely set. I'm cold. I'm scared.

I can't control my emotions as I burst into tears.

"I just want to come home," I cry to Crew. "Please hurry."

"Riley, you need to get to a road and search for a sign. Anything that tells us where you might be."

"No," I blurt out. "I can't walk out of here, not knowing if he's waiting for me or not. It's dark, Crew. I'm so fucking scared."

There's some static before Scar returns to the call. "Babe, it's me. Listen, you have to be brave, okay? You can do this. You're Riley fucking Cross."

"I'm not brave. I'm weak." A sob cracks through me with the omission, finally saying out loud how I've been feeling since the moment I pulled that trigger on the governor. The moment that was supposed to solidify who I was, a guardian and a protector, is the same moment I feel like I lost who I was.

"Are you kidding me? You are a force to be reckoned with. You hear me? Look at everything you've overcome. Now stand up and straighten your crown because no friend of mine is anything less than a vengeful queen. You are going to walk out of those fucking woods and we are going to come get you as soon as we can." She pauses for a moment and I wipe the tears away from my face, trying to believe her. "Oh, and grab a stick of some sort. You may need a weapon."

"I was feeling pretty optimistic until you mentioned using a stick as a weapon." I chuckle softly, letting some of my best friend's strength bleed into me.

I get to my feet and turn the phone toward the ground, using the little light I have to look for the same stick that set me free, then I jerk it away from the logs. "Okay," I tell her, "I've got one."

"I'm on the line with you. You're going to be fine. Walk out the same way you came in."

My feet move in the direction I came, softly—quietly. But, I feel...lost. "Scar," I cry, "I don't know which way to go."

"Talk to me, babe. What kind of road were you on?"

"Um. Gravel. Definitely gravel."

"Okay. Keep walking and I'll keep talking."

Scar's words replay in my mind as I plant one foot in front of the other, willing myself to conquer my fears. *You are a force to be reckoned with.*

I hardly believe it to be true, but it's what she said after that, that really resonated with me. *Look at everything you've overcome.*

I shot a man to defend my friends. I slept with a villain and found his light. I tied my boyfriend up to get free and forged my own path. I fought three men with everything I had, and with a little help, I was able to get away. I'm not weak, I'm a fighter.

I am Riley fucking Cross.

Scar keeps talking, but I don't hear her. All I can focus on is each step in what I hope to be the right direction.

I walk. And walk. And walk until my feet are numb. I could feel the blood on them from the terrain when I sat down, but if I focused on it, there was no way I would have gotten back up again. So the numbness from the cold helps.

"I see a clearing," I whisper-yell. "I think I made it."

"Keep going, girl," Scar cheers me on and hope flutters in my chest.

Walking out of those woods is what I would assume reaching the peak of a mountain feels like. I'm really damn proud of myself. Even more so, I'm relieved to see there's no car in sight.

At least, not from what I *can* see.

"I'm on the road. It's so dark. I can't see much."

"Are you alone?"

My eyes skim the dark area. Fortunately, there's a full moon tonight, so it's not pitch black. "I...I think so."

"Are there any buildings? Anything that can help us find you."

"Yes!" I beam as my eyes latch on to a shape off in the distance. "Yes! There's a farmhouse. I have to walk through a field, but I think I can make it."

"Go to it!" Scars voice is almost a scream and I hear her shuffling around. "Go knock on the door and if someone answers, give them the phone. I'm putting Crew back on."

Before I know it, I'm full-on running to the house. My feet smack against the cold ground, twigs and rocks grinding into my heels, but I don't stop.

There's a chain-link fence with two, maybe three, dogs that are barking and I hope it alerts the owners that I'm here. I also hope they don't greet me with shotguns.

My feet pound against the crumbling wooden steps of the old house, splinters catching my cracked heels. As much as I want to buckle over in pain, I keep myself upright and push forward with everything I've got left.

My heart hammers in my chest as I clench my hand into a fist and furiously begin banging on the metal frame of the screen door. I step back, take a deep breath, and shout desperately, "Help me!" Then I pound on the door again.

Suddenly, the door opens and I'm face to face with a tall, slender man, wearing a straw hat with a big brim. He's got on a pair of jean overalls, adorned with a plaid flannel shirt. His eyes scan my dirty, bare feet before settling on me. "How can I help you, young lady?" His voice is soft as he opens the screen door with an outstretched palm.

"Give him the phone," Crew chirps in my ear.

"I..." I stutter. "I need help." I shove the phone toward him, feeling a bit stunned and speechless.

The man, taken aback, accepts the phone with a confused look on his face. He brings it to his ear and says, "Hello."

His eyes widen as Crew talks his ear off, filling him in on what's going on. Without a word, the man steps to the side and waves me into the house.

I hesitate at first, but when I see a sweet lady wearing a floral apron, her salt-and-pepper hair piled in a bun on the top of her head, I accept his invitation.

The scent of banana bread floods my senses and my stomach growls in response.

Ignoring the man on the phone with my friends, I take the lady's hand that's extended to me and I follow her into the kitchen. "You poor thing. Let's get you some milk and cookies."

The next thing I know, this sweet old lady has me sitting in a chair while she brings me an overflowing plate of chocolate chip cookies.

"Thank you," I say kindly. "You didn't have to go to the trouble."

"Oh, it's no trouble, dear. It's not often we have visitors out here."

I nervously lick my lips and swallow. My mouth feels like cotton, but I feel the hard lump leaving my throat as my nerves settle down a bit. I pick up the glass of milk and drink it all down in one big gulp.

"Where exactly is *here*?" I ask, curious where I am.

The sweet lady refills my milk from a glass canter. "Davenport," she says.

"Davenport? Is that near Boulder Cove?"

She stares off, drawing her finger in the air as she speaks. "Davenport is over here. And Boulder Cove is over here. About an hour away."

I breathe a sigh of relief, knowing I'm not as far as I could have been. Hell, I could have been in another state, for all I know.

"Your friends are on their way," the nice gentleman says as he hands me my phone back. "Sounds like you've been through quite the ordeal. Now, I've agreed not to call the town sheriff for the time being, but you kids could get yourselves seriously hurt by keeping this to yourself."

"Thank you, sir. I appreciate your help." I look at his wife. "Both of you. Really. You've been so gracious and kind."

"You're welcome, young lady."

As my adrenaline begins to fade, my eyes start to grow heavy and the aches in my body begin to set in.

At the time, I forced myself not to think about the pain or discomfort of walking miles through the woods, on a gravel road with no shoes, but the pain starts to set in as I notice blood marking this kind couple's hardwood floors.

"I'm so sorry, do you have anything I can wipe this up with?" I ask in a panic, feeling so rude for barging in here and not taking the time to consider the dirt and blood being tracked in through their cozy home.

"Oh, don't worry about it, dear," the sweet old man says as he grabs a towel and some cleaning spray. "My love, why don't you grab our guest a towel and show her to the bathroom so she can wash her feet?" He studies the cuts and scrapes on my flesh before he adds, "I'll drop the first aid kit off by the door for you. You don't need an infection after everything you've been through."

I nearly choke on a sob. "Thank you," I say as tears stream down my face. "You're so kind."

I wipe the tears from my face as the lady walks me to the bathroom and hands me a towel. Before she leaves, her hand rests over mine for a moment. "Sometimes the hardest cards are dealt to those with the strongest minds." She pats my hand before walking out and closing the door.

I take the time to clean everything and apply ointment and bandages where necessary, and I take a few of the painkillers inside the first aid kit. I'm sure Scar and her boys will be here soon.

As I walk back into the room and take a seat, I'm greeted with more cookies and milk as well as a blanket, and I curl up in my spot to dig in.

All I can do now is sit back and fill my belly while I wait for my ride out of here. Definitely not the worst predicament I've found myself in since the alert went out.

CHAPTER 14
LEV

"TAKE A LEFT AT THE NEXT ROAD," Ridge instructs me, and I scowl at his directions.

"I know where he lives, dumbass."

"I know. But you were different the last time we were here. Wasn't sure if you forgot."

My head shakes in annoyance. "My personality might have been different, but my memory isn't lost."

You know the reaction you get when you mix gasoline with fire? An explosion, right? Well, that's pretty much what driving in a car with Ridge for two hours is like. At least, that's how my fucking head feels right now.

Two hours of nonstop talking, and the most ridiculous shit at that.

An hour ago, he shifted the subject to vampires and how he wishes he was one so he could turn Riley and live eternally with her. The guy is in love, but he's also grossly obsessed.

"You're sure she's okay?" I ask, referring to Riley now that my mind has shifted back to her. It happens so often.

Lately, I find myself thinking about her all the time. I know she's angry with me. I know I have a lot of explaining to do. And I will. In time.

"Maddox said Scar gave him her coordinates and he's on his way to her. They should meet us at his house by sunrise."

It's two o'clock in the morning and we're driving back to our hometown because Ridge is convinced that's where we need to be. The lockdown still hasn't been lifted, and there's no saying when classes will resume now that there was another murder on campus. The search for Riley is still ongoing, and it's safe to say the moment it's suspected we're with her, we'll be added to the wanted list.

Ridge and I have no idea where Riley and Maddox have been, or what they've been doing. He said he'll fill us in when they get here. I just wish I could see her once she arrives. Ridge and I both agreed it's best if I stay at the apartment downtown while they all crash at Maddox's house. His parents are out of town right now—his dad in Boulder Cove with all the other asshole Elders, and his mom in Aruba. It really doesn't matter to me where I stay. Every place is the same in this town. It's depressing as shit and I hate being here. It's probably best if I'm alone because I'll drag everyone down with my 'sourpuss attitude,' as Ridge likes to call it.

The second we pull into Maddox's driveway, I slam the car into park and swing the door open. Curled over, I gasp for air. Ridge just ripped a big one and stunk up the whole fucking car. The stench follows me, burning my nostrils. I wave my hand in front of my face. "You're disgusting, man."

He closes the door and rests his arms on the top of the car. "You're lucky I waited until we pulled into the driveway. I've been holding that shit for ten minutes."

"And you couldn't hold it for thirty more seconds until I

got out?" I flick the latch of the trunk and circle the car to get Ridge's bag out.

"Don't you know it's not good to hold that shit in?" He's at my side now, so I shove his bag to his chest and he lets out a forceful grunt, catching it before it falls.

"You're a damn idiot." I heave a sigh as I close the trunk and walk up the cobblestone path to Maddox's house.

We drag our feet because we're both tired as shit. I catch the camera on the side of the house and nod my head toward it. "Maddox said he shut those off?"

His jaw stretches wide as he lets out a long yawn. "Yep."

Ridge punches in the code on the front door and it beeps before unlocking. He turns the handle and pushes the door open and I follow him inside. It's been a bit since I've been here, but it looks and smells exactly the same. Like apple cinnamon and a hint of sweet tobacco and spice from Maddox's dad's study to the left of the front door. For as long as I can remember, he's puffed on those thick cigars as he works. Come to think of it, I don't even know what the guy does for work, but whatever it is, he makes damn good money.

This house is what I'd consider a modern-day mansion. Everything is neat and orderly and it's not credited to a housekeeper or maid. Maddox's mom does everything herself. She's a regular old Suzy Homemaker, and a good one at that.

My mom was the same way. She never hired nannies or cleaners and always took care of her kids and her house on her own. I always admired that about her. Though, I wouldn't fault her for hiring help. God knows we needed it. Our lives were beautifully crazy.

Now my life is just crazy. No beauty to be seen. Well,

until Riley walked into my life, that is. She reminds me of my mom in a weird sort of way. Soft and tender, yet outspoken and stubborn. Not to mention their undeniable beauty.

As I'm lost in my thoughts, Ridge disappears. I assume he's going to the room he occupied during his years of living here. It's nice that he has that. A family life. Somewhere to go. People who love him. Sure would be nice to have some of the same comforts in life. Standing here now, in this big house full of love and life, I can't help but feel small and insignificant—out of place, even.

With my hands cupped around my mouth, I holler, "I'm out." My voice booms off the high arches of the ceiling.

When he doesn't respond, I see myself out. He'll figure it out when he can't find me.

It's a short drive to the apartment the guys and I lease. We got the place after graduating from Boulder Cove Academy, with the intention of only staying there for the summer until we started our freshman year at the university. Then we decided to keep it so it was ours every summer. We've only got one more summer until we graduate from BCU, then we'll likely give up our lease and go our separate ways. Whatever way that is.

My feet drag as I walk to my car. Coming to this town is never easy for me. It's like a dark cloud rests over Glendale and it's not until I hit the interstate that the sky parts and I'm able to see the sun. If only I were leaving now. Instead, I'm stuck in this hellhole for a bit longer.

It's the dead of night and there's not a sound to be heard, or a person to be seen, and I'm okay with that.

I pull open the car door and drop my ass inside before shutting it.

The next thing I know, I'm parked in front of my childhood home with my car turned off. A new family lives here now. Two teenage boys who are in high school and their mom and dad. This past summer, I drove by and saw the boys in the front yard playing catch with their dad. The smiles on their faces really resonated with my childhood. It's good to know the house is filled with joy and laughter again.

I rest my head back on the seat and close my eyes, listening to the sound of my sisters' giggling as they'd run away from my bedroom door after knocking on it. Their bare feet would pad down the hardwood floor of the hall and I'd jerk my door open to find no one there. They loved messing with me, and even on the days when I pretended to be angry, I loved it too.

I miss them. I miss us.

Swiping away the dew in my eyes aggressively, I turn the key in the ignition and burnout, leaving a trail of smoke behind me.

I'm not sure why I do that to myself, but every damn time I come to Glendale, I do. It's like I have to see this piece of my past to remind myself why we started this fight to begin with. The only reason the three of us pledged our loyalty to The Society was to take it down. Now, with my uncle dead, I can only hope we are one step closer.

CHAPTER 15
MADDOX

THE FIRST TWENTY minutes of the drive to the hotel were quiet. The last twenty were dead silent. Before we left, Riley apologized over and over again for leaving me in that underground room, naked. I told her I forgive her. It's not that I'm angry; I'm just still so worked up after worrying about her for so long. I'm pissed she put me in that position. I want to protect her, but I can't do that if she doesn't let me.

I did, however, manage to get the names of the three guys who attacked her in the woods and I have every intention of handling those boys. At first, I thought maybe I'd give the list to Ridge and let him deal with them, but my gut tells me I need to do this one myself—for Riley.

When I started this school year, I was determined to break out of my comfort zone and stop being a passive participant in life. I refused to be my father's doormat anymore, and instead of going along with the crowd, I'm learning to stick up for myself and Riley.

We're currently in a run-down hotel room that we stopped at because we're both too exhausted to keep going any more tonight, so the plan is to get a couple hours of sleep and then drive the other hour to Glendale. Riley's on the bed beside me, on her side, facing the wall. She's curled into a ball, and I'm almost certain her eyes are open. No matter how heavy my eyelids are, I can't close them. All I can do is watch her.

Each time I blink too long, panic sets in. There's a constant fear inside me that she'll vanish by the time I open my eyes.

Riley rolls over to her other side and our faces align. "Are you mad at me?" she whispers.

My head shakes against the flat pillow. "No."

"I'm sorry."

I wrap an arm around her waist and jerk her body closer to mine. "I know you are. Promise me you won't do that again."

"I've never been so scared in my life, Maddox. I can one hundred percent promise you I will not flee again."

"No more ropes."

She chuckles. "No more ropes."

My lips press gently to her forehead and I pause to savor the moment. "I'm just so glad you're okay."

"Everything is going to be okay, right?"

"Everything is going to be perfect now that you're back where you belong."

As soon as I punish those three boys, and find out exactly who the dead man is who kidnapped her from that girl's dorm room. Because that's what he is—a fucking dead man.

"I'm okay, Mom. And tell Dad to quit freaking out."

I'm cruising down the highway while Riley gets drilled by her parents. Being members, and Elders, they know everything that's going on. They're demanding to know where she is, but she's not giving up her whereabouts. She's still using the burner phone Scar gave her, and I must say, that thing has come in handy.

"I promise you both, I am innocent, and I'm not going to stop until my name is cleared." Her eyes skate to mine and she cracks a smile. We both know she's not exactly innocent, but she's not guilty either.

We're only five minutes from Glendale and I'm anxious to see the guys so we can all put our heads together and come up with a solid plan to end this. Even though I've already got an idea of my own. I just hope everyone is willing to go along with it.

I reach over and place a comforting hand on Riley's lap as she ends the call and violently chucks the flip phone at her feet on the floorboard.

"Didn't go well?" I ask.

A growly sound escapes her. "I love my parents. I really do. But if they think I'm going home so they can take me to plead my case to the board, they're out of their damn minds."

"We're gonna fix this, babe. And I think I know how."

Her eyes widen in anticipation and a smile plays at the corners of her mouth. She grabs my hand and squeezes it, eager to hear what I'm thinking. "What do you have in mind?"

"You said that man wants a confession. Well, we can't give him that, but we can give him a guilty party."

"Who?" she blurts.

"Cade."

"You're a fricking genius, Maddox." She practically climbs into my lap, grabbing my cheeks with both hands while peppering the side of my head with kisses. I fight to keep the car in my lane but smile at her excitement.

She drops back in her seat, a heavy breath of relief bursting out of her. "Why didn't we think of this before? We can frame him for everything, then make it look like he spiraled out of control and took his life before he was caught."

"It's not going to be easy..."

All the hope in her eyes dissipates and she sinks into her seat. "Still doesn't help with the whole governor situation. I'm still guilty, and eventually, I have to confess."

"Not exactly. What if we find out who that man was who kidnapped you. You said he was hell-bent on proving Governor Saint was murdered and you thought it was because the governor knew a secret of his."

"That's how it sounded to me."

"So then we make it look like he's the one who took the governor's life. Either that, or we just kill him."

Her eyes bulge from their sockets. "As in murder?"

"We do what we have to do."

"Wow," she drawls, "I guess I just never took you to be so savage."

"There's a lot you don't know about me, but once this is done, I plan to tell you everything. No more secrets." I pin her with a glare. "And absolutely no more sneaking off."

Her hand smacks my leg and she squeezes. "Deal."

CHAPTER 16
RIDGE

"GET YOUR CUTE ASS OVER HERE," I sing as Riley comes bursting through the front door of Maddox's house.

She runs into my arms and I sweep her up, twirling her around. All of my worries melt away as I kiss the top of her head, burying my face in her hair. Her sweet scent floods my senses and the warmth from her body sends a shiver down my spine.

I squeeze her body so tightly against mine that she feels like a part of me. A limb that I need for survival. "God, I've missed you so damn much."

"I've missed you, too." She buries her head into my chest, but I grab her face and pull her lips to mine.

My tongue slithers in her mouth, intertwining with hers like two ropes trying to overpower the other. I intensify the kiss, wanting to devour every part of her. I feast on her like a starving animal, dragging my teeth across her bottom lip and sucking it into my mouth, only to let it snap free like a rubber band. My lips trail down her neck, to her collarbone, and she lets out a subtle moan.

Grinding myself against her core, I show her what she does to me every time she's in my presence. And especially now, since it's been so long since I've touched her.

With the back of the couch to the left, I spin her around until her back is to my chest. "I need to fuck you, Angel. Right here. Right now."

It's not a want, it's an aching hunger deep inside me. It's as if we're the only two people in the world and she is the only one who can fill the void inside me. I have to have her. Now.

"But Maddox..." She whimpers as I gather a fistful of her hair and tug back slightly.

Her doe eyes peer up at mine. "Maddox who?"

Riley quivers in anticipation as my hands move to her waist, pausing to tug her leggings past her hips. They are so fucking tight that I debate cutting them for a second before I finally get access to her core. They come to a rest on the curves of her tight, round ass and her body jolts as I grab a handful of her meaty flesh, growling headily. "Fuck, Angel." Then I decide to just do it anyway. I take the knife from my pocket, the cold steel making her muscles freeze as I rip the fabric from her body. Goosebumps pebble her body as I run my hand up the inner part of her leg while I stand.

I press two fingers against her entrance and she gasps. Slowly, I prod them inside her, feeling the warmth and wetness as they curl deeper.

Every few seconds, her head turns toward the front door as if she's waiting for Maddox or someone else to walk in. "Don't worry, babe," I assure her. "I'll make this quick."

I push deeper, drumming my fingers in a rhythmic motion against her G-spot. She cries out in pleasure as I continue the motions, now using my other hand to move in circles over her clit.

Her whimpers grow louder and louder as the pleasure inside her builds. "Oh my god." She moans. "I'm gonna come."

Clenching my fingers with her walls, she holds her breath, then spills into my hand, squirting her juices all over.

Before she even comes down from her high, I shove my rock-hard dick inside her. Her body jolts and she gets a tight hold on the back of the couch, digging her nails into the soft fabric.

I dip my hips, pushing into her forcefully until I'm fully seated. With each slick thrust, her walls clench around me and I gasp at the sensation of her tight pussy enveloping me.

The sound of the door opening grabs my attention, and Maddox steps inside as our eyes meet. He closes it slowly, taking care not make a sound as I continue to fuck Riley from behind.

I return my attention to her as he stands there watching me pound into her.

My fingers delve into the skin of her hips and I move her back and forth, rocking her body against mine.

I don't last long. I never do with this girl. Her angelic pussy has the ability to make me come so fucking fast.

A current of electricity courses through my body as I come. I shudder and moan as I feel the warmth of her walls tighten and I fill her up.

Riley lets out a breathless moan before melting into the back of the couch. I lean forward, cloaking her body with mine as I curve my head and kiss her cheek. "I fucking love you, Angel."

Her cheek rests against mine, and she whispers, "I love you, too."

Those words alone triple the size of my heart. I've always known it to be true, but this girl is my sole reason for existing. She is the air I breathe. Every beat of my heart. I will, quite literally, die without her.

Riley inches backward and I slide out of her. Evidence of our orgasms drip down, hitting our clothes and the floor. I tug my pants up, feeling the warmth of the liquid pool against me, then I peel my tee shirt over my head and crouch down to wipe her up with it.

I slide the shirt up between her spread legs, memorizing her form as I do. My fingers drag across her milky skin and there's a slight prickle, proof that she hasn't had a chance to shave in a couple days. I make a mental note to do it for her, and I will, because my number one goal in life is to make her life easier while filling her with so much happiness, and my cum.

Once she's dry, I stand up and spin her around. Her eyes immediately land on Maddox, who has one foot kicked up on the wall by the door and his arms crossed over his chest. There's a look of concern on Riley's face, but when Maddox smiles and crosses the room to us, her emotions quickly shift gears.

"I didn't know you were there," she says to him as he crouches down in front of her. I step to the side as he pulls up a pair of his gym shorts on her that he must have grabbed from his bag.

He remains down in front of her, but tips his chin. "Didn't want to disrupt your reunion."

Riley rolls her lips together. "I know this isn't normal, but I hope it can be *our* normal."

"Normal is boring," Maddox retorts, and I'm in complete agreement. "We are *us*. Doesn't matter what anyone else thinks."

She smiles in response and I find myself doing the same.

Once Maddox is on his feet, he presses a chaste kiss to her lips. "I'll finish getting your room ready. You'll be in the room between mine and Ridge's" His gaze lands on mine. "Ridge, can you show her to her bathroom? She said she wanted a shower."

I nod and take her hand, leading her through to the kitchen, to the staircase on the far side of the house.

Even with everything going on around us, there's a sense of calm inside me right now. It's amazing how much power another human being can have over your emotions.

Still holding her hand, I lead her into the guest bathroom down the hall from the room she'll be staying in. On top of the sink vanity is a towel, along with some bath essentials, such as shampoo, conditioner, and razors.

I close the door and she pauses inside, as if she expects me to leave. Well, she's wrong.

Reaching over, I turn on the bathtub and click the lever to keep the water from draining. "How about a bath instead of a shower?"

A smile draws on her face. "Okay."

I gather the mini bottles of shampoo and conditioner, as well as a new razor, and set them on the ledge of the bathtub. My eyes land on a near-empty bottle of bubble bath on a shelf to the right, so I grab it and squeeze the remaining contents beneath the stream of running water, watching as foam begins to surface.

As the bath fills, I return to Riley. My hands run down her sleeves and I grip the hem of her sweatshirt. I lift up and her arms instinctively rise. Her tired eyes stare back at me and I get lost in them as I toss the sweatshirt to the floor. Still locked on her blue orbs, I lower myself to my knees and take her shorts back down. She steps one foot out, then the other, and I throw them on top of the sweatshirt.

With her hand now in mine, I lead her over to the bathtub. "Join me?" she asks in a near whisper.

"Planned on it."

She steps into the bath, wincing when her feet, that seem to be covered in cuts and scrapes, touch the water. I immediately want to ask her what happened and demand revenge on anyone that caused my girl pain, much less made her bleed. Except, as her body sinks beneath the frothy bubbles, I find myself not wanting to ruin the moment. I undress quickly, eager to join her. I step in behind her, my legs curling around her body as I cage her in.

Riley rests her head back on my chest, and I draw lines up and down her arms with the foam we're engulfed in.

"This is nice," she says. "If only the comfort I feel now could last forever."

"It will," I tell her. "I need you not to worry and let me, Maddox, and Lev do the worrying for you."

Her body tenses and her eyes look up at me. "Lev?"

I nod. "Yes, Lev."

"But he's the reason this happened, Ridge. He's the cause of this mess." She sits up and meets my gaze with questioning eyes. Her forehead creases prominently and her eyebrows cave in. "Do you know where he is?"

I can't lie to her, and I won't. I tuck a strand of hair behind her ear and mutter a barely audible, "Yeah."

"Ridge!" she stammers, her hand sloshing in the water. "Have you known this whole time?"

"No," I say in a harsh tone. I don't make it a point to lie to her, so why would she assume I was? "Not the whole time. After you and Maddox took off, he called me." My tone softens and I pull her into me, forcing her back to my chest as I hold her. "We have a lot to talk about, including where you and Maddox were all this time. And we'll talk about it all. But right now, just soak up this moment with me."

A minute or so of silence passes and she finally relaxes into me. We sit there, soaking in the water, for what feels like hours, but it's still not enough time. I could stay here forever.

Riley begins to stir, then she slides down, allowing her body to fully emerge. I look down at her face through the clear water. Her eyes are closed, her hair spread out like a web that covers my legs.

When she comes back up, she inhales a deep breath and pushes the water off her face.

Picking up the razor sitting on the ledge, I slide the cap off then reach under the water and grab her leg.

"What are you doing?" She chuckles.

"Taking care of you." I stretch my arm out and drag the razor from her knee cap, all the way up to the delicate crease just above her thigh. She watches me, smiling, as I repeat the motions until I've finished the top of one leg.

Without a word, she lowers her leg and lifts the other, allowing me to continue shaving her.

"You're not human, Ridge Foster."

I smirk. "Why's that?"

"Men like you just don't exist. Why are you so good to me?"

"Because, Riley Cross," I raise an eyebrow as I look at her, "I am truly, madly, deeply in love with you."

Once the top half of her legs are done, I instruct her to

turn around until her feet are in my lap, then I shave the lower half with gentle ease, taking care not to nick her skin. Every so often, I swirl the razor in the water, and resume.

When I finish, I gaze deeply into her eyes and take her hand, raising it in the air, and I glide the razor down her armpit.

Her eyes glisten at me as I take her hand in mine and raise it in the air, making sure that no spot is left untouched. I glide the razor down her armpit. Then move to the other, raising her hand and dragging the blade down. After the final stroke, I lower her hand into the water, still holding it in mine.

"I love you, too," she says. "Truly. Madly. Deeply." It's as if she's been holding on to my last words this entire time.

I grab her waist and hoist her onto my lap until she's straddling me. "For life?" I whisper in her ear.

Warm lips press to my ear as she whispers back, "And longer."

CHAPTER 17
RILEY

HALF THE DAY is already gone as I stretch my arms and legs in the bed I'm sprawled out in. Ridge and Maddox ended up sleeping with me—one on each side. This morning, I opened my eyes to find Ridge sitting beside me with a tray of food. He claimed he was only there for a few minutes and didn't want to wake me, but the temperature of the food says it was much longer.

Normally, I'd be a little freaked out about someone staring at me for so long while I sleep, but with Ridge, I kind of like it. Knowing he will always be there makes me feel safe, which is something I haven't felt since killing the governor.

Maddox has been digging around at his dad's corporate office today. He seems to think his dad is harboring a secret that involves Governor Saint. Both he and Ridge have been very tight-lipped about everything going on, but then again, so have I. Ridge still doesn't know I was kidnapped from Temper's room. Or, that he might possibly have a sister scouring all of Boulder Cove University in search of him.

But today, I plan to tell Ridge everything that happened during my time away with Maddox, and after. I can only hope he does the same in return. I need to know where Lev is and why they're protecting him.

A subtle knock on the bedroom door has me scooting up on the bed. I smooth out the blanket over my legs and holler, "Come in."

The door comes open, and Maddox steps inside. "Good morning, beautiful."

He looks sexy as hell in a sleeveless tee shirt and gym shorts. There's a bead of sweat around his hairline that glistens in the sunlight.

"Good morning to you. Have you been working out?"

"Not exactly the kind of workout I wish I was doing. I've been digging through boxes at my dad's office."

"And?"

He shakes his head in disappointment as he sits on the edge of the bed. "Nothing." He exhales heavily. "I just don't understand why my dad won't let this shit with the governor go."

I take his hand in mine, my thumb grazing his knuckles. "Everything is going to come full circle in time. We just have to be patient, and speaking of patience," I begin. "Mine is running thin. I need someone to tell me what's going on with Lev." His eyes shoot wide open and I see his body tense up. "Why do you get so nervous every time I mention Lev?"

Maddox clicks his tongue on the roof of his mouth before dropping his chin to his chest. "Because I haven't been honest with you. Any of you."

"Baby." I place a comforting hand on his back while still holding his hand. "What's going on? You can tell me anything."

Regretful eyes peer up at me and just as Maddox opens his mouth to speak his truth, Ridge walks in the door. Maddox clears his throat and straightens his back, and I realize the moment of honesty has passed us all too soon.

But not if I have anything to say about it.

Ridge plops down on the bed on the other side of me and squeezes my thigh above the blanket. "What's up? You look worried."

I turn slightly toward him, while still giving Maddox my full attention. "Maddox was just about to tell me something important."

My eyes don't leave Maddox. He gulps before darting his gaze from me to Ridge and then back to me. "It's nothing," he says, and I can feel the anger rise inside me.

"No!" I blurt out. "You were going to say something. Now say it. I'm sick of all these secrets. Why the hell are you guys hiding Lev from me? What don't you want me to know?"

Ridge slides off the bed and gets to his feet. He walks over to the window and presses his hands on either side of the frame. "No one's hiding him from you, Angel."

My hands fly in the air. "Then someone tell me what the fuck is going on!"

When no one says anything at all, I lose it. I jump out of bed, nearly knocking Maddox off it, shouting on my way toward the door. "If no one is going to tell me what the hell is going on, then I'll find out myself."

The second my footsteps are out of the room, Maddox says, "Lev didn't kill Cade."

I pivot around and look at him, and Ridge does the same. "Then who did?"

Maddox takes the corner of his bottom lip between his teeth, averts his gaze, and twiddles his thumbs in his lap.

"Noooo," I drawl. "You?"

"What the fuck!" Ridge's mouth falls open. "You killed Cade?"

I'm surprised to see Ridge is as stunned as I am. Of all people, I'd never suspect Maddox. "You murdered someone?" I huff. "No fricken way."

"It's true," Maddox retorts, his eyes still set on his lap. "I'm not proud of it. I thought he assaulted you. Basically," his head finally lifts, "I killed someone for something he didn't even do."

"Whoa," I trek over to him, "don't you dare do that to yourself." I kneel in front of him, taking his hands in mine. "Cade was not a good man. Even if he didn't assault me, we can't forget what he and his dad did to Lev."

"I just can't believe you had the balls to kill someone." Ridge draws his fingers around his mouth from the other side of the room, a look of disbelief on his face. "I guess my boy's a man now."

I can't help the laugh that escapes me. This is no joking matter, but what the hell is this crazy life if we can't crack jokes about the murders of these monstrous men.

Maddox scowls at Ridge, as if he's taken offense to what he said. "Is that what makes a man?"

"Dude, it was a joke."

"Then tell me, are you a man now?"

Ridge's eyebrows furrow together and his lips purse tightly. "What's that supposed to mean?"

"You think this is fucking funny? How about we all laugh at what you've done. Or is that a secret you intend to take to your grave?" Maddox is nearly yelling at Ridge now.

"Hey," I tell Maddox. "It's okay. Ridge told me about what he did as a child."

Maddox's gaze is pinned heavily on Ridge when he says, "That's not the secret I'm talking about."

My head turns slowly to Ridge. "What is he talking about? What other secrets do you have?"

Ridge scratches the top of his head in confusion. "Fuck if I know what he's going on about."

Maddox springs to his feet, shoulders taut. "So that's how it's gonna be?" He huffs as he takes slow strides toward Ridge. "You're just gonna let her go on thinking Lev killed those other four guys and framed her for it?"

Maddox's words seem to have struck a nerve. Ridge's eyes narrow, and slow, controlled anger spreads across his face. He clenches his fists so tightly that his knuckles turn white as he draws in a deep breath through his flared nostrils. "Shut your fucking mouth."

"What is he talking about, Ridge?" I stand there, stunned in disbelief. "Did you kill those men?" I can't believe the words coming out of my mouth. "Did you frame me?"

Ridge's eyes snap away from Maddox and soften as they land on me. "No! God no, Angel." He crosses the room and attempts to take my hand, but I jerk it away. "I would never frame you for anything. That was Lev. You have to believe that."

My head draws back quickly and I can't control the rapid blinking of my eyes. "I don't know what to believe anymore."

I take a step back as this reality begins to set in. Ridge has always been my constant in this group. He's always been there, even when I didn't want him to be. He told me the truth even when it hurt. So what the fuck is happening?

"You lied to me," I say as my bottom lip trembles, but I refuse to give him any more of a reaction.

Ridge jabs a finger in the air in Maddox's direction as he seethes. "So you can forgive him for taking the life of a guy who did nothing to hurt you, but you punish me for taking three to protect you?"

My voice rises to a near shout and I can feel my cheeks burning with anger. "How was that protecting me?"

"Those men knew!" he spits. "They knew you killed Governor Saint, and eventually they would have told someone. They had to go."

Tears prick at the corners of my eyes as I try to process everything I'm hearing. "You killed three men!"

His voice echoes off the walls as he shouts, "I killed three men for you!"

"I..." I backstep, stumbling over my words. "I need some air."

Ridge begins toward me, but I hold up a hand. "Don't. Please," I beg as I nearly trip trying to put some distance between us.

I storm from the room, feeling like everything these past couple months has been a lie. My feet don't stop moving until I'm settling on an old board swing hanging from a towering oak tree in Maddox's backyard. The weathered rope of the swing creaks as I sit down. I don't bother swinging. I just sit there, alone with my thoughts.

Maddox killed Cade. He thought he was protecting me, but in the end, he was actually protecting Lev. I can't fault him for that.

Ridge killed those other men. He, too, was protecting me. How many people have to die for me? Tears spill down my cheeks at the thought of all these lives being taken because of me.

Lev killed Zeke for reasons still unknown. Then he framed me for the other murders, because what, he wasn't in his right mind? Am I so forgiving that I can let that go too?

Minutes pass as I'm lost in thought. I'm not sure how many, but it feels like an eternity because the sun is already beginning to set. Suddenly, my gaze shifts to a shadowy figure moving slowly toward me.

My eyes lift to meet his. "Lev?" That one single word is laced with so much emotion, my heart can barely contain it. It's a mixture of indignation, rage, and pain. "You're here."

With his hands stuffed in the pockets of his black jeans, he strolls toward me. His head hangs low, but his eyes are dead set on mine. I jump up, anxious to see him, but I'm not sure why.

He stops walking, one foot set in front of the other. "You gonna run away from me, Trouble?"

I shake my head no and sit back down on the swing.

He takes a couple more steps until he's pressing his palm to the tree. "The guys are gonna be pissed. But I had to see you."

"I'm glad you came."

His eyes perk up in surprise at my declaration. "You are?"

"Seems I owe you an apology."

The corner of his mouth tugs up. "And I owe you one, too."

"You definitely do. But I'd like to go first, if you don't mind." Lev waves his hand in the air before returning it to the tree, so I begin. "I'm sorry I didn't take the time to listen to you at the cabin. I just...saw your pill bottle and knew it was a match to the one in my room. I'm not saying I'm not mad at you for what you did, but I'm willing to hear you out now."

"I fucked up, Trouble." His hands run through his white-blond hair with his gaze downcast at his feet. "Let me rephrase that. I *was* fucked up."

"I know," I cut in. "I know all about that horrible doctor and your uncle. I'm so sorry they did that to you."

His shoulders shrug. "It is what it is."

"No," I stammer. "That doesn't have to be your response. Be mad, Lev. Be fucking furious. You're allowed to be. It doesn't make you crazy."

"Doesn't it, though? If I react, am I the same man I was when they were drugging me? Will I lose all credibility because I lost control yet again?"

I push myself off the swing and walk over to him. The pain in his eyes slices my heart in two. As angry as I am, I don't want Lev to hurt. I take his hand from the tree and hold it in mine. "You're human. You're allowed to react."

His eyes skate up to mine and butterflies swarm through my belly. "You're human, too, Trouble. You should be angry; you're the one who deserves to be fucking furious. Go ahead and tell me what a horrible person I am for coming into your room and taking advantage of you when you were drunk. And let's not forget, I pushed a man out your bedroom window for my own benefit. Because I wanted it to look like Cade did it. I fucking hated him." His shoulders square as he takes a step back and brings his hands to his chest. "Let me hear it. Give me all you've got."

I slowly shake my head no. "That wasn't you."

"But it was me," he screams, body shaking with anger,

only it's not directed at me. It's directed at himself. "I did those fucking things."

"Stop it, Lev!" I grab both of his arms to hold him still. "You weren't in your right mind. You're not the horrible person you want to believe you are."

Lev closes his eyes and I let go of him as he pinches the bridge of his nose. "Everything's just such a fucking mess."

"No kidding." My voice is almost a whisper as I replay the conversations I had with Maddox and Ridge. "I don't even know where to begin cleaning up any of it."

"You shouldn't have to," he says, eyes now open. "This is our problem—mine, Ridge's, and Maddox's. You shouldn't be worrying about any of it, and it kills me that you are."

"Well, you framed me. So, there's that." A smile plays on my lips and I'm hoping he sees the humor in it.

When he grins back, I'm certain he does. "I take it you know I'm not the one who killed those guys? Or Cade?"

"I know you didn't do it, but I know you did frame me."

"That was my next apology. I didn't know you then, Trouble. Didn't care about anyone or anything. I saw you as a threat because I knew you killed Governor Saint and I knew Ridge's assignment was to investigate his death. Then I saw Ridge going around murdering these men as he was obsessing over you, and my first instinct was to cover his tracks while protecting him from..."

His words trail off, but I know what he was going to say. "From me?"

He draws in a deep breath. "I guess so."

"Do you still feel that way? Like you need to protect your friends from me?"

His response is an immediate, "No." There's a slight

pause before he continues, "The only person I want to keep safe is you."

A warm feeling of contentment flows through me, and I find myself grinning from ear to ear. "But what if the only way I feel safe is *with* all of you?"

"Then I guess it's time we bring some fuckers down." His smile matches mine and I feel like things are finally about to change.

"Together?" I stretch out my arm and he responds by enveloping my hand in his calloused grip.

"Together." Just as the word slips through his lips, his eyes shoot over my shoulder.

I follow his gaze to see Ridge sitting on the bottom step of the porch, watching us.

"He's always there," I tell Lev.

"Yep," he pops the P. "And he always will be. How do you feel about that?"

My eyes roll as my annoyance with Ridge returns. "Right now, I'm pretty pissed at him. Maddox, too."

"Maddox?" He inhales audibly through his mouth. "Didn't know Maddox was capable of doing anything to piss anyone off."

"Ohhhh, you have no idea, do you?"

"Guess not," he quips.

"Well, allow me to fill you in." I gesture toward a small bistro set that's situated between two flowerpots on a gray cement patio.

Lev pulls out a chair for me and the metal legs scrape against the cement. I take a seat, and he settles into the chair across from me.

"I guess there's no easy way to say this." I purse my lips before continuing. "Maddox killed Cade."

Lev's eyes nearly pop out of their sockets before he bursts out in laughter. His hand smacks repeatedly to his leg, as if this is the most humorous thing he's ever heard. "No fucking way."

"That seems to be a common reaction, but yeah, he did. He just admitted it to Ridge and me before I came out here."

"It's true," Ridge hollers from where he's still sitting about forty feet away. "Our boy fucking ended that piece of shit."

"Nosey bastard," Lev grumbles, and I laugh.

After filling Lev in on everything he's missed, we sit outside and talk for what feels like hours. Ridge even brought us out food, while being respectful enough to let us have our privacy, of forty feet. Eventually, though, he did go inside with Maddox.

The sun is completely set now, but there's two yard lamps lit beside us on the small patio.

Lev reaches across the table and he takes my hands in his. Butterflies swarm through my stomach as I relish in the way his skin feels against mine. His mouth opens, then closes, and I watch intently as he struggles to get out the words he wants to say. "I...um. I don't know where we were headed before everything went to shit, but I'm hopeful that maybe we can get back to that place at some point. The truth is," he pauses for a beat, "it's been a long time since I've been scared to lose someone and that might be because I really don't have anyone to lose besides the guys. But the thought of losing you terrifies me, Trouble."

Grazing his thumb with my forefinger, I smile in response as I say, "I'm not going anywhere."

CHAPTER 18
RILEY

LEV RAN BACK to the apartment and grabbed his stuff after deciding to stay here at the house for the remainder of our stay in Glendale.

Maddox and Ridge have been working hard on putting together some puzzle pieces, so we can move to the next phase of our plan. But first, we need to get inside Cade's house.

"Maddox," I call out as my bare feet pad through the kitchen, into the living room. "Where are you guys?"

"In here," Ridge responds. I follow the sound of his voice to an open door off the living room and a familiar scent floods my senses.

I poke my head in the door to see Maddox on the floor beside a desk with a stack of papers while Ridge shuffles through folders in a file cabinet.

"Find anything?" I ask, still unable to shake that scent. I wander into the room, sniffing it out to see what it is.

"Not a damn thing." Maddox clenches his fist as he slams a closed notebook onto the stack of papers. "There's nothing here. Maybe my dad just takes his job as a Guardian very seriously."

I hear Maddox, but I'm not paying him any attention as I approach the desk. My eyes land on a half-smoked cigar sitting in a black marbled ashtray. Without any thought process behind it, I pick up the cigar and inhale the scent.

"Does your dad smoke these?"

"Oh yeah," Maddox grumbles. "Nasty fucking things."

"I don't think there's a day I've seen your dad when he wasn't puffing on one of those tobacco logs," Ridge adds.

I set the cigar back in the ashtray but can't seem to take my eyes off it as memories of yesterday infiltrate my mind.

"Maddox," I say with hesitation in my tone. "Do you have a picture of your dad?"

It may seem like an odd request, but something in my gut tells me I have to see what this man looks like.

"Um, I think there's a family picture of us in the living room on the fireplace mantle."

I don't even say anything before turning around and leaving the room.

"What was that all about?" I hear Ridge ask Maddox, but I keep walking.

Slow, cautious steps lead me to the fireplace, while my heart is nearly jumping out of my chest, seeming to already know what I'm going to find. It's a crazy thought, and I hope I'm wrong, but the minute I lay eyes on the five-by-seven picture, set in a gold frame, my stomach drops.

"No," I mutter under my breath, my knees nearly buckling under the weight of this revelation. *It can't be.*

It's as if the man in the picture is staring straight back at me. Those bluish gray eyes—the same ones that watched me in the rearview mirror while I was bound in the back of his car.

I gasp for air, feeling as though it's all been sucked from my lungs. "Maddox!" I yell, but my voice seems to break. When he rushes into the room, placing a hand on my hip, I realize that in about ten seconds, I'm going to change his whole life. His family may never be the same.

"What is it, babe? What happened?"

My eyes lift to his worried ones as I struggle to get the words out. I point to the picture with a shaking finger and I manage to say, "It was him."

"Him, what? That's my dad. What do you mean, it was him?"

"That's the man who kidnapped me from Temper's room." My body begins to shake involuntarily and I feel like an idiot because the second I laid eyes on that man, I should have known exactly who he was. How could I be so clueless?

"What the fuck are you talking about?" Ridge blurts out angrily. "Who the hell is Temper? And, what's this kidnapping shit you're talking about? Are you guys keeping something from me?"

"Shut up!" Maddox snaps at Ridge before returning his attention to me. "You've gotta be mistaken. My dad isn't capable... He isn't... He..." His words trail off as if he had an epiphany and I don't say anything. Instead, I allow him time to process his thoughts while I process mine.

"Someone fucking answer me!" Ridge growls at my side, nearly making me jump. "Did someone hurt you, Angel?" He grabs my face in his hands and turns me to look at him. "Tell me the truth."

I swallow hard, unsure of what to say.

Maddox snatches the picture off the mantle aggressively

and puts it right in my face. "Look at it again. Please. I need you to be sure. We need to be perfectly fucking sure before we move forward with this." I can't tell if he's begging for me to tell him it was his father, or if he's hoping it isn't as I watch the tremble in his hand right where he's squeezing the frame with all his might.

I stare at the picture, wishing it wasn't true. Hoping like hell I was mistaken the first time, but the longer I look at those eyes, I'm even more certain. "It was him." My tone is low and my words are strained. "I'm sure of it."

Maddox slams the frame to the floor beside us and I watch as the glass shatters into hundreds of pieces. Tears pool in my eyes, but they're not for me or what I went through, they're for him. "I'm so sorry," I whisper.

Ridge steps closer, crunching the glass and the gold frame, having no regard for the photo. It's as if the family Maddox once thought he had is now as broken and as shattered as the shards on the ground. "If someone doesn't tell me what the hell is going on right now, I'm gonna start breaking shit, too."

Maddox growls and runs his fingers along his chin. He turns away with his head hung low as he paces back and forth, his rage apparent, but his pain hidden deep inside him.

"Angel," Ridge says hastily as he grabs both of my arms. My body shakes along with his as his hard gaze sets on mine. "What. The. Fuck. Happened?"

I'm almost afraid to tell him. Scared that he'll go mad and storm out of this house to find Maddox's dad. And once he does, he'll kill him. There isn't a single doubt in my mind after everything I learned tonight.

"I'm gonna fucking kill him," Maddox pipes up, taking

on the role himself. Or at least, threatening to. "He's a dead man."

"Who?!" Ridge screams, the sound so loud that it jolts me. "Who the fuck are *we* killing?"

Maddox stops pacing, his face red hot and his fists clenched at his sides. "My dad."

"All right then," Ridge retorts with a shrug, far less surprised than I thought he'd be. There's not a bit of sympathy for Maddox in his tone and it has me wondering why he isn't questioning this more. Unless, the loyalty these three guys have far exceeds what I ever could have imagined.

"Stop it, you guys," I tell them. "We need to think this through. No one is killing anyone. I think we've all done enough of that for a while."

Maddox's shoulders relax a tad, but it's apparent the anger he's feeling hasn't dissipated at all. "I knew he was hiding something." He looks at me, shaking his head in disappointment. "That's why he kidnapped you. Tell me what he said again about needing a confession."

Ridge grows concerned but holds his composure as I speak.

"He said, um...something about needing a confession within the next couple days, or the governor's sealed records would be handed over to someone." I clear my throat as I try to remember everything, knowing I'm not getting my words exact. "He also said something about a lot of secrets being exposed."

Maddox snaps his fingers. "The governor had something on him. Something fucking huge."

"Fuck the governor," Ridge snaps. "Why didn't you guys

tell me about this? How the fuck could you keep something so damn important from me?"

I run a comforting hand down Ridge's arm. "I was going to tell you. Things have just been so hectic."

"Does Lev know?" he asks, as if in some way it would be a betrayal if I told Lev and not him.

"No," I say as anger rises inside me. "But it's not like I was purposely keeping this from you. Not in the way you and Maddox kept secrets from me."

I know it's not the right time to have this discussion, but if we're laying all our secrets out there, then the feelings that come along with the truth should be revealed too. "I'm hurt that neither of you trusted me enough to tell me what you'd done. And that you let me believe it was all Lev."

"It had nothing to do with trust and everything to do with keeping you safe. And this situation can't be compared. Your life wasn't in immediate danger then. Someone fucking kidnapped you, Angel." He grasps his chest as if the thought physically pains him. "What if something had happened to you? Something...something I can't even fathom." He turns around and bends with his hands to his knees before springing back up. "Did he fucking touch you? I swear to God if he laid a hand—"

"He didn't. I'm fine. He knocked me out, put me in a car and I escaped. The end."

"Knocked you out, how?"

"Chloroform, maybe?" I guess, not knowing of any other drugs that can knock you out from a rag, but also knowing I'm not experienced in that department.

"Son of a bitch," Ridge grumbles. "Yep. He's a dead man."

"They're going down," Maddox chimes in, his voice low

but stern. "Every one of those fucking Elders who have made our lives hell are going down. They will all fucking fall."

It's surreal hearing Maddox speak this way. The harsh words coming from his mouth are far from his usual gentle tone. He's mentioned in passing about how he's always felt like a weak link and I'm proud to see that he's standing up for himself. Even if it is going to be against the man he desperately sought approval from. I can see it in his eyes, hear it in his voice, he's out for blood.

"No one is dying, yet," Ridge pipes up. "In fact, I think I know of a way to use this to our advantage." Maddox and I shift our attention to Ridge as he continues. "First, we need to find out exactly what your dad was so hell-bent on keeping a secret."

A look of defeat washes over Maddox's face. "And how the hell are we supposed to do that? I've searched this place high and low and found nothing."

"Give me five minutes alone with your dad. I'll find out what he's hiding."

"No," I pipe up, a plan already forming in my mind. "I think it's best if we don't let Maddox's dad know we're onto him. If we do this right, we can clear all our names, while bringing down the real villains at the same time."

Ridge quirks a brow. "What did you have in mind?"

"If we're framing Cade for the other murders, what if we give him an accomplice?"

Ridge scoops me off the floor, my feet dangling in midair as he twirls me around. "You're a fucking genius."

As he sets me down, I see Maddox, and my heart splinters. He's on the couch now, elbows pressed to his bare knees as he stares at the floor with a scorned look on his face.

Ridge catches my gaze and follows me over to Maddox's

side. I sit down beside him and rest a comforting hand on his leg. "I know this is a lot to take in."

He jumps up in a state of disbelief, throwing his arms out wide. "He's my fucking dad. How could he do this shit to me, to our family?"

Giving him his space, I remain on the couch while he hovers over the shattered picture on the floor. "Does my mom know about the shit he's been up to, or this horrible secret he's been keeping?"

"Doubtful," Ridge says. "Your mom's a fucking saint."

Maddox's eyes slide up and the pain in them reappears. "I thought my dad was, too. At least, as much as he could be in this world. We're Guardians. We're supposed to protect members, not kidnap them. Whatever the hell he's hiding must be really fucking bad."

"We'll know soon enough," I say softly. "And hopefully, it's not as bad as what you think."

"Well," Maddox says with a sudden shift in his demeanor, "we're not accomplishing anything by standing around here." His eyes dart to Ridge. "Call Lev on that burner phone and fill him in, then we need him to get into Cade's house to put the first part of the plan in motion. After that, let's hear what Riley has planned. I think it's time she knows our endgame here anyways."

"Fuck no. She'll be an accomplice if we fill her in," Ridge says through gritted teeth.

I cross my arms and glower at Ridge. I'm not a damsel in distress that sits on the sidelines, and Ridge Foster needs to come to terms with who the fuck I am.

"I'll be your partner," I say in a condescending tone, moving to stand over him. "If we want this shit to work, we better all get on the same fucking page. First of all, I am not going to sit on the sidelines while the three of you throw yourselves into the lion's den. It's all of us or none of us. And second," I point my finger at both of them to make this very clear, "there will not be another damned secret among us. If you cheated on your math exam in the third grade, I better fucking know about it. No. More. Lies."

Maddox smiles and I can see Ridge debating on agreeing to my terms or throwing me over his shoulder and tying me up to put me in a padded box for the rest of my life where he knows I'll remain safe.

"Deal," Maddox says as we watch Ridge's shoulders sag in defeat.

"Ridge?" I ask, needing to hear him say it out loud.

"All right, it's a deal." He walks over to me and fists my hair. Smacking his lips to mine, he shows me exactly who's in charge here before there's anything I can say about it. He breaks the kiss and looks me in the eyes as he says, "We planned to take down The Society from within, but I feel like you could have probably guessed that by now."

I nod. "I figured as much."

"Well, Angel, now that you've got yourself a harem of murderous psychos willing to go against The Society and exact some revenge, what are you going to do with us?"

The anticipation of what's to come has me feeling light-headed. I hope like hell we can pull this off, because if we don't, we're the ones who are going to take the fall.

CHAPTER 19
MADDOX

CURLING MY ARMS AROUND RILEY, I tug her close while basking in the warmth of her body against mine. "I'm glad you decided not to go."

"Me too. I'd much rather be here with you than out planting evidence," she says while writhing her ass against me.

At this very moment, Lev and Ridge are at Cade's house. Lev was able to confirm his aunt Marta is away with her family right now, grieving the loss of her son and husband. I can't help but feel bad for her. I suppose it makes me think of my mom and how she would feel if she lost me and my dad within the same month. I push thoughts of her alone and sad out of my head. We have enough of our own shit to worry about.

There's an unease inside me that says we shouldn't be letting our guard down and lying in my bed. Even if it is the only place I want to be right now. "We should be doing something," I tell Riley.

"We could make food," she suggests, her voice soft and full of hope at the same time.

A laugh escapes me. "Not exactly what I had in mind. Are you hungry?"

She flips over, lying flat on her back with her hands holding my arm. "I'm always hungry."

I lean down and press my lips to her forehead. "I've got something you can eat right here."

"Oh my god." She giggles. "I'm sure you do."

"Just saying. If you're that hungry..."

A shit-eating grin grows on her face as she pushes my arm off of her. Her body rolls until she's on all fours beside me. "Is that what you want, Maddox? You want me to eat your dick?"

Damn, she's so sexy when she talks dirty.

My hands slap to my sides and I peer down at my erection stretching the sheet. It throbs fiercely with a mind of its own. "Have at it, baby." I give her a wink and I swear her cheeks get even redder.

Seductive eyes watch me as she crawls on top of me, straddling my body. She grips the sheet, pulling it down slowly just to torture me. With her hands skimming up my thighs, she tugs at my boxers, springing my cock free. I'm nearly shaking with anticipation when I give them a swift kick, sending them flying off the bed.

With my arms folded under my head, I lift my hips slightly while her hands caress my body. Her warm fingers close around me and she moves them up and down from the base of my shaft up to the very tip, then back down again.

"Put it in your mouth," I tell her, my voice husky and demanding.

Her eyes never leave mine as she arches her back and closes her mouth around my cock. Sucking in the shallow end, she bobs her head up and down. "Fuck, baby," I grumble while fisting my own hair in an attempt not to come on the spot.

Brushing her lips over the tip of my engorged cock, she continues to stroke with her tightly wrapped fingers. They glide up and down over the bulging veins of my erection. Her tongue follows, flicking and circling as she encases me with her hot, wet mouth. Each suck, each stroke, sends a rush of pleasure coursing through me.

My entire body tingles with desire as she cups my balls and massages them. I reach down, palming the back of her head as I guide her motions. The second her lustful eyes peer back up at me, I lose it. "I'm gonna come, baby. And I'm not ready for this to end yet."

Gripping her hair in my fist, I pull her head back, and in one heady breath, I say, "On your back."

Without a word, she does as she's told. I fucking love her compliance. In a swift motion, I jerk off the boxer shorts she's wearing, exposing her bare pussy.

I drag one hand up her thigh gently, leaving a trail of goosebumps in my path. "It seems I'm a little hungry, too." My brows waggle before I bury my face between her parted thighs.

Her body quivers beneath me as I run my tongue around the outside of her clit and when I suck it between my teeth, she winces.

One hand grips the meaty flesh of her inner thigh as I hold down her leg, her knee pressed to the mattress. The other hand rests on her lower abdomen, and I feel it tighten with anticipation as I move my hand from her thigh to dip two fingers inside her dripping wet pussy. She lets out a muffled moan while keeping her legs open for me as my fingers circle inside her.

Sweat beads on my forehead as I writhe against the sheets. My cock pressing insistently against the mattress while my mouth moves intently at her core.

I work my fingers in and out of her, grazing her velvet inner walls and learning every single spot my girl likes to be touched. Each time I pull my fingers out, she gasps as if she's telling me to put them back in.

Riley grabs my head, using both hands as she forces friction to her core. Her hips roll and she cries out as she fucks my face. I dig my fingers deeper, desperate for her arousal so that I can stick my dick in her and fill her up with my cum. My free hand moves under her and grabs her ass, lifting her slightly, so I can push even deeper with my tongue.

Her cries grow louder and louder as I work vigorously until all her muscles tighten and she releases. Her walls tighten, working my fingers for every drop of pleasure they can deliver. Her legs shake until she relaxes into the mattress, melting just for me. I lick her clean, lapping up every last drop of her orgasm.

I watch her as she comes down, loving how sated she looks over what I've done to her. I keep staring at her as my body slides up hers and in one fluid stroke, my hardness presses into her warm, swollen pussy.

Riley gasps as I ease myself inside, pushing past the tight threshold. Once I'm fully seated inside her, I pulsate in rhythmic motions, moving the shallow end of my cock in and out of her tight hole.

"More, Maddox," she begs as two arms wrap around my neck. I slide my hand up her shirt, wishing I'd removed it before we got started. But now that I'm in, I'm not leaving until I come."

My hips rise and fall and I pinch her nipple between my fingers. Just the sounds she makes has me thrashing into her while our lower halves clap together. Each fall into Riley has her gasping.

God, she feels so fucking good.

"I love fucking you, baby. Let me fuck you for the rest of my life."

"Forever," she chokes out in a breathless voice that makes my heart squeeze with happiness.

Just the word I wanted to hear. *Forever.* It will be my life's mission to keep this girl happy and satisfied, while getting to satisfy myself at the same time.

My heart pounds feverishly as an insatiable need to combust overcomes me, tingles shooting throughout my body. My breathing quickens as I sink deep in her warmth. My cock pulsates as I let go, filling her up with my cum.

I exhale a pent-up breath and sink into her embrace. She holds me tightly, our hearts thumping in sync against one another's.

We're lying there in silence, enjoying the feeling of being so close, when Riley's stomach growls.

"Shit, baby." I lift up, my palms pressed to the mattress on either side of her. "You really were hungry."

She smirks. "Little bit."

I push myself off of her and roll off the bed. "Stay there. I'll get something to clean you up."

A minute later, I return with a warm washcloth. I run it up her sticky thighs, cleaning up the slick mess we made.

Riley watches me, smiling as I drag the washcloth up and down. "You're such a gentleman."

"Only because you deserve it, and more."

Once she's cleaned, we both get dressed—Riley in a clean pair of my boxers and a tee shirt, and me in just a pair of gym shorts.

"Now, let's go get some food." I throw my arms around her lower half and sweep her up, flinging her over my shoulder. Giggles escape her the entire way to the kitchen. And when I finally set her down in front of the stove, she pushes herself up on her tiptoes, thanking me with a kiss.

Riley says she wants pancakes, so we work together to make some. She pours the batter, then I pour the water while she stirs. It's impressive how in sync we move with each other. There's no communication needed as the next steps are taken; it's like we just know.

The frying pan is already sizzling on the stove, so once the batter is clump-free she pours some on. The smell immediately hits my senses and my stomach growls. Riley's eyes shoot over her shoulder from where she's standing at the stove with a spatula in hand. "Sounds like you're hungry, too."

"Fucking starving. For you." I wink.

She chuckles. "You just had me."

"But I can never get enough." I step behind her, wrapping my arms around her, and she relaxes into me. My chin rests on her shoulder and I draw in a deep breath of her scent mixed with the pancakes.

She flips the pancake over, placing the golden side face up, then she sets the spatula on the countertop and turns to look at me. My arms remain pinned to her hips, our noses nearly brushing. "I want to do this every day with you," I tell her. "Sex. Pancakes. Kisses."

Her eyebrows perk up. "Ending the night with snuggles and a back rub?"

"If that's what you want, that's what you get." My voice is honest and sincere. This girl could ask for the world and I would find a way to shrink it just so she could carry it in her pocket.

We finish cooking, then eat the fruit of our labor at the dining room table. I stuff a forkful of syrupy pancakes in my mouth, speaking as I chew. "Good call on the pancakes."

"Pancakes are always the best choice."

We finish eating and put our dirty dishes in the sink, deciding we'll wash them later. Then we do exactly what Riley wants—snuggles and a back rub.

Pure beauty lies flat on my bed. The porcelain skin of her stomach pressed to the mattress and her hands folded under her head.

Straddling Riley's ass with my knees, I squeeze a glob of lavender-scented lotion on my hands and rub them together to warm it up before pressing my fingertips into the center of her back.

I spread the lotion outward in gentle circles, relishing the way her soft skin feels against my calloused hands.

"That feels soooo good," she mumbles, eyes closed and a smile parting her lips.

"It's only the beginning," I tell her as I work my fingers, increasing the pressure while working out all the tension she's feeling.

"I almost feel guilty being this relaxed while Lev and Ridge are out doing all the dirty work."

My hands glide to her sides, fingertips running over the curves of her breasts. "You deserve to relax. You've been through a lot. And don't think I'm not moving to those feet next." Riley's feet have been through hell. Running barefoot through the woods for God knows how long while she was trying to escape, who appears to be my dad, really messed them up. She tries not to let us see her limping here and there, but there was a reason I carried her down to the kitchen. I don't want her hurting, and if I can make up for some of what my father did to her, I have to try.

The thought infuriates me. Finding out your dad is a terrible person should hurt, but it doesn't. Not in the way I would have expected. Instead, I'm silently plotting a revenge scheme of my own. He'll pay for what he's done, and I'm gonna make damn sure he never hurts anyone else ever again.

CHAPTER 20
LEV

WALKING up to the backside of Cade's house, a wave of nostalgia washes over me. The air is suffocatingly thick with trauma and resentment as I look at the house I lived in the years after I lost my family.

It wasn't always bad here. In fact, the first year was surprisingly good. Uncle Austin and Aunt Marta did everything they could to make me feel welcome. But even sweet fruit rots after a while.

Looking back, it's almost as if I can pinpoint the exact day their perspective of me shifted. I was no longer a family member, but their ticket to a multi-million-dollar trust fund. Or maybe it was always that way, and they just put on a show in the beginning. It was a damn good show too.

My second year here is when the verbal abuse began. I was belittled and, many times, forced to eat in my room instead of at the dinner table.

My third year is when things got physical. A slap here, a punch there. My last day here, I'm pretty sure I told my uncle I hated him before he knocked me out cold. I barely remember the details. All I know is, the next day, I fled the house. A week later, a social worker came to school and I was put in foster care with a horrible man—even worse than Uncle Austin.

"You good?" Ridge asks, noticing my reluctance as we approach the house.

"Fucking golden," I tell him.

The truth is, I am fine. I've lived through some shit, but I survived it. I'm still here. It's those sorry bastards who aren't. Austin and Cade got what they deserved. Had they not been taken out, they would have found another way to hurt me and take everything my family left to me.

With the camera in sight, Ridge and I press our backs to the side of the house so we're out of view. Once we're at the back door, I kick up the mat in front of it and retrieve the spare key that's been there since I was, like, six years old, long before I even lived here.

I stick it into the key slot and a second later, the door is open. We walk inside and the scent hits me like a tornado. The smell of leather and money, not that they have much. Austin and Marta pretty much live off The Society. Being a member does have its perks, but I have yet to decide if they're worth it or not.

If my memory serves me correctly, the only cameras are out front and the one we just slipped passed out back. There's no indoor security, so we're good there.

Ridge drops the heavy box he's been carrying to the floor and it lands with a thunderous clap. "Fuck, that thing is heavy."

"I'm not surprised. After all, it holds everything you've collected over the past year on your precious angel." There's a bite of sarcasm in my tone, but I'm actually glad

Ridge was so obsessed with Riley. It's about to come in handy.

"Pick it back up. We gotta make this quick." I walk through the kitchen, taking a left down the hall to Cade's bedroom. I push open the door and step aside. "Put it all in his closet. Make it a shrine that shows his sick obsession."

"Hey," Ridge barks. "It's not an obsession. It's love."

"What-the-fuck-ever." I roll my eyes. "Just make it look like the guy would kill for her."

"With everything in here, it most definitely will. After all, I did."

Once he's in Cade's room, I go across the hall to Austin and Marta's room. I remember a week after I lived here, I walked by this room and saw Austin in his closet, kneeling over an open tote-box full of papers and shit. As soon as he caught sight of me, he quickly threw the lid on it like he was hiding something. Then he jabbed a finger in the air and shouted for me to get the fuck out. So I did.

I approach the closed closet and, with a jerk, I pull it open. Reaching up, I grab the pull string to turn on the light, immediately spotting the same tote from that day. Surrounding it are scattered clothes, shoes, and basically a mess of random shit cluttering the area.

I crouch down and sweep away some of the mess before lifting the lid on the tote. At first glance, it's nothing of use, just more clothes. But when I pull out the worn sweatshirt, I see a stack of papers, some old pictures, and a manila folder labeled *Confidential*. Naturally, I go for that first.

Undoing the clasp on the folder, I flip the lip and pull out all the papers inside. It looks like some sort of report for The Society with The Blue Bloods emblem on top. My eyes scan the first page quickly, but I stop when I see the names Rebecca and Donald Pemberley. *That's my parents.*

This isn't just a report, it's a witness statement from Stanley Crane on the day my family was murdered.

My heart is hammering in my chest as I quickly shuffle through a couple more pages and see a signature at the bottom, and there it is. Maddox's dad's signature—Stanley Crane.

"What the actual fuck," I mumble.

I go back to the first page and begin reading.

> **Detective: State your name for the record.**
> **Witness #3: Stanley Crane**
> **Detective: Mr. Crane, please tell me in detail what you saw that night.**
> **Witness #3: Well, I was walking my dog down Briar Lane when I noticed the front door was cracked open. It was unusual for Donald and Becca to leave their door open, especially at that time of the night. So I whistled for Sammy to follow me up just so I could holler inside and make sure everything was okay. That's when I saw their son standing frozen in the entryway with blood on his hands.**

What? No. I don't remember that. Then again, I don't remember much of anything from that day. I keep reading, hoping something jogs my memory.

> **Detective: Do you know their son's name?**
> **Witness #3: Of course. It's Lev Pemberley. I've known the boy his whole life.**
> **Detective: And what happened next?**
> **Witness #3: I approached Lev, but he was too shocked to speak. He just stood there, staring straight through me with his bloody hands held out in front of him.**
> **Detective: Was he holding any weapons?**
> **Witness #3: Not that I could see.**
> **Detective: It's my understanding that the blood of one of the victims was found on your shoes, is this true?**
> **Witness #3: Yes, sir.**
> **Detective: And how did it get there?**
> **Witness #3: It must have dripped off Lev's hands.**
> **Detective: And a footprint of that same shoe was found in the bedroom of Alana Pemberley?**

I gasp at the sight of her name. *God, I miss you, Alana.*

> **Witness #3: Is that a question?**
> **Detective: It is. Please answer it. Was your footprint of that same shoe found in the bedroom of Alana Pemberley?**
> **Witness #3: That's what I hear.**
> **Detective: And how do you explain that?**
> **Witness #3: I suppose it's possible that I went in there at some point during the chaos. I can't really say. I, too, was in shock by what happened.**
> **Detective: Thank you for your time, Mr. Crane. We ask that you stick around town in case we have any further questions.**

I stop reading there, although there are many more pages of statements from other witnesses.

I don't remember any of this. My eyes close as I try to go back to that day, but my mind won't allow it. I've repressed it so much that I don't think I could remember, no matter how hard I try. I don't think I want to either.

"All done." Ridge's voice comes from behind me.

"Get Maddox on the phone. Now." I slam the papers back into the tote. "Son of a bitch!"

"Sure. Okay." A second later, I hear him say, "Hey. Lev wants to talk." Then he hands me the phone.

I snatch it from Ridge's hand, my mind in a whirlwind. "The night of the dance...*that night*...who all was at my house when you walked there after the dance?"

"Shit, man. I can hardly remember. Um, aside from the police and ambulance, all I remember seeing is your neighbor, who put a blanket over you on the steps."

"Then you called your dad, and he and your mom came and picked you and Ridge up, right?" I ask with panic flooding my veins.

"Yeah. Yeah, I definitely remember that."

"Did your dad act shocked in any way when you told him what happened?"

"Pretty sure it was my mom I talked to when I called, but yeah, they were both beside themselves. Everyone was shocked. Where's all this coming from?"

I reach back into the tote and pull out the entire stack of papers, then I stand to face Ridge. "I think whatever your dad is hiding is somehow connected to *that night*." I shuffle through the papers and pull out the witness statement from Maddox's dad, then I hand them to Ridge.

"No shit?" Maddox sighs. "I thought for sure whatever he was hiding had to do with Governor Saint."

"I would put money on the fact that he was involved with my parents' death somehow and Governor Saint was protecting whatever he did," I tell him. "And if I find out it really did..." As I grip the phone, my hand trembles because I know, in my bones, whatever we are about to find is going to change everything.

"You don't have to tell me twice," Maddox says. "At this point, I'm starting to believe he's just as bad as the rest of them. Finish up there, then hurry up and get back here so we can figure this shit out."

"We're done here. We're on our way." I end the call and gesture Ridge toward the door while I grab the whole damn tote. He walks as he reads with his mouth hung open. I'm ready to get the fuck out of this house. It holds so many of my nightmares but could never touch the worst one. I can feel my heart racing in my chest, my knuckles white from how hard I'm gripping the tote in my hands, knowing they hold the answers to the questions I've been drowning in for the past few years.

CHAPTER 21
RILEY

"THIS IS UNREAL." I shake my head in utter confusion as I pass the papers back to Lev. "How are you doing with all this?" It's a stupid question and I wish I hadn't asked it.

"I'm okay," he says softly.

"No, you're not," I argue. "No one in your situation would be okay." I take his hand from across the table. "I know you're probably not ready, but I'm here if you wanna talk about it."

I fell asleep while getting a back rub from Maddox and woke up to the sound of shit breaking downstairs. When I got down there, I saw Maddox beating the fuck out of everything in his dad's office. Now, Ridge is inside calming Maddox down and I'm sitting in a chair in the backyard with Lev. He filled me in on everything, then handed me proof that Maddox's dad lied in his witness statement. I don't think any of us should jump to conclusions and automatically assume he did something terrible, but we also can't figure out why he'd have Lev's sister's blood on his shoes—and then lie about it.

"He did it," Lev says out of nowhere, his head shaking at his own disbelief. "I can feel it. Maddox's dad fucking murdered my family." Before I can even register what's happening, Lev's chair is screeching across the patio, and when he jumps to his feet, it tips over. The sound of metal colliding with the cold concrete reverberates off the surrounding trees and my body jolts at the loud thud.

I can see in his eyes he wants to run. He wants to fight and kill the man that did this. Hell, I want to do the same. Instead, he clenches his fists then walks back and forth on the patio, from one end to the next, and I wait with bated breath for him to say something. He needs to get out his pain instead of holding it in. After reading through all of this, I'm sure the only thing he can do is let his mind keep replaying that day as he tries to put together all the pieces.

"There's no way he was there," he finally says, his hand running through his hair and his eyes downcast. "I'd remember seeing him. Maddox's parents didn't show up until after the medics and police arrived."

"I believe you," I tell him honestly. "Now we just have to figure out why he was there, and why he lied."

"He was making it look like I did it. That's what he was fucking doing. But somehow, throughout all the statements, he failed."

"Lev," I say his name softly, as if I'm trying to calm a wolf whose teeth are already bathed in blood. His eyes lift and I ask, "Do you really think Maddox's dad killed your family?"

There's not a bit of hesitation when he says, "Yes."

"Then let's fucking prove it and destroy that son of a bitch."

The morning sun beams through the vaulted window of the room I'm in and it takes me a second to realize where I'm at. Turning my head to the left, I see Lev sitting up on the bed, his eyes on me.

"Sleep well?" he asks.

I scoot up until I'm sitting beside him. "Actually, I think I did. How about you?" The bags under his eyes answer my question, but I wait for his response anyway.

"Nah. Haven't slept."

I reach over and take his hand and he watches intently as he twirls his fingers around mine. "I'm sorry I didn't stay up with you."

His eyes bolt to mine. "Don't apologize for sleeping. You've been through hell and need the rest."

A lump lodges in my throat and I fight the tears that threaten to break free. I hate that he's hurting. "So do you." My voice is almost a whisper.

"I'm just glad you stayed with me. It's been a while since I've had anyone care as much as you do."

"Lev," I say sternly as I turn my whole body toward him, "so many people care about you."

"Oh yeah? Name a few."

"Me, Ridge, Maddox…"

"And the list ends there. Face it, Trouble. I've got nobody. Which is fine. This is my life. It's been this way for years."

"Well," I squeeze his hand tightly, "I'm not going anywhere and neither are Ridge and Maddox, so you've got us for life."

The corner of his mouth twitches with a smile. "You mean that?"

"Hell yes, I do. We're all in this together. For the long run."

There's a beat of silence before he looks at me and says, "I know I fucked things up—"

"Stop it," I spit out. "Don't even go there. We've all fucked up."

"True. But I was going to say, I know I fucked things up, but I really like where we were headed before I did."

His words pull at my heartstrings, eliciting a smile to my face. "I did, too."

Lev leans in slowly and presses his lips to mine. It's gentle and soft, and not at all like any other kiss I've shared with Lev.

My eyes close and I bring my hands around his head, cradling it in my palms so he can't pull away. I want this feeling to last. The butterflies in my stomach. The tingles shooting through my core.

Lev turns more toward me then lowers his body down on mine, blanketing me with his warmth. One hand glides up my side beneath my shirt and goosebumps break out on my skin.

My insides quiver in anticipation of what's to come, and God, I hope something more is coming. Then I feel his erection pressing into my thigh and I'm certain he wants this is as much as I do.

The timing is terrible, but maybe this is exactly what we both need. We deserve to feel love and happiness despite the hell around us. Isn't that who we are to each other? The calm in the storm, the breath of fresh air after a wave sweeps you under. And there's nothing I want more than to breathe him in until he's as much a piece of me as my heart is.

I run my hand down his back then move it around his

waist, dipping my fingers beneath the waistband of his boxers. My heart is hammering in my chest as I slide lower, feeling the silky smoothness of his head and the cool steel of that piercing I love so damn much. The feeling alone is enough to have me panting already.

Lev lifts his head, bright blue eyes peering down on me. "I need you, Trouble."

I respond by wrapping my hand around his girth, stroking in slow, subtle motions and flicking his piercing with my thumb when I twist. He lifts his hips, giving me room to work.

His mouth trails lingering kisses down my neck and jawline. A wave of heat floods through my body as his hot breath touches my skin.

I keep stroking him, feeling the metal of his piercing graze against my palm. I forgot how big Lev is, and he is really fucking big. My pussy clenches at the thought of him being inside me. It's both terrifying and exciting at the same time.

I've had sex with Lev before, but it was a time when there wasn't much passion. Right now, I feel every emotion surface. He lifts his body off of mine and I'm forced to let go of him.

Before I have time to complain about his heat not being on me, he grips the hem of my shirt and rips it off in one motion, tossing it across the room. I'm not wearing a bra or panties, and I'm thankful for that because I don't want to waste a single second. My insides are literally screaming for him to fuck me.

I watch him keenly as he kicks out of his boxers then bites the corner of his lip, his gaze lost on my naked body. He fists his dick in his hand, pumping it as he looks down at me with a sinful expression that has me trying to press my thighs together. "You're so fucking beautiful," he says breathily.

My cheeks flush with heat at the compliment and I reach out, grabbing him by the waist and pulling him back down to me. "So are you." He is. Lev is so damn beautiful. And sexy—mysterious, crazy. He's perfect.

I fist my hand in his hair as his body presses to mine. "Now fuck me."

He tsks. "So impatient." Then he slides his hand down my stomach and I suck in a deep breath. Shivers dance across my skin as he parts my legs and his hand explores the wetness between my thighs. His lips cover mine and our tongues dance in a rhythm I feel like we've always known.

The tips of his fingers prod at my entrance and my hips rise off the mattress, desperate for him to push deeper. My heart rattles against my rib cage as he continues to tease me, rubbing circles around my pussy without giving me what I'm craving.

I growl into his mouth and he lifts his head, breaking our kiss, a devious smirk on his face. "What is it that you want, Trouble?"

My response is immediate. "You."

His face buries into my neck and as he sucks on my delicate skin, he says, "I'm gonna need you to be more specific."

"I want all of you," I tell him breathlessly. "First your fingers, then your dick."

The next thing I know, he's knuckle deep inside me and I'm crying out, nails dragging down the skin of his back. "Oh, fuck. Oh god." My back arches in a mixture of pain and euphoria while his eyes stay glued on me, soaking in every ounce of pleasure he gives my body.

Curling his digits, he hits just the right spot, driving in

over and over. I can feel my walls start to grip him. His pace picks up and my jaw drops open in bliss...so much so that I see stars. My body is not my own as I come undone within a matter of seconds since he entered me. I can't control the trembling in my body that builds with every thrust. Suddenly, I'm swept away, lost in a whirlwind of pleasure, as proof of my orgasm gushes out of me like it never has before.

"Fuck, Trouble. You're fucking soaked," he says in a mixture of awe and surprise.

As I come out of the state of ecstasy he put me in, my cheeks flush red. I've never squirted like that before. I know it's a thing, and I've always made a little bit of a mess, but never to the point that it sloshes up onto my stomach. "I'm sorry." I don't know what else to say.

"Are you fucking kidding me?" He grabs my face with the same hand that's covered in my arousal. "Don't you dare be sorry. It's sexy as hell. And," he pauses as he spreads my legs wide and slips his enormous dick inside me, making me gasp, "it feels so damn good around my cock."

My hands fly out to my sides, gripping the sheets as he slides in and out.

Lev pants and groans as his chest rises and falls rapidly. His grip on my face moves to my throat and it tightens while he presses his other hand to the mattress, bracing himself. I watch the contours of his abdominal muscles as he works himself inside me, each roll of his hips and every thrash against my core.

"Fuck, Trouble." He growls. "You feel so good."

He pounds into me harder and faster, and I feel his head swell inside me while my walls envelop around him.

His mouth falls open and he holds my gaze as his fingers tighten and black spots dance in my vision. The silence between us filled with only his short, sharp breaths as he releases.

My head falls back, and suddenly, I'm floating in another universe as another orgasm bursts out of me, coming right along with him. He releases me just in time for me to moan his name and cry out in pleasure.

His hot breath fans my skin and he thrusts one more time before collapsing on top of me.

A minute later, his body softens as he rolls onto his side, one arm flung around me. I turn to face him and push a strand of hair out of his face before planting a kiss on his lips. Contentment begins to settle into me, and I know I'm right where I'm meant to be.

CHAPTER 22
MADDOX

IF SOMEONE WOULD HAVE TOLD me a week ago that I'd be luring my dad to his own demise, I would have laughed in their faces. It's the middle of the night and I'm standing outside the gate at Boulder Cove Academy, alone. He's on his way from the hotel he's been staying at in the city and, hopefully, none the wiser to our plan.

I know me, Riley, and the guys agreed that we were in this together—no more secrets and all that shit. But this is something I have to do on my own. I need answers and if Ridge and Lev are here, they might kill him before he gets a word out.

All my life I've bent over backward to appease this man. I've cried. I've sweated. I've bled. I did everything in my power to gain his approval to the point that it broke me. It's a sad day when you learn the person you admire most is nothing but a worthless scumbag. It's almost empowering in a way, though, knowing I no longer have to live up to his expectations. I feel like a new man.

A pair of headlights come into view, illuminating the

snowflakes that are falling. I stick my phone back in the front pocket of my jeans and walk toward it.

The car comes to a stop as I approach the driver's side door. Dad rolls down the window and I fold my arms and lean into the open window.

"Where the hell is she?" His tone is laced with both anger and eagerness. Of course his first words are about *her*, instead of asking if I'm okay, or if I'm safe. *She* is useful to him; whereas, I am not.

Selfish fucking prick.

I reach through the window, my expectant eyes never leaving his as I hit the button to unlock the other doors. Without a word, I circle the car and pull open the passenger side door, then I plop down on the seat.

"Head east," I tell him. "We need to park the car and walk."

His fingers white-knuckle the steering wheel and his teeth grind. "Where the fuck is she, Maddox?"

"I told you I'd take you to her, but we can't drive. We need to ditch the car somewhere safe and walk."

"It's three o'clock in the fucking morning and you wanna go on a goddamn hike?"

Fighting the urge to lash out, I draw in a deep breath and hold my composure. "It's a short walk."

Dad slams the car into drive and whips a sharp turn, traveling the opposite way he just came.

While he's distracted by the drive, and his anger issues, my eyes dance around the car, looking for any proof that Riley was in here. It's possible he didn't even use his own car to kidnap her, but I find myself looking anyway.

There's nothing out of the ordinary, except something that keeps rolling into my feet. I reach down and pick it up nonchalantly, taking care not to draw attention. It's hard to see what it is, but the buttons on the side and the speaker on the front lead me to believe it's a recorder.

I sit up and casually slide the object into my pocket. If by some chance it is a recorder, it may come in handy when I get his confession. Could use my phone, but it'll be more of a slap in the face when I use his own device to bring him down.

A minute later, the warehouse comes into view. "Take a left."

"What the hell is this place?"

"Just do it." He's really grating on my nerves, but if I don't keep it together, I'm sure to raise suspicion. I'm never disrespectful to my dad, but I'm finding it really hard not to be right now. Knowing what he did to Riley, and possibly Lev's family, has me ready to end him now. If only I didn't need answers first...

Without even flicking the blinker, he turns down the gravel driveway to the warehouse.

"Drive around the back," I tell him. "There's a pole barn back there."

The car bounces over mounds and rocks, making its way down the beaten path, Dad huffing and puffing the entire way.

He steers the car to a stop in front of the pole barn and I hop out, instructing him to stay as I open the door. Once it's high enough for him to get in, I wave him through, directing him to park right next to the car I keep here.

A second later, he's growling as he slams his car door shut. "This better be worth it, boy."

"It will be," I assure him. "I've got her secured somewhere and she's willing to confess everything."

I grab a couple flashlights off the mantle in the barn, handing him one. We walk out and I pull the door down, hiding the vehicles inside.

It's a good twenty-minute walk to the cabin where Riley and I were a couple days ago, and it's not a pleasant one. During our short hike, my father doesn't hesitate to tell me what a screwup I am. How I'm the worst Guardian in The Society, and how I will basically fail at everything I try to accomplish.

What he doesn't know is, those words don't hurt me anymore. He's worthless in my mind, a piece of shit player in a fucked-up game. My respect for him went out the window the second he laid his hands on my girl. It only got worse when I found out he hurt people I loved—and children, at that.

So instead of lowering myself to his level, I don't respond. I just take it all in, knowing that before long, he's going to eat his words.

I slow my steps as we approach the cabin and Dad gives me a sideways glance. "This is it?"

I nod. "Yep. She's inside."

He picks up his pace, heading straight for the front door of the cabin.

"That girl has been a fucking thorn in my side. Running and hiding while I have the whole goddamn Society on her ass. This ends now."

"That's right," I say as I follow closely behind. "It ends now."

Dad rips the front door open, exuding confidence and authority as he enters the cabin. His light skates around the room, but what he's looking for isn't here. "Where the hell is she?"

My fingers grasp the edges of the trapdoor, feeling the wood's splinters under my skin. I flip the adjoined boards up and they hit the floor with a thud.

I look over my shoulder at my dad, eyebrows raised. "She's down here."

"I've heard of this place," he says as he kneels beside me, peering down into the hole.

"And now you get to see it." In one fell swoop, I give him a shove, sending him down the hole and into the underground room.

Surprisingly, there isn't an ounce of remorse as his body crashes against the concrete floor. Even his grunts and groans don't faze me.

I grab the trapdoor and steady it against my shoulder, so it closes as I go down.

When I reach the bottom, I see my dad curled over, babying his shoulder. "What's wrong with you? I need a paramedic, son. I think it's broken."

"Good," I huff as I crouch over him. My right hand trembles as I reach into the inside pocket of my coat and pull out my dad's pistol. His eyes widen, body stiff, as I press it to his temple. "Maybe it will motivate you to answer my questions."

"Son," he chokes. "Wha...what are you doing?"

"What I should have done a long time ago." I give him a swift kick to the ribs and it's so satisfying that I do it again. "If I'd known then, what I know now, you bet your sorry ass I would have. Now get yourself off this fucking floor and stand up like a man."

He curls into a ball like a little bitch, moaning and crying.

"I said get up!" I shout. I reach into my pocket and pull out the recorder while still pointing the gun at him.

"I can't. I think my shoulder is shattered," he sputters and whines as he tries to push himself up to no avail. "I think my leg is broken, too." Hopeful eyes peer up at me, as if he thinks I might actually help him. "Call an ambulance, son. I need help." Then he cries out even louder. "God, help me!"

A devilish grin spreads across my face. "No one can save you here. Not a paramedic, and not even God."

I kneel beside him, knowing there's no way in hell he's getting off this floor. I press the gun back to his temple and grit out, "Is this yours?" I show him the recorder. "Is this what you planned to use when you kidnapped my girlfriend and tried to scare a confession out of her for something she didn't do?"

"She did do it, though. She shot Governor Saint and she needs to pay for her sins."

"And who the fuck are you to play God with her life, or anyone else's, for that matter?" I hit the record button on the side of the recorder. "What was your connection with Governor Saint, anyway?"

"I...I barely knew the guy. He was a Blue Blood, just like all of us."

"You're lying."

"Son, I need help."

"You're gonna need help when I'm done with you. I'm just not so sure anyone will care enough to save you." I dig the gun deeper into his temple. "Tell me what he has on you? Is it proof that you killed the Pemberley family?"

His eyes widen in surprise, bottom lip quivering. "No. No, I didn't do that."

"What if I told you I have those files that you so desperately wanted to remain sealed, and I know everything?"

"That's not possible. Those records won't be handed over for two more days. And even then, the contents remain classified for months, maybe even years."

"Do I look like a guy who follows the rules, *Dad*? I mean, after all, I did learn from the best." He doesn't respond, just lies there trembling while pleading with sorrowful eyes. "I know you did it, and soon, everyone else will, too. The question is, why? Why the fuck would you murder that poor family? Those sweet girls?"

Suddenly, there's a shift in his demeanor. He breaks into a sob as he tries again to get up, only to fall right back down on the concrete while letting out an unrestrained whimper. "I didn't wanna hurt those little girls. His family was in the wrong place at the wrong time and it will haunt me for the rest of my life."

It's true. He did it. My eyes brim with tears at just the thought of what he did to Lev's sisters, or any of them, for that matter. But I push the sadness away because I can't dwell on that at the moment.

"What the fuck, Dad? How could you?"

"He fucking took her from me," he cries out. "Donald killed the woman I loved."

My gut wretches at his confession. All these years I've been living with a complete stranger. A man I looked up to. I would have cut off my arms for my father, if that's what he asked me to do. I would have done anything for his approval.

I'm completely dumbstruck. At a loss for words. "Mom's alive and well. What the fuck are you talking about?"

"Not your mother. I love her dearly, but our love was no match for what I had with Helen."

"Helen?" My voice squeaks. "Ridge's mom?"

His eyes well with tears, his cheek pressed to the cold concrete. "She was everything to me, and Donald was assigned to take her out. I begged him not to do it, but he did anyway."

"Are...are you saying you and Ridge's mom were having an affair?" I can hardly believe what I'm saying, let alone what I'm hearing. "You're fucking married to Mom!" I can't control the jerky movements of my head or my shaking hand as I grind the gun into his skull. "How the hell could you do that to her?"

"Love, son. It makes you do crazy things."

"But you love Mom?"

"I do. Very much."

None of this explains why the governor was helping him, or protecting his secret. He killed members of The Society for no reason other than sheer anger and hatred. It was unprovoked and not part of an assignment or punishment.

My head is spinning and I need to get a grip if I want to get the rest of his confession. I need it all to clear Riley's name. Somehow, I need to make it look like he killed the governor to protect himself.

I inhale a deep breath because I can't crumble right now. "How did the governor find out what you did?"

"I messed up. Didn't cover my tracks, and I cracked. Told him everything and we struck a deal..."

"What kind of deal?" *Fuck. I don't even know if I wanna hear this.* A deal with Governor Saint can't be good. "What else did you do, Dad?"

"I..." He sputters and cries, but continues as if he's confessing his sins to a priest in search of forgiveness. "I killed his wife for him. Hit-and-run. It was easy and quick."

I nearly topple over as the words leave his mouth. He speaks as if he's talking about a history test. *Easy and quick?* Who the hell is this guy?

"You killed..." My words get lodged in my throat, my voice barely audible. "You killed his wife?" I set the recorder down while it's still going and run my fingers through my hair, feeling dizzy and off-balance. "You're a fucking monster!" I spit out. "The worst of the worst."

My entire life I've been living with a serial killer. And not the kind who killed the bad guys. He killed the good ones.

Mustering the courage, I ask the question weighing heavy on my mind. "Does Mom know?"

"God, no." He sobs. "She doesn't know any of this. Please, son. Please don't tell her. I'll do anything. I'll...give me that gun. I'll end the madness right here and now. Or you do it. But please, you can't tell her."

"Oh," I force a laugh, "she's gonna know, and so will everyone else." My head shakes in utter disappointment. "You're nothing but a fucking worthless scumbag, you know that? Now I have to go and break my mother's heart while I tell her what you did. I hope you rot in hell."

I stand up, letting the gun drop to my side as I swing my leg back, body tensing with anticipation. With a grunt, I thrust my foot forward and deliver a barreling kick right into his ribs.

I reach into my pocket with a jerky hand and pull out my phone. Tapping on Ridge's name, I then press the phone to my ear. He answers after the second ring. "Get Riley and Lev, and get to the room in the underground tunnels beneath the cabin owned by Scar's parents. I've got him, and I've got the confession."

"Are you fucking serious?"

"No, I'm lying, dipshit. Yes, I'm serious. Hurry your asses up." I end the call and drop my phone back in my pocket.

"Maddox?" He says my name as a question. "You don't want to do this, son..."

"Don't!" I stammer. "Don't you dare call me son. I am no longer your son and you are no longer my father!"

"But I love you, Maddox." He bawls and sniffles. "You're my flesh and blood."

This man who treated me like a pawn my whole life, who just a few minutes ago was telling me how worthless I am and how I could never live up to who he wants me to be, is now trying to tell me he loves me. I call bullshit. If this is what love is to him, I don't want it. "Well, I fucking hate you. I wish I could kill you. Unfortunately, I think someone else deserves that justice. So instead, you get to live for a few more minutes."

CHAPTER 23
RIDGE

"SLOW DOWN," Riley huffs as I move quickly down the trail. It's been almost two hours since Maddox called and there's no saying what might have happened between then and now. It was a shitshow getting here. Cell service is sketchy as fuck. Not to mention the gates to The Academy were locked, so we had to drive around the backside of the property, and so far, we've walked two miles through the woods, with about a quarter mile to go.

Riley's been in a mood. She's pissed that Maddox snuck off and did this shit without us after we all agreed we're in this together and there will be no more secrets. I told her that this was something he had to do for himself. I get it. I probably would've done the same thing.

Fortunately, she fell asleep halfway and was able to get a little bit of shut-eye. She's only been sleeping for a few hours here and there and you can tell her body needs more rest. Lucky for me, it was with her head on my lap. And yes, I was in the back seat with her while Lev drove. I couldn't let her sit back here all alone. I don't think there's a man on this planet who would pass up the opportunity to have this girl's head on his lap.

The loud snap of a branch in the distance has Riley practically jumping into my arms. "What was that?" she whispers into the sleeve of my hoodie.

"It's okay, Angel. I've got you. It was probably just a squirrel, or a raccoon."

Lev takes her other hand, sticking close by. In the last twenty-four hours, something changed with the two of them. I was worried it might take Riley a bit to get past some of the shit he did, but surprisingly, she forgave him quickly. I suppose she did the same for me when she found out what I'd done. I'm just glad all four of us are on the same page now. We're a team—a family. A fucked-up one. But family, nonetheless.

Another branch snaps, followed by the sound of crunching leaves. Lev and I share a look when we all stop walking. I click my flashlight off then nod at his, my way of silently telling him to kill the light.

"What's going on?" Riley shivers at my side. "Is someone out there?"

"Nah. We're good," Lev tells her. "Just playing it safe."

"Shhh," I murmur, listening keenly to any and all sounds, aside from Riley's heavy breathing.

The sound of footsteps comes closer and closer and I wrap my arm around Riley's waist, pulling her close. "Who's there?" I call out. "Show your fucking face, coward." I pat the pocket of my leather jacket where my knife is, making sure it's there if needed.

"Hey," Lev hollers. "If you're there, come out. Otherwise, we'll come find you and it won't be pretty when we do."

The sounds stop completely. We wait a minute, and still nothing.

"I think they left," Riley whispers.

"Probably," I grumble. "Fucking pussies." It's possible no one was even there, but I say it just to voice my opinion if they were.

I click my light back on and Lev does the same. Riley opted to keep hers off since she's holding on to both me and Lev.

We take a left and I keep my wits about me, knowing that there is a good chance we're being followed. Lev knows it, too. I can tell by the way his eyes keep darting around the woods. Every now and then, he looks at me, eyebrows raised. We don't say anything, though. It would scare the hell out of Riley and that's the last thing either of us want.

"You guys," Riley says softly, "there's something you both should know."

My eyes snap to her and I stop walking, forcing her to stop with me. "What?"

I watch intently as her throat bobs when she swallows and it causes my blood to pump faster because I know it's something serious. All I can think of is, who am I killing next and how the fuck will I cover it up this time?

"Let's walk and talk," she says. "We can't waste any time." I nod in response and we all start moving again. "When I left Maddox in that room, I ran into some people out here."

"What people?" I grit out. "Guys? Did they fucking touch you? Did they hurt you?"

Riley crosses her arms over her chest and her lips purse into a white line. "Can I talk, please?"

"Well, who the hell was it?"

My skin is crawling in anticipation. I swear to everything if someone laid a finger on her...

"Three guys."

"That's it," I snap as I drop Riley's hand and reach into my pocket for my notepad and pen. "They're fucking dead. Give me names."

"Dude," Lev scoffs. "Let her finish. Jesus Christ."

I release the notepad, letting it settle back in my pocket, then I take Riley's hand again. "Sorry. Go on," I tell her, attempting to gain some sort of composure, even though my body is ready to go into kill-or-flight mode at the moment.

"I don't know who they were, but they didn't hurt me. They tried, but someone helped me. She was like this dark angel that appeared out of nowhere."

I don't give a damn about the girl. I need to know who these guys are. "Does she know who they were? Can she tell us their names?"

"I'm sure she does. They all go to BCA together. But Ridge, this girl—"

Her words are cut off by the sudden sound of someone running...right toward us. In a knee-jerk reaction, I grab my knife out of my pocket and flip the blade open. "Come get some, fucker!" I howl with the blade pointed outward.

"It's me." Maddox steps into the beam of light, hands up in surrender. "Put the knife down."

We all exhale a sigh of relief, and I put my knife away. "What the fuck are you doing out here? Where's your dad? Don't tell me he escaped."

"Or that you let him go," Lev chimes in. "I have plans for that fucker."

"He's there. Slightly unconscious. Can't walk. Can barely talk. But it doesn't matter." Maddox curls over to catch his breath as he digs something out of his coat pocket. "I've got it all on here." He holds up a recorder, waving it in the air with one hand while the other remains pressed to his knee.

Riley steps forward and grabs it from him. "This is the same recorder he had when he kidnapped me. I bet my voice is on here."

Maddox straightens his back and looks at Lev while I shine the light on him. "I'm sorry, man," he says, his tone laced with empathy. "It was him. He confessed to it all."

Riley hits Play on the recorder and the sound of Maddox's voice rings in our ears. It's not Maddox's typical soft tone. No. He's fucking pissed. I'm actually pretty proud of the way he stood up to his dad. I'm proud of him for taking all of this in his own hands. Maddox is a good guy, but even good guys need to be bad sometimes. And this is one of those times.

I watch Lev as we await the confession. For that one pivotal moment we've all been waiting for when Maddox's dad says, "I didn't wanna hurt those little girls. His family was in the wrong place at the wrong time and it will haunt me for the rest of my life."

There it is. The truth. And while it hurts now, I'm hopeful one day it will set Lev free.

"Keep listening," Maddox says, his eyes now on me.

I listen intently to Maddox's dad. "Not your mother. I love her dearly, but our love was no match for what I had with Helen."

I snatch the recorder from Riley and hit Stop. "Helen?" I spit out. "Tell me he's not talking about my mom."

"It's true," Maddox tells me. "They were having an affair. It was a revenge tactic because Lev's dad killed your mom. Then, Governor Saint found out and blackmailed him into killing his wife."

"Neo's mom?" Riley's eyes shoot wide open as she looks at Maddox. "Your dad is the one who hit her?" She drops her shaking head. "This is too much."

"I don't even know what to say." My hands fly in the air. "This is unreal."

We all stand there for a few moments in shock as we try to process everything. When suddenly, I notice one of us is missing. "Where's Lev?"

All eyes skim the area around us, but he's nowhere in sight. With my hands cupped around my mouth, I holler, "Lev!"

"Fuck." Maddox scoffs. "We need to get to the cabin before he kills him. Get my mom on the phone," he tells me, before turning his attention to Riley. "Your parents, too. It's time."

CHAPTER 24
LEV

MY BLOOD FEELS like fire running through my veins. My feet can't move fast enough as I shimmy down the ladder, skipping the last three steps and jumping down. I see him immediately. Stanley Crane lying in a fetal position with a few spots of blood on his side. He's holding his shoulder, knees to his chest.

The toe of my boot strikes his back. "Wake the fuck up."

He grumbles and moans a few inaudible words, but his eyes remain closed, so I kick him again. "I said, wake the fuck up!"

When he still doesn't wake up, I grab the collar of his shirt and jerk his head off the floor. "It's doomsday, you son of a bitch, and I'm going to fucking destroy you!"

His eyes flutter open and I give him a second to register who's looking back at him. "Lev?" he croaks.

"That's right. Now take a good, long look at my face because it's going to be the last one you ever see." I throw him back down and his head ricochets off the concrete floor.

He wails in agony while curling his body into a ball, as if that will protect him from what's coming.

The sound of the others coming down the ladder grabs my attention, but I ignore their presence as I swing my leg back and kick this asshole right in the face.

"Stop it!" Riley cries out as I position myself to kick him again. "Please, don't do this, Lev."

With my foot hanging in midair like an unhinged beast, I glance to the left to see her covering her face with her hands in disbelief.

She takes two steps toward me and reaches her hand out. "Not like this. Please."

A sense of calm washes over me. Just looking at her makes everything better. I put my hand in hers and say, "Go back up the ladder. I don't want you to see this." My eyes dart over her shoulder to Maddox and Ridge. "All of you. Just go."

"Not yet," Ridge says. "You'll get your revenge and he will pay, but let's do it the right way. You don't need The Elders gunning for you, and we still need to officially clear Riley's name."

"No!" I shout, my eyes back on the piece of shit at my feet while my hands tremble with rage. "We do this my way!"

"Lev," Maddox says all too calmly, always the peacemaker. Except there's no peace to be had here. My eyes land on a gun sticking out of the front of his jeans. It's tempting to grab it from him and shoot the piece of shit lying on the ground.

I nod toward the gun. "Where'd you get that?"

"It's my dad's. Took it from the house before I came out here."

"Give it to me," I demand, knowing the poetic justice of him dying by his own fucking weapon.

"Not yet, man." He places a hand on my back. "In about thirty minutes, you can do whatever the hell you want with him. We just need him to stay alive a little bit longer."

I scoff. "For what? So someone can come down here and drag his ass to a hospital where he'll live to see another day? No. Fuck that!"

"My mom's on her way," Maddox whispers. "She deserves her peace, too." There's pain in his words, and suddenly, I feel like the selfish asshole in the room. Of course Maddox and his mom deserve peace. I wasn't the only one affected by this man's heinous acts.

"Then what?" I ask, needing to hear the plan so that I believe him. I need to believe I'll finally get to make the man pay that took away my entire family, that ruined my whole fucking life.

"My parents are on their way, too," Riley says and my eyes connect with hers, knowing that she can ground me. "Maddox told them there's proof he was working with Cade and killed him, and that he killed Lev's family. He also told them he has a verbal confession of him talking about how the governor knew his secrets and how he killed the governor's wife. It's enough motivation for him to also be punished for the governor's murder. As a Chapter chairman, he's getting approval to appoint your duty as a Punisher. Your first assignment—Stanley Crane."

My already wide eyes stretch in disbelief. "Are you serious?"

They all nod in response. I roll my eyes to Stanley. "You hear that, dipshit?" I crouch down to where he's sobbing uncontrollably. "You're gonna be punished, and I get to do whatever the fuck I want with you." A maniacal grin splits across my face as I watch his eyes widen in pure fear.

It's unreal, staring at the man who ruined my life all those years ago. For a while, I gave up hope that I'd ever find out who did it. There was also a point in time when I didn't even care because I was numb to all emotion. There was a time when it was nice, not feeling anything—not caring. But as I watched relationships bud around me, I was desperate to feel normal again. Once upon a time, I thought Doc Edmonds was the key to happiness, or any emotion, really. I was so certain he'd fix me. Instead, he just broke me even more.

Except now that I'm here, my boys at my side along with my girl, I realize he never stood a chance. I'm back and I'm ready to exact revenge on the man who wreaked havoc on my life. Then, I'll finally be free to live.

"Are you okay?" Riley asks, noticing how quiet I am as I hover over Stanley.

I look up at her, my expression stoic. "I'm fucking great."

Her lips press into a thin line. "I'm here if you need me."

I reach up and take her hand, smiling. "Thank you." Those words aren't enough; they will never be for her. She has this way of bringing me back to the present. Instead of continuing to fill my head with rage and anger, she reminds me what's real. I can see why Ridge is so obsessed with her, if she does the same thing for him too. I watched him sitting on the edge, hardly able to balance his mind, much less his temper. The lengths he goes to are utterly insane, but I can see them from a better perspective now that I know just how amazing Riley is.

Leaning down, she presses her lips to mine, then says, "I'm gonna go up and call Scar so she can fill Neo in on what's going on. He needs to know what happened to his mom. After all this time, he might finally be able to get closure, too."

I nod in response, thankful for that. I'm not Neo's biggest fan, but I know how heavy the burden of unanswered questions is.

"I'll go with her," Maddox says. I'm glad he's going because no one wants to see their parents endure the torture I'm about to bestow on this man, no matter how much they hate them.

Riley goes up the ladder, followed by Maddox, and once their feet leave my sight, I swing my hand back and slap Stanley hard across the face. "You're lucky they showed up when they did or you'd be coyote food right now."

Ridge joins my side, grinning from ear to ear. "May I?"

"Have at it," I tell him, stepping aside so he can have a piece of the action.

He crouches down, teeth grinding as he grabs him by the shoulders, lifting his upper body off the floor. He puts emphasis on the shoulder Stanley's been babying by digging his fingertips into his flesh. The pathetic excuse of a man cries out in pain, which only encourages Ridge to hurt him more.

"You touched my girl, Mr. Crane, and I don't take kindly to people touching what's mine." He throws him to the ground and when his head hits the concrete, a sickening thud echoes throughout the room.

Stanley's eyes close and it appears he's lost consciousness. "That's enough." I grab Ridge by the shoulder and pull him back. "Let's wait until his wife gets here. She might wanna rough him up a bit herself."

Ridge growls and spins around to face the opposite direction. "What's your plan? You gonna let him get medical treatment then torment him some more, or you just gonna end him the minute you get the assignment?"

"Fuck no, he's not getting any treatment. As soon as I get the okay, he's done for."

Like a menace, Ridge paces the room as if it's torture not to kill this man. I get it—I feel it, too. His eyes snap from his watch then back up. "What's taking everyone so long?"

"Riley's parents have a good hour drive, and who knows where Maddox's mom was. It could be a while. Why don't you take my car and drive Riley back to BCU, so she doesn't have to be around this shit. It's safe for her to return now. I'll get a ride with Maddox."

"Thanks, man. I think I will. She's been through enough and this is all probably triggering for her." Ridge heads up the ladder, stopping halfway. "You need anything before I go?"

"Actually, I do." I walk over to the bottom of the ladder and look up at him. "I want Stanley's gun that Maddox has. I'd bet money it's the one he used *that night,* and it's fitting he goes out with the same weapon he used to take an innocent family out with."

"You got it. I'll get it from Maddox before I take Riley out of here." He disappears out the trapdoor, only to return a minute later with the gun.

With it gripped tightly in my hand, I stare at it for what feels like an eternity.

The next bullet to leave this gun is gonna be for them. Justice will finally be served.

CHAPTER 25
RILEY

"MOM!" I fly into her arms, squeezing her tightly as tears stream down my face. "I'm so glad you're here."

Her grip on me is just as tight. "Oh, Riley. We've been worried sick about you."

"Seems you've been busy, kiddo," Dad says, and I let go of Mom before throwing myself at him. He hugs my head to his chest. "We're just glad you're okay."

"I didn't do the things they're accusing me of. I swear." It's partially the truth. In reality, I was only being sought after for the murders around campus. It was only Stanley Crane who was pushing for me to get sentenced for the crime I actually *did* commit.

"We know you didn't. We've got members at Cade Pemberley's house now. They've found evidence that links him to a lot of crimes."

My parents have been briefed on our version of the story and The Society's press will be releasing the exclusive story in the morning. It was the only way to clear my name and stop the manhunt while also showing the rest of the world who was to blame for the crimes committed.

It's not all true, but no one needs to know; they just need a person to blame. Mom hands me her phone to read the email containing the article that will be published.

Manhunt Ended, Former Guardian to Blame

The manhunt for Riley Cross has ceased.

The events revealing the perpetrator of the murders across campus and through The Society are still unclear, but what is known is Stanley Crane is to blame.

His crimes go many years, the first major one being the Pemberley family murders. It was found that Donald killed Helen, Mr. Crane's mistress, and he was seeking vengeance when the family was caught in the crossfire. The seven-year case has now been officially closed and the murders solved. May the remaining family and friends be able to find peace knowing the murderer has been brought to justice.

In the investigation, Mr. Crane also admitted that Governor Saint knew the truth about the murders and held it over his head. In exchange for his silence, the former governor asked Mr. Crane to murder his wife. Mr. Crane followed the

governor's orders, resulting in a hit-and-run while continuing to be under the governor's thumb until he eventually snapped and killed him too.
Investigators were also able to tie Mr. Crane to Cade Pemberley's murder. A shrine of Riley Cross was found in Cade's home, where we can only assume he kept the items he stole from her over the years while stalking her. We believe he also killed Zeke Martin, according to a handwritten note found in the shrine. There was also evidence proving that Cade and his father both physically and mentally harmed their nephew while he was in their care and even after. He was unavailable for comment, but his loved ones have said that he will need time and space to process all of this information.
Cade Pemberley was working for Mr. Crane but drew a line when Crane wanted to pin Riley as the primary suspect of the murders. Mr. Crane then decided Cade was too much of a risk and murdered him just one mile from campus. This should serve as a warning to all students to be more aware of their surroundings and to always stay in groups when possible.
As for Riley Cross, she has been absolved of all charges and will be returning to

school to resume her studies shortly. The entirety of the events has shaken her and her family and they ask for time and space at this time to get back to their new normal.

All in all, it's a sad day to hear that a Guardian, one of our protectors, was really just a weak man who made a lot of bad decisions. If there is anything that we can hold tight to at the end of the day, it's that The Society will reign and justice will be served. Mr. Crane has received the full punishment for his crimes. May we learn from his mistakes.

I had to try and keep myself from shaking while reading the draft sent to the involved families for approval. It's a whole fucking mess, but it seems like everyone will buy it. Which in turn, gets me and the guys off scot-free. My insides are literally dancing with excitement that this nightmare is almost over.

"Honey," Mom says, stroking my hair from behind me. "We think it's best for you to come home for a few days. You need to relax, rest, and regroup."

"No!" I blurt out as I spin to face her while handing her phone back. My eyes move back and forth from her to my dad. "I want to go back to my dorm with Scar. I'm fine now. I promise." The idea of leaving my guys after everything we've been through actually makes my heart ache.

My parents share a look of concern before my dad finally nods in agreement. "Okay," Mom says. "I suppose since

Thanksgiving break is only a week and a half away, you can stay in your dorm."

"Thank you, Mom." I hug her again, shivering as snowflakes fall down on us.

"Let's get you back to campus while your dad handles business with your friends."

My eyes perk up. "What kind of business?"

"It seems I've got an assignment to hand out to Lev Pemberley, and a few words for Stanley Crane before I do." I stop in my tracks and turn to face him.

"What happens after that? Lev, Ridge, and Maddox? Will they be safe?"

"Have they done anything wrong?" Dad asks, and I shake my head no while my insides are screaming at me to play this cool so they can't tell I'm lying. He buys it, considering I never lie to my parents. They must give me the benefit of the doubt here and just assume my nerves are on edge, which they totally are. "Everything will be handled officially at their next Chapter meeting. But they shouldn't have anything to worry about."

A smile draws on my face. "I love you guys."

All three of us join for a tight embrace when the sound of feet shuffling in our direction has us breaking apart. I look over my shoulder to see Ridge.

"Hey," he says softly with a slight wave before dropping his hand to his side.

"Mom. Dad. This is Ridge." I keep my eyes on him and a smile on my face. "My boyfriend."

Dad clears his throat but doesn't say a word.

"It's nice to meet you both." Ridge offers his hand to my mom first and after they shake, then he extends it to my dad. I'm literally holding my breath in anticipation as I wait for my dad to stop being such a dad and shake the guy's hand.

Finally, he does and I exhale a sigh of relief.

"Thank you for taking care of our daughter," Dad says, and I can't help the giggle that escapes me. Ridge has most definitely taken care of me, in more ways than one.

"Of course. I'd do anything for Riley." Ridge hooks an arm around my shoulder. "Which is exactly why I'm here." He peers down at me. "I was wondering if I could get you out of here and take you back to your dorm at BCU." Questioning eyes land on my dad as he looks at him for approval. "If that's okay with you, sir."

Sir? I want to laugh, but I don't. Who is this guy and what has he done with my chaotic boyfriend, Ridge? It's enlightening to see him kiss ass, though. And even better that it's my dad—the only man in my life until Ridge, Maddox, and Lev came along. The only man the three of them will actually have to foster a relationship with.

"Actually," Dad says, "I think it's best if her mother drives her back. With all the chaos going on around us, we can't be too safe."

"I'm safe with Ridge, Dad. I swear to you he'd never let anything happen to me."

"Oh, honey," Mom says with a gentle hand on Dad's back. I already wanna kiss her cheek because I know she's going to side with me. "Let him take her. The perpetrator is in custody. They're safe now. Besides, I'd like to be here for Gail when she arrives. She's going to need a friend."

Gail is Maddox's mom, and I agree. She's definitely going to need a friend in the days to come.

"Thanks, Mom." I lean into her, resting my head on her shoulder.

Dad narrows his eyes. "You call me the minute you get back to your dorm, understand?"

"You got it, Dad." I say as I wrap him in a hug. I wouldn't say I'm a daddy's girl, per se, but up until I met Ridge, Maddox, and Lev, he was the most important guy in my life.

"No pit stops at the student center or coffee shop. You go straight there." He looks down at me and I can feel the tension in his voice, the worry and concern for my safety evident. I put my hand on his chest as I make him a promise.

"Yes, Dad," I say as I step away from him, about to tuck myself back under Ridge's arm, when my father responds.

"Good." He opens his arms wide. "Now, come give your dad another hug. I've missed you so much."

My heart doubles in size as I step into his embrace. "I love you, Dad."

He kisses the top of my head and his voice reverberates in my ear. "I love you, too. I'm glad you're safe and you found someone who protects you."

I step away from my dad and take Ridge's hand. As we walk away, I blow a kiss over my shoulder at them, making my mother beam with happiness as she returns it.

"So," Ridge begins, his thumb grazing my fingers as we move quickly to get out of the cold. "How'd I do?"

"With my parents? Honestly, I'm pretty impressed."

"What?" He huffs a laugh. "That I was nice? What do you take me for, some deranged psychopath?"

"Do you really want me to answer that?" I give him a playful grin.

"No. Please don't." He shakes his head at me and I smile even wider.

We both laugh as we continue walking, hand in hand. Fortunately it's a short walk to Lev's car, but it's still far enough from the cabin that we're out of eyesight from everyone else.

It doesn't matter, though. Even in the dead of the night, with snow falling and critters foraging around us, I've never felt safer. Ridge has a way of making me feel like the most important person in the world. I know, without a doubt, he'd lay his life on the line for me. But as my feelings grow stronger and stronger, I'm beginning to think I wouldn't want him to. I'd want to be the one to lay my life on the line for him. I'd do anything for him, for all of them. Which is exactly why I need to tell him the truth about the girl I hid out with the day I was kidnapped.

The only audible sound is the crunching of leaves beneath our feet and a couple coyotes howling in the distance. But the thoughts in my head drown out any forest noises. How do I tell the guy who thinks he has no family that he might have a sister? I guess that's not the part I'm struggling with. How do I tell a guy that his sister is the reason I was kidnapped in the first place? That she gave me up just so she could get a ride to BCU, where she thought she'd find Ridge. Curiosity has me wondering if she made it back to The Academy safely. I shouldn't care. Especially after what she did to me. I can't help but wonder, though. If Temper does turn out to be a relative of Ridge's, I may have to suck it up and forgive the girl, even if I never get an apology.

My mind swirls with thoughts of what she could have been thinking selling me out like that. She had to know it wouldn't go well. Was Stanley that good at manipulating people that he made her actually believe he didn't want to hurt me? Could this all just be a misunderstanding on her part?

We make it to Lev's car, and Ridge opens the passenger door for me. I climb inside, cupping my hands around my mouth for warmth.

Ridge gets in the driver's seat and closes the door before bringing the engine to life. He looks at me, eyebrows raised as his hands run around the steering wheel. "I can't believe he's letting me drive his car. He'll have my head if I fuck this car up."

"In that case, drive slow. Very, very slow."

"Nah." Ridge smirks. "You only live once." He shifts into drive and slams on the gas, kicking dirt up behind him as he whips down the trail.

I can't help but laugh because he's like a child with a new toy. I'll set aside my fear of crashing into one of these nearby trees and let him enjoy it while he can. The calm before the storm. The storm that I have to bring.

A few minutes later, we're on the paved road and he's slowed the pace of the car a bit. He reaches over, his hand resting on my lap.

It's now or never. I have to tell him.

"Ridge?" My voice is almost a whisper. As if I don't want him to hear me. I sort of don't because then I won't have to say what I'm about to say.

"Yeah?"

Here goes nothing... "Remember earlier I tried to tell you and Lev something, but we were interrupted when Maddox showed up on the trail?"

"Oh yeah. Sorry, Angel. What was it you needed to say?" His thumb rubs circles on my leg.

I place my hand over his and gulp. "There's a small detail I left out when Maddox's dad took me." I pinch my fingers together, squinting my eyes. "Just a really small thing.

I couldn't say anything before because I was afraid it would distract us and I didn't want a little thing to distract us." It's a lie. This is a huge thing. Bigger than huge.

"Well, what was it?" He chuckles. "What's this super small thing?"

"When he took me, he took me from a dorm room."

His eyes widen and he glances at me before looking back to the road. "Whose dorm room?"

"It wasn't a guy, if that's what you're worried about?"

"Better not have been. I've killed enough people this semester."

I squeeze his hand, wanting to play on his joke, but this really isn't a joking matter. "It was a girl. Her name is Temper."

"Okayyy." He drags out the word like he's confused. "So what's the big deal? Sorry," he corrects himself, "small deal."

"This girl helped me out of a sticky situation and agreed to let me hide out in her dorm. Once I got there, we started talking, and it turns out she lost her dad, too."

"Lots of people lose a parent or two, Angel. What are you getting at?"

I inhale sharply, speaking on the exhale. "Her dad's last name was Foster."

Ridge's eyebrows pinch together and he pulls his hand off my leg. "And she's a member?"

"Well, yeah. She attends BCA. She said her dad was a member and now he's not. She just learned of him a couple years ago."

"There are no other Fosters that are Blue Bloods. Our lineage was short. My ancestors are all deceased. It's just me and my dad. Well, now it's just me. That's impossible."

"Do you think..."

"Do I think she could be a relative? Fuck. I don't know." He runs his hand through his hair. A mix of excitement and dread pooling in his features.

"Before you get too excited, there's more. And I don't want this to hinder your idea of her because if she is your sister, or a relative at all, I want you to reach out to her. But, she's the one who gave me up to Maddox's dad. She told him where I was in exchange for a ride to BCU...so she could find you."

"So she's a fucking rat?" He swerves the car a bit, jerking toward me, and I brace myself against the side of the car.

"Well, no. She was just trying—" He swerves back into his lane and my heart skips a beat.

"Don't defend her." His voice rises. "In fact, don't even say another thing about her." Ridge grips the steering wheel tighter, all the blood draining from his knuckles. "Fuck her. Anyone who hurts you is worthless in my book."

I run my hand down his arm, happy that he's so protective over me, but also a bit concerned that he doesn't care to know more about the girl who might be his sister. This could be the only living family member Ridge has left. I don't want to be the reason he misses out.

"She was really sweet," I tell him, hoping to change his mind. "Funny, too. And like I said, she helped me out of a sticky situation. She scared off the guys I ran into."

"You mentioned those guys. And I still haven't gotten names."

I don't dare delve into detail about what happened with those bastards. If I told Ridge the extent of what those guys did to me, he'd be whipping this car around and adding names to his list of victims before we've even fully dealt with the issue at hand. I believe karma will give them exactly what they deserve, so I'll keep the details to a minimum.

"I don't know their names. Buuuut, I know someone who does."

"That Temper chick?"

"Uh-huh."

"Is this your way of trying to get me to talk to her?"

"Maybe." I raise my shoulder, trying to play it off with a shrug.

"Well, it's working. I'm gonna find out who those guys were and make sure they know they don't fuck with my girl." His hand returns to my lap and I lace my fingers between his.

My heart flutters. I love it when he refers to me as his girl. And I'll never admit it out loud, but I love knowing he would kill for me.

"I'm just saying, think about it. I'm willing to move past what she did, if you are. There could have just been a misunderstanding. Stanley is a manipulator, we don't even know what he said to her."

There's a beat of silence before he asks, "Is she a junior or senior?"

"Must be a junior. She wasn't there last year when I attended. Oh," I blurt, "she goes by Temper Rose. Said it's her mom's maiden name. Just in case you decide to look her up or go find her."

"We'll see what the future brings. Right now, all I care about is getting you back to your room and keeping you safe."

It's not a no, so I can rest easy on that. I want this so badly for Ridge. And if by some chance she turns out not to be his sister—or a relative at all, for that matter—that's okay. He's still got me, Lev, and Maddox.

Ridge turns the volume up on the radio and "Better Man" by Pearl Jam plays through the speakers. The adrenaline of the day and telling Ridge about his sister has worn me out. I've loved falling asleep with my guys these past few days, but I have to admit, I am excited to get back to my own space. To see my friend. I let out a yawn and lie back in my seat, turning to face Ridge and watch him hum along with the music.

CHAPTER 26
LEV

SCREAMS COMING from Stanley's wife can be heard from where I'm standing above ground. She's talked, cried, and punched him a few times, and now she's shouting at the top of her lungs.

I'm waiting rather impatiently for Mr. Cross, Riley's dad, to decree my new assignment. This is a special one—a personal one—and I'm thankful it's being handed to me and not just some other member whose punishment will be a life of misery. Stanley Crane doesn't deserve a life, period, but it's only with Maddox and his mom's approval that I will fulfill my oath and punish Stanley to the fullest extent.

With the gun in my back pocket, I walk toward Mr. Cross as he, too, closes the space between us. "Is it finalized? Do I get the assignment?" The anticipation is eating away at me. There's a chance The President of my chapter will handle this a different way, even if Mr. Cross voices his reasoning on why the assignment should be given to me.

The second he says, "Raise your right hand," I release all the air I've been holding in my lungs.

I do as I'm told, lifting my right hand in the air with my fingers pressed tightly together. I've taken this oath three times, so I know the drill, and I begin without him telling me what to say. "I, Lev Pemberley, solemnly swear to keep the secrets, oaths, and promises of The Society. To protect our antiquity and to abide by all rules. I understand that failure to do so will result in my abolishment, never to enter The Blue Bloods' society again."

"Thank you, Mr. Pemberley. I trust you won't let us down." Mr. Cross hands me a notebook with my name engraved on the front. Without hesitation, I flip to the first page to read my assignment.

Punish Stanley Crane. Report any pertinent information found during your investigation to The Elders.

I close the notebook and bite back a smile. "Thank you, Mr. Cross."

Mr. Cross steps closer, slaps a hand to my shoulder, and whispers, "Off the record...make that son of a bitch pay."

"Will do, sir."

My eyes land on Maddox, who's sitting on a log with his elbows pressed to his knees and his face in his hands. I walk toward him slowly and the sound of me approaching has him lifting his head. "You got it?" he asks, pain and betrayal lacing his voice. I know it's not aimed at me, but it still hurts to see him like this.

I pat the notebook in my palm. "Yeah." Taking a seat beside him, I allow the silence to engulf us while waiting for him to speak first. Maddox is the gentle one. Ridge and I talk with our fists or we yell. Maddox, on the other hand, needs patience.

He grabs the notebook from me and opens it up to read the passage in the front. "If you're seeking my permission, you've got it."

"You're sure? Because I can handle this in a different way. There are other options." I don't like those other options. Any option where Stanley leaves this place breathing makes my body actually want to vibrate with anger. But Maddox is my boy. I have to make sure this won't break him.

He hands the notebook back to me. "The man on that floor is already dead to me. I feel nothing toward him. Go do what you have to do. And if you don't, I'll do it for you." My fingers graze over the gold letters of my name, biding time as I wait for him to recant what he said. To tell me not to do it. But he doesn't. "Well. What are you waiting for?"

"Once it's done, there's no going back."

"Then you better hurry your ass up." He shoves me forward and I see the resolve in his eyes.

I smile widely, finally having the reassurance I need. "All right. Guess I'll see you in a bit."

"I'll be here."

The climb down the ladder is indescribable. Everything is falling into place and happening at exactly the right time. Had this all happened last year, or even a month ago, I wouldn't have the emotional capacity to even understand why I was doing what I was doing. Now, my mind is clearer than ever and I'm feeling an array of emotions surface.

Heartbreak for my family who left too soon. Sadness that I lost so much time with them because of a ridiculous man and his vendetta. Relief that I can finally pay back the fucker who took them from me. I feel it all, aside from a few emotions that one might have in a situation like mine—remorse, empathy, and regret.

Standing on the middle of the ladder, I see Mrs. Crane knelt beside her husband—who's on his back. She's gritting out profanities and shouting about how she hopes he goes straight to hell when he leaves this earth. I leap down from where I'm at and my boots hit the ground with a thud.

Mrs. Crane's eyes lift. "Please tell me it's time."

I'm a bit surprised she's so adamant on her husband meeting his maker. Not that he will where he's going.

"Whenever you're ready," I tell her. "If...you are ready?" It's a question more than a statement because I need to be certain she wants this, too. I'm not a good man, but my empathetic bone has fused back together for the people I care about. Since Maddox is one of those people and this is one of the few family members he will have left after this, I need to be sure this isn't going to break something between the two of them.

She stands up, sweeps her hair off her shoulder, and says, "As far as I'm concerned, you're late. He doesn't deserve to breathe our air for another minute."

It's true that The Society members are ruthless, but I'm beginning to realize just how ruthless we all are. Secrets, lies, murder. None of us are innocent. Not even the woman in front of me who, on any other day, I would describe as warm and gentle.

Mrs. Crane walks toward me with tearstained cheeks and bloodied knuckles. She stops at my side, placing a gentle hand on my shoulder. "Make him hurt." Then she disappears up the ladder.

I watch Mr. Crane for a second, waiting to see if he begs

for his life. His cold eyes are dead set on me. Every couple seconds he blinks, making it known he's still alive.

I take a step toward him, then another, still watching. Still waiting. He finally opens his mouth to speak. "Well. What the hell are you waiting for?"

I shrug my shoulders, one hand gripping the gun in my pocket. "Just trying to decide if I wanna make this quick, or torture you a bit first."

He turns his head and hacks up some blood, then spits it straight out in front of him. "Or maybe you're just too much of a coward."

I pull the gun out, my hand trembling as I raise it in the air.

"Go ahead," he taunts me. "Pull the trigger."

With a jerky finger set on the trigger, I count down in my head.

Ten.
Nine.
Eight.
Seven.
Six.

A raspy laugh climbs up his throat. He coughs and spits again. "Seems I forgot the most cowardly Pemberley member of all when I took the others out. Always knew I should've tracked you down and put a bullet between your eyes." The venom in his tone is enlightening. It settles any question in my mind I could have had about my decision here. He means every single word. They aren't out of desperation to die; they are out of a sickness within him.

With the cold steel gun in my trembling hand, my arm stretches outward, pointing directly at his heart. I've killed before, but never with such a personal connection. "Too bad you missed your chance." My tone is stoic—empty of any emotion.

One.

I watch as the bullet fades into his chest, a pool of blood spilling out onto his shirt. His eyes go wide before settling into a blank stare. "How's that for a coward?" I ask his corpse.

It's finally over.

CHAPTER 27
MADDOX

Three Days Later

STANLEY CRANE IS GONE. The nightmare has ended, and I don't feel an ounce of sadness. Will I miss the man I thought he was? Of course, I'm only human. But that man didn't exist. He was a figment of my imagination, built on manipulation and lies. The world is a better place without him in it, and I'm a better man without him in my life.

After Lev fulfilled his assignment, there was just one more thing he had to do, and being his best friend, I accompanied him. Stood by his side as he used the last bullet in my dad's gun to end the life of Dr. Edmonds—another monstrous man who was a waste of skin and air.

Lev finally got the justice and closure he's sought so desperately for, for years. The book of his past is closed, and we're all ready to live in the present while soaking up each moment we have with our girl.

"Do you hear them?" Riley says, speaking about the

students who fill the coffee shop. "They're all looking at us. Laughing and whispering. We're a fucking joke to them."

News traveled fast about everything that went down. How my dad went on a killing spree and we were all tangled in his web. It's only natural that people would gossip and begin to spread their own versions of what happened. Hell, I'd do the same. But it's still annoying as fuck.

"Just ignore them," Lev says. "Give it a week and they'll be gossiping about something else."

Ridge sticks a forkful of pancake in his mouth, talking as he chews. "I can give them something to talk about. A new murder mystery to try and solve."

"Don't you dare." Riley scoffs. "It's way too soon to jump into that ring of fire again."

"Fiiiiine." Ridge drags out the word. "I'll be on my best behavior." He gives her a wink. "For now."

Riley leans over and kisses him on the cheek. "That's all I ask."

We all continue eating, and I can't help but notice Riley's eyes dancing around the coffee shop as the hushed voices and unwanted stares resume. She drops her fork down on the glass plate with a loud clank and I stiffen in my seat.

"Don't worry about them, babe," I tell her, knowing a bomb is about to explode.

"No," Riley grits. "Fuck them. They want something to talk about, I'll give them something to talk about." She nudges my side and pushes herself up on the seat. "Let me out of the booth, please."

"Uh-uh," Lev waves her back down, "they're not worth it."

"What I have to say will be." She pins me with a hard glare. "Now please let me out."

"Let her the fuck out." Ridge grits. "If she has something to say, let her say it."

My eyes roll and I slide out, giving her the space she wants. But once I sit back down, Riley sticks two fingers in her mouth and blows out an ear-splitting whistle.

"Do you all think we don't hear you? Your laughs and whispers. Your fears that we're all just a bunch of crazies over here? We hear you, and guess what? We don't fucking care. The truth is, we're all a little mad here. Each and every one of us, including all of you." She stands up taller as she meets their eyes, her finger pointing at them as she continues. "We're Blue Bloods. We're a society comprised of selfish assholes who would feed their own families to the lions just to save themselves. But we're also a unit. There might be some bad apples in the bunch, but there's still some good. So sip on your coffee and whisper about how we were all involved in The Society's latest scandal, but be careful. Come tomorrow, you yourself might be the latest gossip." The entire room is silent. Not a sound to be heard as everyone listens to Riley.

She shrugs her shoulders, the tension settling a bit. "I guess what I'm saying is, watch your backs because half of the students in this room are crooked." She goes to sit back down but stops herself. "Oh, and if any of you have a problem with anything I just said, you can take it up with me or one of my three boyfriends."

I bite back a laugh as she swats my arm, the vein in her neck protruding. "Lemme back in."

Ridge starts a slow clap. Then Lev drops his fork and says, "Screw it." Then he joins in.

My face turns beat fucking red because I hate the attention laser focused on us, but I drop my chin to my chest and clap along with them.

Unfortunately, it ends there. No one else joins in, and no one cares about anything Riley just said. Some laugh. Some become quiet. And some still whisper and stare. But, Riley is smiling, pleased with herself, and that's really all I care about.

"So," I begin, hoping to say something that will slice through the tension at the table. "My mom invited everyone to our house for Thanksgiving dinner. Who's down?"

"I promised my parents I'd come home for break," Riley says. My shoulders tense slightly, thinking about spending a holiday without her. "But I never said how long I'd stay. I can probably get away after our dinner and come to Glendale for the remainder of break."

"Count me in," Lev chimes in. "No way in hell I'm missing your mom's blueberry pie."

All three of us look at Ridge. He holds his fork in the air as he swallows down his food. "I'll get back to you on that."

We're all taken aback by his response, but I'm the first to voice it. "What else do you have to do?" It's a good question because Ridge has been with my family for the holidays since he lost his mom. He hasn't missed a single one.

Ridge zips his fingers across his lips, but I notice Riley nudging him underneath the table. There's something they're not telling Lev and me.

"What happened to no more secrets?" I ask.

"No secrets," Ridge retorts. "Just need to figure something out before I can commit to anything."

I have no idea what he could possibly be talking about, but I decide to let it go...for now.

We finish eating and we're heading out of the coffee shop

with our heads held high when some jackass sitting at a high-top table by the door decides he's got something to say.

"Yo," he calls out, and we all snap our heads in his direction. "When you guys are finished with her, pass her this way. Pussy is pussy. Loose or not."

My jaw locks as I lunge at him, going right for his waist. His chair crashes into the ground, me on top of him. Ridge and Lev jump in, and fists are being thrown in every direction. I take a blow to the side of my face and I can't even tell if it was the asshole or one of my friends accidentally punching me.

Sounds echo through the room. People shouting—some chanting. My adrenaline is pumping so fast that each voice is nothing but muffled static.

I see Lev get pulled off the guy first. He pretty much flies backward then disappears. Ridge is now straddling the big-mouthed asshole's lap, whaling him in the face over and over again like a lunatic. I stumble back onto my ass and just sit there watching as the guy's face gets rearranged.

"Ridge!" Riley howls. "Enough!"

As if she is the only one who can snap him out of the trance he fell into, he immediately stops, his arm poised to strike again if she commands.

He looks over his shoulder, his bloodied hands at his sides. When she shakes her head, he gets off of the guy who's definitely unconscious.

I push myself off the floor then grab him by the arm. "Come on. We all need to get the hell out of here."

Ridge follows suit and all four of us haul ass out the door. All I can think about the entire jog back to our dorm is, I hope like hell we didn't just kill the guy. We're supposed to be getting on the straight and narrow for a while. It's only been three days since we got our lives back.

"That was fucking epic," Ridge beams with his adrenaline still pumping. He balls a fist and punches it into his palm. "We knocked that dickwad out."

I look at Riley, noticing her caved-in eyebrows and creased forehead. She crosses her arms tightly over her chest and walks steadfastly as we all try to keep up with her.

The guys and I share a look as we jog up to her side.

"Angel?" Ridge says.

Then I place an arm around her waist. "Babe?"

"Trouble, what's wrong?"

She exhales deeply through her nose and shakes her head. "I can't take you guys anywhere."

"Sure you can," Ridge tells her, but when he looks at me and Lev, he cracks a smile. "We're good boys."

"You're all hellions," she gnashes, then throws her hands in the air. "We're all hellions."

I squeeze her waist and pull her side close to mine as we continue walking. "Better to raise hell than be in it, right?"

Lev jumps up to her other side and throws an arm around her shoulder. "Fuck that guy. He got what he deserved and half of the people in that coffee shop would agree."

Ridge comes barreling behind Riley and grabs her waist, scoping her up and away from us. He throws her over his shoulder and starts running down the sidewalk. "We're all a little mad here."

Riley lifts her head and starts laughing. "Help me, guys. He's lost his damn mind." We all laugh as we chase after them. Ridge swerves around a tree then back on the path, and Riley's hair is thoroughly tangled by the time Ridge comes to a halt. He carefully sets her down, then looks at her like he's actually worried. "Are you mad at me, Angel?"

Lev and I pick up our pace and Ridge finally sets her down.

"You're fucking crazy, Ridge Foster." She slaps his shoulder.

"Crazy about you," he responds, pulling her waist to him and planting a kiss on her lips.

"And I'm crazy about all of you." Her eyes dance from one of us to the next. "No matter what happens in this lifetime, we're in this together. I love you, guys."

"I love you, too," I tell her, while Ridge and Lev say the same.

Somehow, we all end up in a cheesy group hug with the blood on Ridge's hands getting all over us, but I don't mind much, not when the center of our attention is the most beautiful girl in the entire world. Seeing her smile while sandwiched among all of us, all the worry and fear she had been holding on to since the day I met her gone, that alone makes my heart beat faster.

EPILOGUE
RILEY

One Week Later

MY GAZE DANCES around at the many different dishes Maddox's mom has made. Maddox said she stress cooks, and this has obviously been a stressful time for her. Tack on Thanksgiving and she's been cooking up a storm. The windows and the sliding glass door in the kitchen have a milky film of fog covering them from the three pots of boiling water on the stove.

Lev and I just left dinner at my parents' house, then made the two-hour drive to Glendale, so we could have dinner with Maddox's mom. I'm still stuffed from the first feast, but I saved a little room for more.

My eyes land on the three pies, fresh out of the oven, and my mouth waters. "Everything smells delicious, Mrs. Crane."

"Thank you, dear," she says as she sticks a wooden spoon into the casserole. She lifts it up with her hand underneath to catch anything that falls, and she brings it toward my face.

"Oh. Okay. Thank you." I open my mouth and she puts the tip of the spoon in, feeding me a taste of the cornbread dressing. "Wow," I say. "That is *really* good."

"It was my great-grandmother's recipe—one of Maddox's favorite holiday dishes. The secret is to double up on the celery."

I lick my lips and swallow down the bite. "Are you sure I can't help with anything?" I glance around at all the dishes that are complete and those still cooking. The least I can do is help her clean or cook.

"You can get those boys to quit wrestling in my living room." She cracks a smile, just before a crashing sound hits our ears.

We look at each other with wide eyes before rushing to the doorway of the living room. Maddox and Lev are standing innocently in the middle of the large space with their hands at their sides and a look of worry on their faces.

"It fell," Maddox quips, and when I look at their feet, I see what he's talking about. Lying in three pieces is a blue-and-white vase.

Mrs. Crane scowls with her hands on her hips. "Maddox Crane! How many times do I have to tell you boys not to wrestle in this house." She tsks as she looks at me. "I swear they're like toddlers, no matter how old they get."

Maddox crouches down and picks up the remnants of their roughhousing, careful not to cut his finger as he handles the larger pieces. "Sorry, Mom."

Lev helps by grabbing the base of the vase that broke. "Yeah. Sorry, Mrs. Crane."

"You boys are lucky I hated that vase." She taps my shoulder. "Come on, Riley. Let's get back in the kitchen while these Neanderthals clean up their mess. My potatoes are boiling."

As we're walking away, I shoot the guys a smile over my shoulder, and Maddox waggles his brows at me. It's nice seeing Maddox and Lev in this environment. I've only ever seen them at school and the many places we hid out. This feels nice—it feels normal. My only wish is that Ridge was here.

He said he's going to try and make it, but he's in Cedarville having dinner with his sister. That's right. A few days ago, Ridge went back to BCA and talked to Temper. They hit it off immediately, and by that night, they were in Cedarville, where Temper's mom lives, and she told them all about their father.

Ridge and Temper have a plan to track him down and hear his excuse for leaving, but Temper's mom doesn't want them to get their hopes up. There hasn't been a single trace of him for years. From what she heard, he assumed a new identity and is living down south. But those were just rumors and no one knows for sure. I hope one day they find him, if only for some peace of mind.

Ridge also got the names of the three guys I met in the woods that day. I now call them the Three Bad Wolves. And Temper, well, she was a modern-day Little Red Riding Hood that night. So helpful and sweet, until she wasn't. Only, Temper hates the color red and she's certainly no damsel in distress.

An hour later, we're all being summoned to the dining room table, where we find Mrs. Crane standing at the head of it. "I want to thank you all for coming here. I know how dear you are to Maddox's heart and it means the world to me that you can be here for him during this trying time." Her eyes are downcast and she runs her fingers down the dew of her wineglass as she continues. "I'd also like to apologize for the actions of my late ex-husband." She lifts her glass in the air and smiles. "May he rot in hell."

I'm a bit shocked by her words, but then again, I shouldn't be. Stanley Crane was a horrible man who did horrible things. According to Maddox, his mom isn't hurt as much as she is angry. In time, I have no doubt that she will be just fine. Maddox will, too. The past is in the past and we're all moving forward, one day at a time.

A familiar voice comes from behind me. "I think we can all cheers to that." My eyes shoot over my shoulder and I see Ridge and Temper entering the dining room.

His gaze sets on mine and I smile back at him. Contentedness washes over me, having all three of my guys here at the same time is an indescribable feeling.

"Hope you all don't mind that I brought...my sister," Ridge says as he looks at Temper.

Mrs. Crane pulls out a chair to the left of her, then the one beside it. "Not at all. The more the merrier. Have a seat, you two."

Ridge takes the seat across from me, his feet brushing softly against mine. Temper sits beside him, wearing a black lace dress and black knee-high boots. Her sleek black hair is down, flowing around her face. She looks beautiful...and happy. She and Ridge both do.

"So, what'd we miss?" Ridge asks.

I take a sip of my water and say, "Lev and Maddox got in a little bit of trouble."

Ridge's eyebrows rise. "Who are we fighting now?"

I give him a teasing kick while everyone laughs. "Not

that kind of trouble. They just broke a vase. No one needs to fight."

"It was a horrid vase," Mrs. Crane cuts in. "It was a gift from Stanley's wretched mother." We all keep our mouths shut and our eyes on our empty plates while trying not to laugh. She quickly changes the subject for us, freeing us from having to decide how to react to that statement. I swear, I like her more and more each minute. "Dig in, everyone. Eat before it gets cold."

"Actually," Maddox pushes his chair back and stands, "there's something I'd like to say first." He looks from Lev, to Ridge, to me. "Thank you all for being the best friends a guy could ask for. No matter where life takes us all, I know we'll all be together." He raises his glass. "Happy Thanksgiving."

"Happy Thanksgiving," we all say in unison.

We fill our plates with food and eat while talking about the present and the future, leaving the past where it belongs.

Once we finish eating, Temper and I help Mrs. Crane clear the table. "Ugh," I grumble as I walk into the kitchen with a half-empty platter of mashed potatoes. "I am so stuffed."

"Me too," Temper says. "Everything was delicious, Mrs. Crane. Thank you so much."

I'm setting the platter on the counter when I feel a hand on my shoulder. "Can we talk?" I turn around to see Temper with her mouth curved in a frown.

"Sure," I tell her as I wipe my hands on a kitchen towel. I set it down beside the mashed potatoes and take a deep breath. "What do you wanna talk about?"

"I'll give you girls some privacy," Mrs. Crane says before she dips out of the room.

Temper's shoulders slump in defeat. "I owe you an apology, Riley. I'm so sorry."

"Really?" My eyes perk up. "For what, exactly? Hiding me then disappearing, or telling a serial killer where he could find me?"

"All of the above." She shrugs with a half-smile on her face, reminding me so much of Ridge, I might actually hit him just because it makes it that much easier to trust her again.

"Listen, Temper," I say with a bout of grace in my tone. "I'm really fucking pissed at you for what you did. But, I love Ridge so much and I'm so happy he's got a sister. It's literally the best thing that's happened to him."

"Not really," she says, and I squint at her in confusion. "The best thing that's happened to him is you, silly."

"Okay." I chuckle. "Now you're just kissing my ass."

"Maybe." She shrugs. "Or maybe I'm telling the truth. My intuition about people is pretty spot on and I knew the minute I saw you in those woods that you were one of the good ones."

"You obviously don't know me, or my boyfriends."

The corner of her mouth lifts up in a crooked smile. "I don't. But I hope to get to know all of you. So what d'ya say? Think you can ever forgive me?"

I roll my lips together, studying her. Wondering if I could truly ever trust this girl. Then, I remember the things I've done in the past and how I'd hate for my actions to be held against me. So I say, "I guess time will tell."

"I can work with that. I swear I'm going to make it up to you, one way or another."

"I actually know how you can start."

"Do tell."

"Don't let your brother kill those three guys. They're disgusting jerks, but Ridge doesn't need any more blood on his hands. And those guys are going to learn the hard way that karma is a fucking bitch."

"Ohhhh," she drawls. "Don't you worry about that. All three of those guys are about to get exactly what they deserve."

"Is that so?" I tsk. "Is it safe to assume you have something to do with that?"

Temper waggles her brows with a mischievous grin on her face. "No one fucks with my friend Riley and gets away with it."

"Oh, Temper." I put an arm around her shoulders. "Something tells me we're going to be good friends."

"Well, yeah." She huffs. "We're practically sisters now."

"Whoa now. Let's not get ahead of ourselves." We laugh in unison and I can already feel how close we are. I feel connected to my boys, but somehow with Temper, I feel like she's the little sister I never had.

Ridge walks into the room wearing a smile. "Look at that. My sister and my girl becoming besties."

"You shush." I tease. "Baby steps."

He curls his fingers at me, calling me over. "I'm gonna need you to baby step right over here because I've missed you."

I drop my arm from Temper's shoulders and eat up the space between Ridge and me. On my tiptoes, I press my lips to his. "I missed you, too."

Lev and Maddox come into the kitchen and Maddox slithers up to my side. His mouth finds the crease of my neck. "Having fun without me?"

"Just talking," I tell him, but the way the heat of his

breath is riding down the V of my shirt makes me think I could certainly go for some fun.

Lev comes up behind me and his hands rest on my hips. "I think it's time to say good night to Mrs. Crane and go back to our apartment."

My insides quiver with excitement. It's been so long since I've been alone with all three of my guys. Aside from tonight when I'm sure Temper will be there and Maddox will be here, we have the rest of break together. Netflix and chill, with a whole lot of spice.

"You all go," Temper says as she scrubs a dish in the sink. "I don't know this lady from Eve, but I suppose I can stick around and help her clean up."

Maddox takes a step back as he gestures to the wine cabinet. "Crack open a bottle of wine and you two will be best friends by the end of the night. My mom loves to talk."

"Oh joy," Temper says, her voice laced with sarcasm, but she heads to the wine cabinet anyway.

"It's settled then." Ridge pumps his fist in the air. "Best fucking sister ever." Then he scoops me in his arms like a baby. "Take my car and I'll text you directions to the apartment. Give us an hour."

"Two," Lev says, then scans the rest of us. "Maybe even three."

Three hours? All my holes are begging for that to be a joke. "Wait a minute, you guys. We can't just leave her here alone."

Temper sweeps her hand through the air, holding up a bottle of red and a bottle of white. "It's not a big deal. Besides, I owe you."

"Good point," I tell her, taking advantage of her kindness

because I have an odd feeling it won't last forever. "Ridge, take me out of here."

He squeezes my ass with his hand that's cradling it and I wince as he carries me out of the kitchen, through the massive house, and to the front door. Maddox pulls the door open, then hollers, "I'll be back in a couple hours, Mom."

Maddox decided it was best if he sleeps at home tonight. He's been worried about his mom being alone, but fortunately, his grandma is arriving in town tomorrow, so she'll have company for a while.

Mrs. Crane comes rushing into the living room and I try my best to hold my skirt down so I'm not flashing her while Ridge holds me. "Y'all are leaving already?"

"Riley isn't feeling well," Ridge lies. "We've gotta get her to bed."

"Oh no," Mrs. Crane grasps her chest. "Was it something you ate?"

"Cramps," Lev spits out and I wanna slap his face off.

"Yeah, Mom. Riley's bloated and has cramps. So...we gotta go. Love ya." He goes to step out the door, but I reach out and grab the sleeve of his hoodie.

My cheeks flush with heat in complete embarrassment for not only what they're saying, but also the way they're behaving like a bunch of horny teenagers—which they are. "I'm so sorry to rush out, Mrs. Crane. Thank you so much for being so generous. The food was amazing and I look forward to seeing you again before we head back to BCU."

"Anytime, honey. And if that son of mine gives you any trouble, you let me know."

I smirk at Maddox as I say, "I sure will."

The guys thank Mrs. Crane, then Ridge carries me out

the door, and the minute it closes, I tear into them all. "Cramps!? Bloated!? You're assholes."

Lev shrugs. "No one else was saying anything, so I went with the first thing that came to mind."

I roll my eyes while trying not to laugh because it is pretty funny. "You didn't give anyone else a chance to say anything," I point out.

Ridge finally sets me down and we all pile into Lev's car. It's a short five-minute drive to the apartment they lease and my nerves are on edge the entire time.

When I walk inside the small space, I'm actually pretty surprised at how clean it is. I take that to be Maddox's doing because Ridge and Lev sure as hell don't know how to pick up after themselves. It smells like a mixture of all three of them—sandalwood, sea salt, and spiced pine.

As my eyes are skating around the space, taking it all in, Maddox takes my hand and leads me down a short hallway and into a room. Almost immediately, I know it's Ridge's room. Not because of the king-size bed, but because of the gothic decor and slew of clothes scattered on the floor. Also, because there's a picture of him and a woman, who I take to be his mom, sitting on a dresser.

As Maddox is leading me over to the bed, Ridge and Lev come through the door and Ridge closes it, then clicks the lock. Maddox steps behind me with his back to the bed. He sweeps my hair to one side and trails kisses down the nape of my neck.

"Expecting company?" I ask Ridge with raised eyebrows.

"You just never know in this town," Ridge says. "Crazy psychos everywhere."

Lev peels his shirt over his head and drops it to the floor. "That's rich coming from you."

Ridge ignores the jab and strolls toward me with a grin on his face. "I got the girl, didn't I?"

His hands run down my sides and he grips the hem of my shirt before lifting it up. "That you did." I bite the corner of my lip anxiously. "You all did." His hands gather behind my back and the next thing I know, my bra is falling at my feet.

Maddox steps out from behind me and drops his jeans to the floor while Ridge lowers me to the bed, settling between my legs. Eagerness surges through my body. This will be my first time with all three guys and the thought sends a tingle down my spine.

Ridge leans in, his warm breath tickling my skin. Slowly, his hand moves from the back of my knee to my thigh. His fingers graze over the fabric of my damp panties before resting at my entrance.

"You ready to be fucked by your men, Angel?"

Heat courses through me at his words and I let out a raspy, "Yes, please."

Lev rests into the mattress on my left side, and Maddox to my right. Both are on their sides watching me. Staring like I'm some rare art piece worth millions. I've never felt so wanted in my entire life.

I extend my hand and stroke Maddox's cheek before forcing his lips to mine.

Lev cups my left breast in his hand before sucking my nipple between his teeth. My back arches off the bed, and just as it does, Ridge pulls down my skirt and panties and replaces them with his face between my thighs.

I spread my legs wider, letting them fall to the sides, and my back arches off the bed.

Two fingers circle at my entrance before pushing deep

inside me. I whimper into Maddox's mouth and he adds pressure to our kiss. His erection grinds against my side, and I know I need to do something about it.

I break our kiss and say, "Get on your knees."

His eyes grow wide in response to my request and he jumps up without hesitation. "You don't have to tell me twice."

Maddox's body hovers over mine. One of his knees presses against my shoulder while the other slides behind my head. I feel the heat of his body radiate against me as I take his stiff length in my hand. Dragging my fingers slowly down his cock, my mouth salivates at the sight and the velvety surface ripples beneath my touch.

Lev's weight shifts on the other side of me and I look over to see him getting off the bed. I slow my strokes on Maddox and lift my head to see where Lev's going. But when he stops and watches Ridge finger-fuck me, I pick up my pace and stroke Maddox faster.

Ridge continues to work his fingers inside me, then he presses his hands to both of my knees, spreading me wider before he buries his face in my sex. His tongue circles around my clit, sending a ripple of electricity through my body.

I lift my head again, only this time, it's angled at Maddox. I gesture at him to come forward and when he does, I trail my tongue from the base of his shaft up to the tip. When I reach his head, I swirl my tongue and feel him shudder with pleasure.

He leans into me and I wrap my lips around his girth while his palm cradles the back of my head. His hips glide back and forth as he feeds me more and more of his cock. I continue to circle my tongue around the head, using my hand to create friction at the base, then I begin to pump him in tandem with my mouth.

"Fuck, baby." He growls as he slows my pace and trails his fingertips through my hair. "God, you feel so fucking good. You keep that up, I'm not gonna last much longer."

"Trouble, I think we need you on your hands and knees," Lev says, so I slide Maddox out of my mouth while he moves back, so I can reposition.

"Okay," I say breathlessly. As I go to turn onto my stomach, Lev lies down and pulls me on top of him.

Ridge grabs my hips and jerks my lower half upward. His fingers trail feather-like marks down my legs before running between my ass cheeks. When I glance over my shoulder to get a look at him, he levels his face with my ass, then spits before raising his eyebrows with a smirk. His fingertips prod at my asshole before going in fingernail deep.

I turn my head to find Maddox in front of me, stroking his cock, and it's so damn sexy, all the tension in my body at the idea of what's to come melts away. "Isn't that my job?" I tease.

"Well, then open up, baby, and get to work."

He guides his cock into my mouth while I brace myself with both of my hands. And he's the one who ends up doing all the work. Rolling his hips and fucking my mouth while fisting my hair.

Lev grabs my hips while Ridge pushes my ass down gently, guiding me onto Lev's cock that slips inside my pussy with ease. The cold metal of his piercing sends a chill down my spine. I'm grateful he's the one in this hole because I can't imagine him stretching the tight muscle of my ass with that metal.

Continuing to bob my ass up and down on Lev's cock,

Ridge does the work while his fingertip slowly moves inside me farther and farther. I moan in response, feeling the rumble climb up my throat, vibrating against Maddox's cock.

The next thing I know, Ridge is pulling his finger out and I hear the sound of him spitting again, followed by a warm liquid coating my asshole. He positions his head against my hole. "Take a deep breath for me, Angel."

Eyes wide, I inhale deeply with Maddox's length practically touching my tonsils.

Ridge enters slowly, inching the head of his dick inside me, and it literally feels like I'm being ripped apart by a red-hot torch. I'm forced to stop sucking off Maddox until the pain subsides.

"Tell me if you want me to stop, Angel." Ridge's voice is raspy and thick and the last thing I want is for him to stop. I want this so damn bad. I will endure all the pain, just to get to the rapture because I know this is going to feel amazing if I can just get past this point.

Lev grips my cheeks in his hands and pulls my face down until our noses are touching. "Focus on me, Trouble." He lifts his hips slightly, then drops them, repeating the motion as he fucks me slowly. His hand moves between us and when he starts rubbing my clit, I'm lost. There's no pain, only pure intense pleasure.

I sink into Lev, relishing the way his size completely fills me up. My walls stretch around him, tightening with each thrust.

Before I know it, Ridge has slid all the way inside me and the pain I expected to feel is only bliss.

"You doing all right, Angel?"

I nod in response before reaching out and wrapping my

fingers around Maddox again. I guide the shallow end of his cock into my mouth, while stroking the lower half. With each thrust from Ridge, I pant around Maddox's cock. And with each lunge from Lev beneath me, I cry out in pleasure. Before long, I don't recognize the sounds escaping me.

Each guy picks up his pace until all my entrances are rapid-firing with a zing of electricity.

"You're fucking amazing, Trouble," Lev rasps as he bucks his hips. The feeling of them both working together inside me has my pussy taut with tension. I swear they make me feel so full, I could explode at any given second.

"So damn good." Ridge growls as his fingertips delve into the meaty flesh of my hips. I wish I could see him. Watch his face while he works.

Instead, I peer up at Maddox and take in the way his mouth forms an O as he fucks my throat.

A rush of heat spreads through me. All my muscles clench as my mind enters a state of ecstasy. I cry out, practically screaming as I come undone. My sounds only arouse the guys further and each one of them fucks me harder, faster, forcing another orgasm to take over my body. I'm a shell of a human and I'm certain my soul has left my body.

"I'm gonna come," Maddox says just as his head swells in my mouth. I take him in as far as he'll go, feeling the warmth of his orgasm shoot down my throat. He pulses against my tongue, leaving a salty and bitter taste behind as he pulls out. I look at him as another orgasm hits me when Lev pinches my nipples. Maddox's eyes stay pinned on mine, his thumb grazing my lower lip.

"Oh god," I roar.

"That's right, Angel. Come for us." Ridge groans.

And I do. I come again and again. By the time I start to

come down from the high, I'm certain I've had at least three orgasms. Or one really big one. I don't even know. All I know is it felt fantastic and I can't wait to do it again.

Lev thrusts once more, then pauses, holding me in place as he comes inside me. "Fuck," he moans airily.

At the same time, Ridge moans and does the same thing, halting his movements as he fills me up.

Lev's body relaxes onto the mattress and I collapse on top of him. His arms wrap around my waist and our sweaty bodies melt together like hot wax.

"I'm pulling out now, Trouble," Ridge warns me. I hold my breath as he slides out slowly, but the pain of his exit is nothing compared to his entrance. He drops down on the bed beside us and Lev slides over a tad and folds his arms under his head. Maddox lies on the other side and a whole new wave of emotion hits me. I've never felt more at home in my entire life. I lean down and kiss Lev's lips and he doesn't even hesitate to reciprocate my kiss after I just sucked Maddox off.

"I love you," Lev says softly into my mouth.

I smile against his lips. "I love you, too."

"I don't know what I'd do without you guys." I turn to Ridge, and he strokes my cheek with the back of his hand.

"You've got my heart, Angel. Always and forever. You'll never have to find out."

I turn to the left to Maddox, who's on his side with his head propped up. His fingernails drag gentle lines down my back, leaving a trail of goosebumps. "You all complete me."

"You complete us," Maddox says with a smile.

Lying here in bed with all three of my guys, my heart feels like it's tripled in size. This night was more than anything I could have ever dreamed up. And the reality is, this is the first night of the rest of my life with these guys. Each one of them is a puzzle piece that connects with my heart, and with them, I am complete.

With them, I feel like I can take on the world. I can't wait to see what the future brings for all of us, because we're in this together. For life or longer. My boys and me.

As I doze off to sleep, I remember the promise they made to each other, the promise they made to me, and I feel it in the depths of my soul.

We will reign.

The End.

Thank you so much for reading! If you liked the Wicked Boys of BCU Series, be sure to check out Scar's series Bastards of Boulder Cove!

ALSO BY RACHEL LEIGH

Bastards of Boulder Cove

Book One: Savage Games

Book Two: Vicious Lies

Book Three: Twisted Secrets

Wicked Boys of BCU

Book One: We Will Reign

Book Two: You Will Bow

Book Three: They Will Fall

Redwood Rebels Series

Book One: Striker

Book Two: Heathen

Book Three: Vandal

Book Four: Reaper

Redwood High Series

Book One: Like Gravity

Book Two: Like You

Book Three: Like Hate

Fallen Kingdom Duet

His Hollow Heart & Her Broken Pieces

Black Heart Duet

Four & Five

Standalones

Guarded

Ruthless Rookie

Devil Heir

All The Little Things

Claim your FREE copy of Her Undoing!

ACKNOWLEDGMENTS

Thank you so much for reading They Will Fall. I hope you enjoyed Riley and her boys!

A special thanks to my wonderful team for all the hard work you put into helping me create this book: My dedicated PA, Carolina Leon. All my girls for your support, friendship, and advice. My Street Team, the Rebel Readers for your help in getting the word out.

Thank you to my beta & alpha readers:

Taylor, you helped me tremendously. Your flexibility with my time crunch means so much to me. You played such a big part in helping me tell this story the way it should be told. Thank you so much for everything!

Drita. I appreciate your feedback, as well as your friendship.

A big thanks to…

Y'all That Graphic for the amazing cover and graphics!

Fairest Reviews Editing Service for the beautiful edit and for your encouragement and patience through this. You helped me more than you will ever know!

Rumi Khan for proofreading and being so flexible!.

Greys Promo for spectacular PR Services.

XOXO Rachel

ABOUT THE AUTHOR

Rachel Leigh is a USA Today and International bestselling author of new adult and contemporary romances.

She loves to write—and read—flawed bad-boys and strong heroines. You can expect dark elements, a dash of suspense, and a lot of steam.

Her goal is to take readers on an adventure with her words, while showing them that even on the darkest days, love conquers all.

Rachel lives in Michigan with her husband, three little monsters (who aren't so little anymore) and a couple of fur babies. When she's not writing or reading, she's likely lounging in leggings, with coffee in her hand, while binge watching her favorite reality tv shows.

- facebook.com/rachelleighauthor
- instagram.com/rachelleighauthor
- bookbub.com/profile/rachel-leigh

Made in the USA
Middletown, DE
22 September 2023